THE CINEMATICS CLUB

They started a filmmaking club.
Then they became their own heroes.

THE CINEMATICS CLUB

A YA NOIR

RENEE WINDMAN

The Cinematics Club
Copyright © 2024 by Renee Windman

Published in the United States by Renee Windman

Library of Congress Control Number: 2023922512

TheCinematicsClub.com

Cover, book, and illustration design by Renee Windman

Printed in the United States of America

First edition, 2024

ISBN 979-8-9894737-0-0 (hardcover)
ISBN 979-8-9894737-1-7 (paperback)
ISBN 979-8-9894737-2-4 (Ebook)

For my mother and father

1

Palm Trees and Moonlight

Life is NOT a movie…

That is what her mom always says exasperatingly when Sophie speaks with fervor and passion about life. Sophie's mom, Sarah, grew up during the wartimes of films like *Casablanca*—a world of black and white, light and shadow, where endings didn't always wrap up nicely with the boy and girl flying off into the sunset. But Sophie has turned sixteen this summer, and her life is colored by the golden sunshine of Los Angeles.

Sophie Alexander walks along Ventura Boulevard on a Saturday afternoon. Wearing an oversized white shirtdress, a black vest, and black Unisa flats, she gazes at the shop windows. It is that time of year when summer starts to fade into fall, and the 1985 school year at Noble High will be starting Monday. The sun casts long shadows on the pavement with silhouettes of the palm trees. Though she feels sad that the summer is over, Sophie is excited to start her junior year. She has passed being the awkward new freshman and has formed a small group of friends.

The main Valley boulevard is a vibrant mix of trendy stores and clothing boutiques. The jewel of the block is La Luna, the single-screen movie theater where Sophie works on the weekends as a ticket booth cashier. The theater was built in the late 1930s and was fashioned after the grand movie palaces downtown. She gazes at her watch, which reads four thirty p.m.—she'll be right on time for her five o'clock shift.

She walks past the usual stores. Popsicle is a trendy gift shop filled with T-shirts, funky toys, and bins of jelly beans and every flavor, shape, and color of gummies. Giant blow-up clouds hang from the ceiling, and there is a pristine feel to the sparkly white interior that makes all the colorful merchandise pop.

Sophie continues past Video Vault, where a giant cardboard cutout of *The Terminator* stands guard. The store is no bigger than a living room, but it is filled from floor to ceiling with racks of VHS boxes. One can find every video imaginable there, from *Star Wars* to midnight movies. *Ghostbusters* is playing on the TV screen mounted on the wall behind the cash register. The front of the store features new releases, and there is a small section in the back stocked with X-rated films. There are handwritten signs posted along the partition announcing, MUST BE AT LEAST 18 YEARS OLD TO ENTER!

Sophie peers through the door to see if Charles James is working. CJ, as he prefers to be called, is a black teenager with a love of ska music and style. Just before he spots Sophie standing in front of the shop, CJ blurts out, "Hey, get back to the cartoons!", busting some kids peering into the X-rated section. He is dressed in a Video Vault T-shirt, skinny pinstripe slacks, suspenders, creepers, and a black trilby hat.

"Sophie," CJ calls, "I just got in David Lynch's *Dune*!"

Sophie smiles with excitement and replies, "We will have to watch that! I'll check if Su is still working. Catch you later."

Just a few steps later, Sophie smells the unmistakable aroma of sugary batter being poured into a press to make waffle cones. The scent leads her to Ciao Gelato, the first gelato shop to open amongst the frozen yogurt stores that dot the boulevard. There is a crush of teenagers and suburban moms lined up to get into the store. The walls are painted teal and pink with large black-and-white prints of Italy and chic people on Vespas. The décor invites each customer to grab a cone, sit at a tiny metal table, and dream that they are living la dolce vita for a while.

Sophie sees her friend Susan carefully crafting a double scoop of pistachio and vanilla on a freshly sculpted cone from the waffle press. Sophie catches Susan's eye and points to the right, indicating that she is walking toward the movie theater for her shift. Susan nods that she understands—she will meet Sophie at the theater when both of their shifts end at nine. Susan hands the cone over to the eager college girl in a hurry to join her friend at one of the last tables by the front window. Those tables are in high demand for those who want to be seen by the passersby walking along the boulevard.

Sophie comes to the last store before the theater, which pulls her attention away from the street's blur of crimped hair, Day-Glo, and Live Aid T-shirts from the concert in July. Chelsea Loft is *the* place to find all the latest fashions. This store has floor-to-ceiling windows and a warehouse-style interior with exposed vents and beams. The center of the store features a large staircase that leads to an elevated circular platform, where a DJ with spiky platinum-blond hair is spinning records. Sophie circles around the racks of long paisley-patterned blouses as The Cult's "She Sells Sanctuary" pulses through the store. She loses herself for a few moments, then realizes she needs to hurry up to make it to her shift at the theater.

The concrete sidewalk transitions into a mix of turquoise and azure terrazzo tiles, similar to how the bricks turn into the yellow brick road in *The Wizard of Oz*. La Luna Theater rises from the boulevard, its neon marquee topped with a glowing moon. Sophie walks fast passing the Art Deco gold-and-glass ticket booth and pulls open the lobby door. She veers to the left of the concession stand and opens the door marked MAN-AGER. Sophie pulls open the metal desk drawer to retrieve her sparkly name tag. She hurries out of the office as she affixes it to her vest. When she looks up, Sophie sees Robert Garcia, the theater manager, walking over to her with a roll of red tickets.

"Sophie," Robert says, revving with excitement, "we are premiering *The Bride* with Sting tonight. It is going to sell out fast—just look at the line out front."

Robert started working at the theater twenty years ago when he was a teenager and has worked his way up from cleaning the place to managing it. The owner, Max Greenfeld, comes by now and then. He is in his sixties and looking to retire soon. Max remembers when a movie ticket cost only fifty cents and everyone dressed up in hats and gloves to attend. Back in the fifties, every day was a red-carpet event.

A tall, confident guy in his early twenties walks into the lobby, coming back from his break. Dylan Peters takes his sunglasses off and slides them into his dark brown hair. He's attending film school and works as La Luna's weekend projectionist. He sees himself as the next big action director, inspired by James Cameron and George Miller.

Dylan calls out to Sophie, "Hey, Moonlight." The nickname refers to the fact that she's not your typical tanned, aerobicizing SoCal girl. He proceeds to put on an exaggerated British accent and playfully teases Sophie for her love of classic romantic period dramas. "Oh, is it teatime? Oh, where is my castle?" Dylan cracks himself up as he grabs a bag of popcorn off the concession counter and continues, laughing, to the projection room door.

Sophie hurries out of the lobby, opens the rear door of the box office, which she quickly locks behind her, and places her purse under the counter. She checks that the roll of red paper tickets is in place and scans the line of beach-blond girls with fluorescent sunglasses and jelly shoes. Sophie turns the sign on the window from CLOSED to OPEN, slides open the speaker, and says, "Welcome to La Luna. How many for the six p.m. show of *The Bride*?"

By five thirty, the last ticket is sold. A husband and wife rush up to the booth, and Sophie tells them, "Sorry, the six p.m. show is now sold out." The wife is grief-stricken at the thought that she won't have two hours in the dark with Sting. The husband flashes a gleeful grin, which she doesn't see, then says, "Bonnie, I know how much this means to you, and I am *just* as upset. Let's not ruin our movie night, though, since your parents are watching the kids. *The Return of the Living Dead* is showing at the Valerio 3." Bonnie sighs as she walks away with her now-beaming husband.

Sophie places a SOLD OUT sign in the box office window and closes the speaker. She gathers the cash box, counts the money, and writes down the amount on the receipt slip. Bending down below the counter, she grabs her purse and drops it into her lap. Retrieving her yellow Walkman tape player, she fixes the headphones so that they disappear into her wavy hair. Sophie pushes the play button and hears the echoing synthesizers of Eurythmics' "Love Is a Stranger." Mouthing the lyrics, she pulls out her compact.

Suddenly a figure comes up to the window. Sophie is applying her red lipstick when she hears knocking on the glass and muffled words. When she glances up from her reflection in her compact, her hazel eyes meet his blue eyes. The boy's lips stop moving, and they both stare, transfixed, for a moment. Then Sophie realizes she didn't hear what he said. She puts her lipstick and compact back in her purse, pulls the headphones away from her ears, and opens the speaker. "Sorry, but the six p.m. showing of *The Bride* is sold out. The next showing will start at nine."

Confusion crosses his face as his choppy hair falls across his eyes. Pushing his hair back away from his face, the stranger says with the hint of an accent, "Is this not the Majestic Theater playing *Year of the Dragon*?"

Sophie decides that this time she will give a strong and sophisticated response. "This is the *magnificent* La Luna Theater. To get to the Majestic Theater, go two blocks down to Willow Street and then take a left near the market." She smiles confidently with her freshly painted lips, sure she has made an impression. The stranger thanks her, looks down the street in the direction she has indicated, and walks swiftly away.

Sophie watches as he disappears down the boulevard. The sun is setting, and the Santa Ana winds are starting to kick up. Sophie gathers her belongings, locks the tiny door, and emerges from the box office into the evening. Taking one last look down the boulevard, she wonders who the stranger was. The neon marquee of La Luna lights up the deep blue sky.

Sophie walks inside the theater, secures the cash box in the manager's office, and places her name tag back in the desk drawer. She smiles as she spots the framed poster of *Blade Runner* that hangs on the wall. Her shift is now over, and she meets up with Susan, who is waiting for her in front of the theater.

"Sophie," Susan says as she hugs her best friend, "I can't believe I got gelato on my new Esprit jumpsuit!" Exasperated, Susan points to the multicolored stains on her cotton jumpsuit and brushes off the remaining waffle cone crumbs. "I hope you had a better night. Were there lots of cool people going to see the movie?"

Sophie instantly remembers that moment when her eyes locked with the stranger's. Susan slowly looks up to Sophie and sees that she is in a haze.

"Hello?" Susan calls, "Earth to Sophie. Did the sight of Dr. Sting Frankenstein put you under a spell?"

Sophie laughs. "Yeah, I'm under a spell…you could say that."

CJ drives up on his midnight-blue Vespa and slows next to where Sophie and Susan are talking under the glow of the neon lights. He pulls his camera from his bag and snaps a picture of them. "Do you need a ride?" he asks.

"Thanks, CJ," Susan replies, "but Steven is picking us up tonight. We'll see you on Monday for the first day of school!"

CJ nods and rides off, secretly wishing Susan had taken him up on the offer. He imagines riding down the boulevard into the night with her on the back of his scooter.

Steven Tran pulls up in his shiny red Toyota Supra, head-lights beaming. He is Susan's older brother, a recently gradu-ated aerospace engineer who works at DynaRocket. Steven is the image of success for Susan and her middle sibling, Andrea, who is taking premed classes at UCLA. He just purchased the car, and the new paint gleams. The window rolls down, and Steven leans over the passenger seat to call, "Are you ready to go home?" He's dressed in his all-white tennis outfit of a polo shirt, shorts, socks, and sneakers.

Susan and Sophie walk over to the car, and Sophie squeezes into the pristine back seat of the hatchback next to Steven's racquet bag.

"Thanks for picking us up," Susan says as she buckles her seat belt.

Steven drives off down the boulevard and glances in the mirror. "Sophie," he says, lowering the radio volume, "I saw that *The Bride* is playing at your theater." He shifts into gear and continues, "Too bad. I really want to see *Year of the Dragon*."

Sophie sighs as she looks out the window, hoping she might catch another glimpse of the stranger. The car speeds down the boulevard as the stereo plays Depeche Mode's "But Not Tonight."

2

A Noble Start

Beep… beep… beep…

Sophie hears her alarm clock going off, but her eyes remain shut. Slowly she pulls the blue graphic Marimekko blanket down from over her eyes. Looking out her bedroom window, all she sees is a gray, overcast sky. This is not the "jump out of bed to blue skies and do somersaults" first day of school that always appears in movies. Sophie is excited to start the new school year but is also anxious about doing well in her classes. She knows that her academic achievements this year are key for her college applications.

Sophie throws off the covers and hits the button on her alarm clock. She looks around at the art on her periwinkle bedroom walls—Van Gogh's *Café Terrace at Night* and posters of U2 and INXS. The night before, she put together her outfit for the first day of school: a khaki dress with a bright orange tank and olive military belt that wraps around her waist twice.

Sophie gets dressed and does her makeup—just a quick sweep of natural eye shadow and blush. She opens her bedroom door and makes her way down the hall lined with family photos to the kitchen. She passes Martin's bedroom door, her older brother who is away at college studying physics. There is still a sign tacked to it reading ENTER AT YOUR OWN RISK.

"Morning, Sophie," her mom says as she cooks scrambled eggs. "Are you having breakfast?"

Sophie grabs a piece of bread. "I am going to have some toast and juice. I already packed my lunch. I'm getting a ride to school with Susan. She and Andrea are coming by to pick me up in a few minutes. We want to get there together."

The kitchen is painted bright yellow, and Sophie's dad, Simon, is sitting at the round white Formica table. He is finishing up his breakfast of toasted rye bread with cheese and a cup of coffee. He lifts his head from the newspaper and says, "Oh, I thought I was going to drop you off before I go to work." He is a serious father who wears his role as the family bread-winner and caretaker like a badge of honor, since he lost his family during the Holocaust. Simon always dresses in navy-blue pressed pants and a striped shirt with a pen protruding from the pocket.

"That's okay, Dad," Sophie replies, "Susan should be here any minute."

Hearing the blare of a car horn, Sophie peers out the kitchen window to see a white Honda Accord pulling up to the front curb. She grabs her lunch bag from the fridge, says goodbye to her mom and dad, and rushes out to the car.

Sophie opens the rear door and slides in behind Susan. "Morning, thanks for picking me up." The new wave music of Shere Thu Thuy perks up the morning ride.

The musky scent of Poison perfume overwhelms the car. "My sister had a date with Keith last night." Susan rolls down the window.

Andrea is dressed in an oversize blue plaid shirt, a wide black belt, a vest, and leggings. Her long jet-black hair flows down her shoulders while her bangs defy gravity with hairspray. She is the second person in their family to attend college after Steven.

Andrea playfully pulls the perfume bottle from her LeSportsac bag and sprays it at Susan. "Don't you want to make the boys go wild on your first day of school?" They all start to laugh.

The Honda turns into the parking lot of Noble High and stops in front of the main entrance. Noble High is a sprawling campus with a main two-story Art Deco–style administration building surrounded by bird of paradise. "How I love seeing my alma mater," Andrea exclaims, peering out from behind her Ray-Ban sunglasses. "Have fun!"

Susan and Sophie get out of the car and wave as Andrea drives off.

Sophie opens her blue Trapper Keeper, checks her schedule, and says to Susan, "We have Mr. Hart for chemistry first period. It's in the science building, room 201." Sophie looks over to Susan, who is brushing her hair to the side.

Susan gives a sigh of relief to be standing with Sophie. Even though she loves her family and understands the sacrifices her parents made to leave Vietnam and create a new life for their children, there's a lot of pressure on her to succeed like her older siblings. At school, at least, she feels a sense of freedom to express her individuality. She has trimmed her black hair from a shoulder-length bob to an asymmetrical, angular cut. She opens up her buttoned-up shirt to reveal a Cure T-shirt.

"We better hurry," Sophie says at she looks at her wrist-watch. "The reminder bell just rang, and we have ten minutes to get to first period."

Sophie and Susan breeze through the administration building. A sea of students and teachers whiz past as they emerge into a freshly mowed green quad. Passing the quad, Sophie and Susan make their way into the gray-and-white checkered hallway lined with lockers.

"Room 201," Susan proclaims as they walk through the door. The room is filled with high two-person lab tables. Susan and Sophie walk toward the front of the classroom and pick a table to share. The classroom quickly fills up with students. Some of them they know, and some are new. When the round wall clock above the blackboard reads eight o'clock, Mr. Hart strides in.

Greg Hart is an athletic man with a brown beard. He is known for his love of hiking and leads the Noble Hikers Club. One can often spot him wearing his Members Only jacket, Lacoste polo shirt, and Nike shoes. His short stature—he's barely four foot five—is overshadowed by his giant goofy personality. He loves teaching and sincerely wants his students to excel.

Mr. Hart hears the bell ring and closes the classroom door. Without saying a word, he walks behind his lab desk and presses play on a boombox. The theme from the movie *Weird Science* starts to play. All the students know the words, and Mr. Hart encourages them to sing along. He then stops the music and proclaims, "Welcome to chemistry one! My name is Mr. Hart, and I will be teaching you about the exciting properties of matter." He pulls down a huge chart and continues enthusiastically, "You will learn about the periodic table of elements and participate in many exciting lab experiments! Our first order of business is to take attendance. You can greet the student seated at your table, since they will be your lab partner for the semester."

Roll call begins, and the fidgety class settles in for the first lesson. Mr. Hart's left eyebrow quirks up playfully. He unzips his jacket and reveals a T-shirt that says HEART OF AU. "Which of my brilliant students knows what my shirt means?"

Susan raises up her hand, knowing the answer from the endless prep quizzes Steven has given her. "Heart of gold."

Mr. Hart, impressed with the quick response, throws Susan a granola bar. "That's correct! Heart of gold." He scans his seating chart. "Susan Tran. Are you Steven and Andrea's little sister?"

Susan nods, cracking a forced smile as she shrinks beneath the weight of her famous older siblings' reputations.

The end of the hour quickly approaches, and Sophie and Susan have different classes for the rest of the day.

"I'll meet you on the quad for lunch," Sophie says as she starts to walk down the hallway. "If you see CJ, let him know!"

"Okay," Susan yells out as they drift apart.

The lunch bell rings at twelve thirty, and students flood out of every door. The sky that started out gray this morning has turned light blue and sunny. Sophie walks out of the foreign language building, carrying her notebook and lunch bag. She squints at the sunny sky, walks out into the quad, and surveys the scene. The usual cliques have gathered in the places Sophie remembers from last year. The cheerleaders and jocks have staked out their prominent spot at the top of the lawn where the stage-like steps are located. This is where major school announcements take place. The metalheads with their long hair huddle by the snack shack, and all the other ethnic and inter-est-based groups form small circles that dot the grassy quad.

Sophie makes her way toward the front of the school. She spots Susan and CJ already sitting on the ground in the shade of a tree with their lunches. "Hi!" Sophie exclaims. She makes a seat on the cement with her textbooks so her outfit doesn't get dirty. She feels a sense of comfort in her little group, knowing that they share a common bond as first-generation Americans. They are trying to navigate a new world—to grab the American dream and do better than their parents—and also fit in with the look of successful popular students. Between friends, they want to define themselves.

CJ is dressed in skinny pants, creepers, a short-sleeved shirt, and a pullover argyle vest from the sixties. "Sixth period I have Mrs. Martinez for AP Spanish." He pulls out a burrito from his paper bag and asks Susan and Sophie, "What classes do you have?"

"I have Ms. Kahn for modern art history," Sophie replies. She bites into her cheese sandwich.

Susan waves her schedule and says with glee, "I have Mr. Weber for AP English!" Pulling a box from her backpack, she opens the lid to reveal a carefully crafted lunch. Susan proclaimed herself a vegetarian this summer, to the bewilderment of her family. Her lunch box has one compartment for salad, a container for dressing so the salad doesn't get soggy, carrot sticks, and spring rolls, which her mother always makes.

"Look what Oscar gave me in the hallway. He drew the flyer." Susan passes a folded piece of paper to Sophie.

Sophie opens the orange paper, which reads: NOBLE HIGH HALLOWEEN DANCE: SATURDAY, OCTOBER 26. There is a black ink drawing of a skeleton dancing. Sophie and her friends smile with excitement and exclaim simultaneously, "What should I be?"

A group of cheerleaders walks by in their blue-and-gray Noble Knights uniforms and white Reebok sneakers. Sophie looks over at one of the girls, Brittany Meadows.

Sophie and Brittany met when they were in elementary school. They shared their first crushes and had sleepovers where they danced to their favorite bands' records—Culture Club for Brittany and The Police for Sophie. During the summer of 1983, they had a stupid fight and ended up drifting into new circles of friends when they started high school in the fall.

Brittany has cut her long brown hair into a short, feathered cut and bleached it blond. She looks away and keeps talking with the rest of the cheerleaders as they ascend the cement stairs leading to the quad stage.

"Hello!" Amber, the head cheerleader, screams out to get the attention of all the students on the quad. "My name is Amber Cummings, and on behalf of Principal Patterson, I want to welcome you to an exciting new year at Noble High!" Amber kicks her leg up and clasps her hands. "We will be having *so* many great events this year, starting with homecoming this Friday at seven. Come out and support our Noble Knights football team! Yay!" Amber squeals as she looks around the quad. "The first school dance is going to be *so* awesome because it is our epic Halloween costume party! Pick up a flyer in the office or at the snack shack."

Principal Parker Patterson jogs up the stairs to join the cheerleaders. Dressed in a loose-fitting suit with a crisp shirt and tie, he is a fit man in his fifties with salt-and-pepper hair. "Thank you, Amber and our Noble cheerleaders! To all of our students, I want to welcome you to an incredible year. In order to give each of you the opportunity to excel, we expect every student to sign up for an after-school club. Become a member of one of our established clubs, like hiking or debate, or be a leader and start your own. Have a great year!" The cheerleaders behind Principal Patterson clap and cheer as they leave the stage.

Sophie, Susan, and CJ look at each other, their brains working in unison.

"Hey, we should start our own club," CJ says, slurping up the last of his drink. "We all like movies. Why don't we start some kind of a film or moviemaking club? My uncle Will works at the *Los Angeles Daily Tribune* as a news photographer, and he also knows about movie cameras. He's always encouraging me since I like taking photos. I can ask him if he'll be our club mentor."

Susan thinks about it and responds, "I can join, but I also need to sign up for the chemistry club for my college applications."

Sophie nods and says, "Of course, Su. We can make the club about film appreciation, film history, moviemaking, whatever we want. It will be more artistic than the AV Club, since they just videotape the school events."

They finish putting away their lunches as the bell rings. "I have trig now," Sophie says, grabbing her books from the pavement. "Let's meet in the photography room after school!" She walks toward the math building.

CJ asks, "Su, I'll walk with you to the gym, since I have volleyball." He holds his hand out to help Susan up off the ground.

"Here's a snack for you." Susan places one of her spring rolls in his backpack, which is decorated with patches of The

Untouchables, Fishbone, and The Specials. Susan and CJ walk off together into the flow of students.

3

Starry Night and Day

Finally, the last class of the first day of school.

Sophie settles into her desk and opens her notebook to a clean sheet of paper. The classroom is decorated with prints of artwork hung in chronological order—from the Impressionists to the pop art of Keith Haring. A petite woman in her late forties walks to the front of the classroom and gives a warm smile. Ms. Beverly Kahn is channeling her inner hippie, wearing a flowing skirt and top with her curly short hair wrapped in a scarf. "Hello," she says. "My name is Ms. Kahn, and this is modern art history. We will start with the Impressionist period and end by studying current art trends. All of our lectures will include slides, so please take notes. We will have quizzes every Friday along with a midterm and a final exam. Okay, let's begin."

Ms. Kahn switches the lights off and takes her place behind the slide projector. A single beam of light pierces the dark classroom, filling the screen on the wall. Ms. Kahn transports the students into the world of Impressionists Monet and Renoir with their dreamlike use of color and brushwork. Halfway through the period, she shows a slide of Vincent van Gogh's self-portrait. Ms. Kahn lectures about the Dutch painter's tragic life and his profound expression through his art.

With a click of her remote, the carousel advances to a slide of *The Starry Night*. Sophie is mesmerized by the artwork and starts to sketch it in her notes. Ms. Kahn describes the painting in an animated tone: "*The Starry Night* was painted in 1889. Imagine, almost a hundred years ago. Look at the swirling brushstrokes and the wonderful blues and yellows. The moon… the stars…the night sky comes alive!"

Sophie is furiously sketching when someone walks into the room and stops right in front of the projection screen. The figure, looking down at a card, is bathed in the painting. The boy looks up at Ms. Kahn at the back of the room, squinting past the light obscuring his vision, and says, "Sorry, is this modern art history?"

Sophie suddenly stops sketching. *I know that voice*, she thinks, searching her memory. She lifts her head to see the figure emerge and disappear into the brilliant painting.

Ms. Kahn walks over to her desk and looks at her list of students. "Hello, are you Matthieu Bernard?"

"Yes. I am sorry that I'm late," the boy responds as he steps out of the painting. "The counselor wrote the wrong classroom on my schedule."

Ms. Kahn points to an empty desk next to Sophie and says, "Why don't you sit there. Please see me after class and I can go over what you missed."

Matthieu walks over to the desk and sits down. He glances over at Sophie and her drawing of the Van Gogh painting. In the darkness, Sophie tries to focus on the lecture, but she is intrigued by the stranger who is sitting beside her. Then, with the feeling of being jolted from a dream, the lights of the classroom turn on.

"Students." Ms. Kahn walks to the front of the classroom. "We will continue with Van Gogh and the Post-Impressionist painters tomorrow. Please see me with any questions."

Since it is the last class of the day, the students quickly gather their belongings and rush out of the classroom.

Ms. Kahn starts to move the slide projector cart and sees that Matthieu and Sophie are the last students remaining. "Matthieu," Ms. Kahn calls out, "I would like to go over the classwork with you before you leave."

Matthieu gets up from his desk. In what seems like slow motion to Sophie, she turns her head in his direction. She gazes at his lips as he says, "I like your drawing." Without lingering, he walks to the front of the classroom to meet with Ms. Kahn.

Who is he? He has an accent. What is his story? Sophie is intrigued by the possibilities.

Sophie walks from Ms. Kahn's class down the hall to art room 104 and peeks through the door. The room is partitioned—one side is filled with long art tables, and the other side is set up as a darkroom. CJ is busy writing names on the blackboard with a small piece of chalk: PHOTO-TASTIC, CAMERA OBSCURA, FILM AND MOTION, FREEZE FRAME. Sophie walks in and places her books and purse on a table.

Susan soon follows, unloads her books next to Sophie's, and sighs. "I already have a week's worth of homework tonight." Lowering her head onto her books like a pillow, she says, "Can we change this to the nap club?"

Seeing that CJ is still busy at the chalkboard, Sophie leans close to Susan and whispers, "Su, there is a new guy in my art history class. He has dark hair, blue eyes, and some sort of accent. His name is Matthieu. Have you seen him?"

Susan sits upright with immediate interest and replies, "No. Did you talk to him?"

Sophie opens her notebook to her sketch of Van Gogh's *The Starry Night*. "He said he liked my drawing, and—"

CJ gets frustrated that they are whispering and not paying attention to what he is writing on the chalkboard. "Hey, remember why we are here?" he calls. Sophie scribbles quickly on a piece of paper, tears it off, and places it in Susan's hand. Susan reads, *I'll tell you more later!*

CJ asks, "Okay, should our club meet every Monday from three thirty to four thirty?"

Sophie nods. Susan responds, "Yes! I have Chemistry Club on Wednesdays, so that works well for me too."

CJ, relieved that the first decision was an easy one, feels that things are going smoothly. "Next, look over the names I came up with and our mission for the club."

Sophie and Susan read the chalkboard:

MISSION: THE (NAME HERE) CLUB PROMOTES CREATIVE EXPRESSION AND AN APPRECIATION OF VISUAL STORYTELLING AND CINEMATIC IMAGES.

CLUB NAMES:
PHOTO-TASTIC
CAMERA OBSCURA
FILM AND MOTION
FREEZE FRAME

Susan walks up to CJ, takes the chalk from his hand, and crosses out Photo-Tastic and Freeze Frame. "Photo-Tastic sounds *so* corny. And every time someone says Freeze Frame, they are going to start singing that J. Geils Band song." Susan sings, "*Freeze frame...doot...doot...*"

CJ concedes on those points. "Okay, so how about Camera Obscura or Film and Motion?"

Sophie shrugs, not feeling these either. "Sorry, CJ, but where is the drama? I thought we were going to be avant-garde and cool."

CJ thinks. "Well, we are looking to be *cinematic*?"

Susan chimes in with the first thing that comes into her mind. "How about the Cinematic Breakfast Club?"

They all laugh, and then Sophie blurts out, "Su, you've got it!" Susan and CJ both look surprised that Sophie seems serious. Sophie walks over to the chalkboard, picks up the eraser, and erases all the names. Then she writes across the board in large letters:

THE CINEMATICS CLUB

CJ, Susan, and Sophie all take a long look at the name. They all nod, and smiles form on their faces as they realize they are starting something new, entirely their own creation. Sophie takes a piece of plain white paper from her notebook and starts to sketch a flyer.

The Cinematics Club
Every Monday from 3:30 p.m. to 4:30 p.m.
Art Room #104

Love movies and photographs?
Join our club and learn about creating your own with
an expert professional photographer mentor!

Club Leaders:
Charles James, Sophie Alexander, and Susan Tran

"I'll work on the artwork tonight," Sophie explains. "Then I'll make copies to post on the quad bulletin boards."

Susan glances at the clock; it is already four thirty. She feels energized. "Time flies! Sophie, thanks for doing the flyer. CJ, let your uncle know about our club and see if he can be here starting next Monday. I'll work on our meeting notes."

They all grab their stuff and head out. As they emerge at the front of the school, the moon hovers in the late-afternoon sky. It may be only the first day of school, but Sophie senses that this year will be something completely different.

4

Rewind and Hit Play

No. That sucks. Ugh.

Sophie turns to a blank page in her sketchbook. She has been drawing different logos for the Cinematics Club and is not happy with any of her designs. Sitting at her bedroom desk, Sophie has already finished that day's load of homework, which is neatly stacked on the floor.

Need some inspiration.

She flips through some of her magazines—*Interview, Seventeen, Art News*. Sophie imagines a life beyond high school, the life of exciting art gallery openings and fashion shows that she sees in the magazine spreads. She is planning on pursuing museum studies and has been researching colleges on the East Coast.

Sophie's attention meanders up to her bulletin board, where there are photos of her family and friends. They capture the happiness and freedom of past summers: her dad swimming in the Mediterranean Sea on their family trip to Europe; her brother doing a cannonball into their pool; the reggae festival she, Susan, and CJ went to for her birthday.

Looking at the photo of the three of them, Sophie feels a shared bond beyond their friendship—something deeper, since they are all first-generation Americans. All of their parents came to the U.S. looking to start new lives. Sophie's Jewish parents emigrated from Europe in the 1940s, Susan's parents fled Vietnam during the war in the 1960s, and CJ's parents met in Kenya and left during the military upheaval in the 1950s. They lived in England temporarily before making a home in Los Angeles. Sophie feels like she is living somewhere between the turbulent past of her parents and a hopeful future that is not yet written. It's like looking at a Polaroid picture that is just starting to reveal the full image.

Sophie goes over to a shelf stacked with records and books. Flipping through her albums, she pulls out one by UB40, reminding her of the summer concert. The needle hits the vinyl on "Don't Break My Heart." Sophie starts to dance and grabs books about the art of the 1920s and 1930s, scanning the pages. She loves this period. The ideas start flowing, and Sophie finally hits upon the mark—*I've got it!* She pulls out a fresh piece of paper and sketches a flyer for the Cinematics Club. Inspired by the asymmetrical designs of El Lissitzky, the logo cuts across the paper on a diagonal: two interlocking C's, a symbol for the creative eye.

Then the phone rings. She hears her dad's voice and then his footsteps getting louder. Sophie turns off the stereo as a knock comes at her bedroom door.

"Sophie," her dad says with a stern tone, peering into the room, "Susan is on the phone. It *is* a Monday, so don't be on all night."

Sophie knows her dad takes study time seriously and wants to reassure him. "Oh, I am *sure* she has a question about the chemistry homework. I won't be long. Thanks." She closes the door, picks up the phone in her room, and waits to hear the click that means her dad has hung up the phone in the kitchen.

"Hi, Sophie?" Susan whispers. "Sorry for calling so late, but I want to know more about this Matthieu."

Sophie grabs the phone from her desk, moves it to the bed, and starts to recount the events. "I first saw him on Saturday at the theater, not knowing I would ever see him again." Lying down on her bed, she twirls the phone cord around her fingers as she looks around her room. Her eyes catch on her Van Gogh poster. "But then he appeared again out of a Van Gogh painting!"

Confused, Susan asks, "Wait, what? Did you say he came to life from a painting?"

Sophie realizes it sounds completely ridiculous, but the picture in her mind has not faded. "Yes, well, umm…at least from the projection of a Van Gogh painting in art history class. I'll get to see him again tomorrow, so I'll let you know more!"

"I'm intrigued." Susan says.

Before putting the phone down, Sophie adds, "I finished the flyer for the Cinematics Club. You and CJ are going to love it! Night, Su!"

5

Going Clubbin'

The first week of school at Noble High has finally come to a close. The palm trees sway furiously back and forth across the blue sky. Students leaving school, shielding their hair from the gusts of wind, are losing the battle. The mousse and hairspray they have applied are no match for nature.

In the administration building, a flock of teachers seeks refuge in the teachers' lounge. Sophie finishes pinning their club flyer on the announcements board. Principal Patterson hurries past her, speaking into his walkie-talkie: "What do you mean my car is covered in shaving cream?"

Sophie buttons up her oversized black blazer and exits the building. She forges ahead through the gusty wind. Excited to announce their group, she makes the rounds, posting the Cinematics Club flyer around campus.

Sophie comes to her last stop—the bulletin board outside the arts building. Stacking her books and the flyers on the ground, she pulls out a sheet to pin to the board. Another gust of wind comes up and blows the flyers down the walkway. A boot lands on one, and then a hand grabs the rest. Sophie turns away from the bulletin board and realizes it is Matthieu who has captured the flying papers. Walking toward her, he reads one of the sheets. "The Cinematics Club. Is this your creation?"

Sophie thinks, *This time our meeting is no coincidence.*

"Yes, this is a new club I'm starting with two of my friends." She extends her hand to collect the flyers and says, "Thank you for catching these. I'm Sophie, by the way."

Handing her the flyers, he says, "Hi, I'm Matthieu." He picks up her belongings from the ground and asks, "Was that you working at the movie theater ticket booth?"

Sophie nods as she takes her things.

"That's cool. You must see a lot of great movies."

"I work at La Luna on the weekends." Sophie checks the time on her watch. "I have to get going. I'm getting a ride to work with my friend Susan. Do you want to walk with me?"

"Sure." As they walk through the campus, Matthieu says, "I love films like *Mad Max*. My dad works on movies. He's not an actor—he's behind the scenes. So he works a lot."

Sophie and Matthieu arrive at the school entrance and Susan waves from the front seat of her sister's car.

"That's Susan." Sophie points her out. "She's my best friend, and she's also in the club."

Seeing that their time together is abruptly ending, Matthieu asks, "Can I have one of your flyers? I'm interested in seeing what your club is about."

Sophie hands him a flyer. Walking toward the car, she turns back and leaves him with a final thought. "See you on Monday, Matthieu. We *are* the Cinematics Club."

******

Andrea's car comes to a stop in front of La Luna Theater. Sophie and Susan get out. "Thanks, Andrea," Sophie says. "My mom is picking me up later, so we'll drop Susan at home."

It's a Friday night, and Andrea is preoccupied with her plans. While looking over her face in the rear-view mirror, she casually replies, "Oh, okay. That sounds great. Have fun. I am running home to change. Keith is taking me out to this new dance club called the Metro! Bye!"

Susan and Sophie laugh as she drives off. Susan heads toward Ciao Gelato, and Sophie walks into La Luna. She enters Robert's office as he hangs up the phone. Movie posters cover every wall—*Tron, Caddyshack, Cheech & Chong, Raiders of the Lost Ark*. He clears a few stacks of papers off his desk and starts to scribble on a sheet marked SCHEDULE.

"Sophie," Robert says as he writes, "Oscar is running late today. I am not cutting him any slack because he's my nephew, but my sister is at the dentist and out of it, so Oscar is driving her home. I am going to cover the box office for you. Can you cover the concession stand until he arrives?"

"Of course, Robert," Sophie replies, retrieving her name tag. She walks over to the concession stand and assesses the state of the counter. The candy shelf is cleaned out from the matinee, and she needs to get the popcorn machine running. At least there is time before the next movie.

Sophie cleans the counters and restocks the shelves, putting aside the broken candy for herself and the other workers. After loading the popcorn machine, she folds up the cardboard candy boxes and places a candy bar in her back pants pocket. Walking past the entrance to the theater with its rows of velvet seats and brilliant blue carpeting with stars, she takes in the beauty of the empty space. Then she pushes open the exit door with her back and heads out into the alley. She puts the boxes in the dumpster and spots Dylan, smoking a cigarette as he anxiously paces back and forth.

"Hey, Dylan. Are you still waiting for the film delivery?" Sophie asks. She walks over and gives him the candy bar stowed in her pocket.

"Thanks, Moonlight. Yeah, Rikki was supposed to be here thirty minutes ago!" Dylan responds as he glances down the alley. "I need the reel for tonight's first showing of *After Hours*."

As he takes a bite of the candy bar, they see a vehicle speeding toward them. The van, decorated with the company name Reel World Ltd., comes to a screeching halt. The side door slides open, and a guy with long permed black hair jumps out with the film reels.

"*Dude*, sorry I'm late. The van got a flat tire, and I couldn't find a pay phone," Rikki Russo says, handing the canisters to Dylan. Rikki delivers film reels to movie theaters during the day and is the lead guitarist in a local hair metal band called Searing Magmä at night.

"Are you coming to my show Saturday night at Pete's Hitching Post?" Rikki asks. "Here are our rad new stickers!" He shoves the oval decals into Dylan's shirt pocket. They are decorated with a drawing of the Norse mythological fire giant Surtr emerging from a volcano, raising a guitar up into the lightning sky.

"Sure, I'll see if I can make it." Dylan grips the reels and runs up the back fire escape stairs, a quick way to get to the projection booth. Rikki jumps into his van and speeds off down the alley.

Sophie returns to the theater and checks on the popcorn maker. She scoops up a cup of popcorn, pumps on a splash of buttery liquid, and sets it on the counter. The candy is nicely organized, and the aroma of fresh buttered popcorn fills the lobby.

Everything is ready.

A line of movie-goers peers through the glass front doors, eager for the show. Sophie pops into the ladies' room to freshen up before the crowd descends on the concession stand. Grabbing her black blazer from the lounge chair, she discovers a torn piece of paper in the right front pocket. She unfolds it.

Sophie,

There is a trail near my house. Do you want to go for a walk on Sunday afternoon?

—Matthieu

6
Fire Road

Matthieu pulls up to Sophie's house. The silver convertible, a two-seat 1980 Fiat Spider, looks very sophisticated and adventurous compared to the neighborhood's suburban station wagons. The car was handed down to him by his dad when he turned sixteen. This is the first time Matthieu is seeing where Sophie lives, and he is a bit self-conscious about meeting her parents. He hopes that an afternoon walk will seem less like a date and will prevent her father from putting him under a microscope. He is dressed simply in jeans and a plaid shirt over a plain white T-shirt.

Before Matthieu gets all the way up the walk, the front door opens. Sophie's dad, Simon, appears.

"Hello, Mr. Alexander, my name is Matthieu." He extends his hand toward Sophie's dad, hoping to make a good impression. With a firm handshake, Matthieu continues, "I am in Sophie's art history class. I thought she might like to go for a walk, since the trails around my house have a nice view."

Simon, being a protective father, examines the stylish convertible, which reminds him of his dating days. "Hello,

Matthieu. It is nice of you to come by. I am glad that we can meet." Sophie's dad pulls a piece of paper and a pen from his shirt pocket and hands them to Matthieu. "Why don't you write down your address and phone number. I'll come by tonight at six o'clock to pick up Sophie. I always enjoy driving in the canyon."

Sophie comes outside as her dad tucks the pen and paper back into his shirt pocket. She is dressed simply in jeans and a long T-shirt with a wide black belt that nicely cinches her waist. A colorful scarf is tied around her wavy hair. Sophie's mom, rounding out the Alexander Review Committee, also comes out to meet Matthieu. She is used to making sure everyone is attended to. "Hello, I'm Sophie's mom, Sarah. Would you like to take some sodas or snacks with you?"

Matthieu shakes her hand and smiles. "Thank you, Sarah. That would be nice."

Sarah is pleased and dashes back inside, then reappears with cans of sodas and small bags of chips.

Sophie and Matthieu walk to his car, and he opens the door for her. Sophie's mom smiles, excited by the sight of her daughter growing up, while her dad takes a deep breath, eyeing this boy in a convertible with his little girl.

✳✳✳✳✳✳

The Fiat turns off the busy main canyon road onto a narrow street: Windswept Canyon Way. The tall trees form a canopy that provides deep shade from the afternoon sun. Matthieu shifts the car into a low gear and makes the ascent up the steep driveway. He parks under a low-slung carport. Sophie realizes that this is no ordinary ranch-style home.

"Ever since my dad saw the movie *Mon Oncle*, he always wanted a modern house. This one, built in the 1950s, is an architectural Case Study home," Matthieu explains as he leads Sophie to the door.

When they step into the living room, they are surrounded by floor-to-ceiling glass. Sophie is mesmerized by the sight of such a unique place, from the stone floors to the wood-paneled walls. Spinning around, she says, "This is a cool hideaway!" She notices how quiet it is. "Is your family home? I would like to meet them."

Matthieu walks Sophie to the kitchen. "My dad is out with my stepmom and little brother, Leon. They should be back later. Are you hungry? We can take some food with us on our walk. There's a bench overlooking the Valley."

Sophie eagerly replies, "Sure! My mom already gave us the sodas and chips."

Matthieu puts together goat cheese sandwiches and gathers everything into a khaki military-style canvas backpack. He grabs his jean jacket and his house keys, which hang on a hook by the door.

Matthieu and Sophie climb up to a trail above the house. The cool shade of the trees soon gives way to the bright afternoon sun. The Valley fans out below, a sea of houses in every direction.

"These trails are called fire roads," Matthieu says as they walk along the canyon. "Firefighters use them to get up to the hills if a fire breaks out. I like coming up here."

A few people pass them on the road—girls in neon leotards and leggings and an older couple in polo shirts and shorts.

Matthieu spots the bench he'd mentioned. He offers his hand to help Sophie up the steep steps carved into the hillside. Once they settle on the wooden bench, he pulls out the food and drinks from his backpack.

"That's a cool bag," Sophie says. "Where is it from?"

"It's an old British military bag. My dad found it at a French flea market," Matthieu says.

Sophie takes a bite of the creamy cheese sandwich. "France—is that where you are from?"

For the first time, Matthieu feels at ease with Sophie and slowly lets his guard down. "Yes. My father was born there, but he grew up in England." Matthieu opens a bag of chips and continues, "He went back to Paris after college. He met my mom on a movie called *Transporteur*. She was a costume designer."

Matthieu turns away and looks out at the view. He attempts to hold back his feelings, but his voice cracks slightly as he says, "She was driving to the set and was hit by a drunk driver. I was nine years old." He tries to clear his voice by drinking some soda and continues, "My dad just wanted to leave after that and moved us to New York for work. He met my stepmom there, and they had Leon. This summer he got a job here."

"I'm so sorry about your mom," Sophie says compassionately.

The late-afternoon sun gives way to dusk. Sophie looks out over the suburban landscape, then turns back to Matthieu. "Do you know what it is like to feel everything? I mean, *everything*?"

Matthieu looks into her eyes and understands. He leans in and kisses her. It seems like a sudden impulse, but he feels an undeniable connection to her.

The sky has transitioned into a peaceful watercolor palette of blue grays, the last orange light of the sun illuminating the horizon. It is peaceful as they walk past the native plants, and the city lights spread out across the Valley below. Sophie shields her arms from the cold that has arrived with the setting sun. Matthieu takes off his jean jacket and gives it to her to wear. When they approach his home, they see the headlights of a car driving up the hill. Sophie's dad watches them with a hawklike presence from his blue Peugeot sedan.

"Hi, Dad. I'm coming," Sophie calls out, and hands Matthieu back his jacket.

Sophie and Matthieu forgo the usual parting words like *thanks* or *I had a great time*. Sophie just gives him a smile, and he answers it with his own.

Simon's car slowly maneuvers down the driveway. Matthieu lingers in the night before going inside.

7

A Circle of Friends

It is three fifteen on Monday, and CJ is the first to arrive in art room 104 with his uncle William, who is dressed in a suit and a tie. Susan and Sophie, both juggling their school books and poster boards, make their way into the art room next. Students run past them, laughing, on their way out of school.

The classroom still exhibits signs of the last class of the day—the smell of photographic chemicals and prints that are hanging on a rope to dry.

"Susan, Sophie, this is my uncle William," CJ says.

"Nice to meet you," William says, shaking their hands. He was the first in their family to emigrate from Kenya, which helped CJ's parents when they applied for their visas to the United States. He has brought a cardboard box filled with photography samples and various photo and film cameras to demonstrate.

"Is this the whole club?" William asks with surprise.

"I posted flyers all over the school," Sophie replies assuredly. "It is not quite three thirty; I am *sure* more people will come. We need at least six students to form an official club."

Sophie positions the poster boards against the chalkboard, displaying the club logo along with CJ's mission statement.

"Hey, Sophie, thanks for inviting me," Oscar Garcia says as he enters the noticeably empty room. "Looking forward to being in the club!"

Oscar is a short Latino boy with a slim frame. His shiny black hair is slicked back with gel, and his clothes are nicely styled. He started working at La Luna over the summer around the same time Sophie was hired by his uncle Robert. Oscar takes a seat and looks around with his usual large grin, which helps hide his nerves in new situations.

Sophie posts the club sign on the door. *Only four people... maybe I should have put up balloons or something?*

A new girl walks in to the classroom holding a flyer. She has long dark hair pulled back in a braid.

"Uh…hi, I am here for the club," the girl announces shyly while looking at everyone in the room. "I am Anisha Patel."

Susan instantly recognizes Anisha and waves her over. "Hi, Anisha! Aren't you in Mr. Hart's chemistry class?"

Anisha is surprised that Susan remembers her, since she sits on the opposite side of the classroom from her and Sophie.

"Yeah, I am in your class," she says softly. "You are *so* lucky to be lab partners with Sophie. This boy, Naveen, sits at my table and stares at me every class like we are boy-friend-girlfriend."

William has set up a variety of film cameras and a video camera on a table. "I think we should get started. Hello, every-one, my name is Mr. Omolo, and I am your club mentor. We will be meeting every Monday from three thirty to four thirty."

Sophie's mind starts to race, wondering why Matthieu hasn't shown up. *He was in art history, and he didn't look sick.*

She comes to a disappointing realization—*he isn't going to show up after all.*

Just then, Ms. Kahn walks in with Matthieu and introduces herself to William.

"Hello, I'm Beverly Kahn, the art history teacher. Matthieu was helping me put up a Gauguin poster in my classroom. He told me that he was coming here next, and I am very excited to hear about this club."

"Nice to meet you, Beverly," William replies warmly. "I'm William Omolo."

"You have very bright students here, and I know that they will create some incredible work." As she adjusts her kimono-style jacket, Ms. Kahn smiles and says, "If you need anything, I'll be just down the hall."

Sophie beams with satisfaction that this club is becoming a reality. *Matthieu came through after all.*

"Okay, we have hit the magic number of six students," Mr. Omolo says with a sigh of relief. "Let the Cinematics Club begin!" Loosening his tie, he says, "First I'll tell you a little bit about myself and the types of cameras I've brought. Then each of you can tell us about yourself and what you want to create as a group project."

Mr. Omolo walks over to his box of photographs. He has a natural confidence and is warm and genuinely interested in inspiring the students.

"We are all creators," he says. "Each of us has talent and a point of view that can be shared. In this club, we will express ourselves through photography and film."

He holds up a newspaper and explains, "I work as a news photographer at the *Los Angeles Daily Tribune*. In my job, I travel all over this city capturing the happiest and saddest events, from fires and deaths to everyday people doing extraordinary acts."

He picks up his Nikon film camera with pride. "This is my camera of choice, but you can use an instamatic film camera, such as this Kodak, or even a Polaroid. Your final group project will be to make a film that we can present at the school's winter assembly. I'll teach you to use a sixteen-millimeter film camera and the latest technology, an eight-millimeter Sony home video camera.

"What I want to leave you with is that these are the tools. It is important to know what each can do. But ultimately, it is you, *each of you,* who will bring something to this project that no one else can see—who will make it special."

Now that he has captured their attention, William says, "Okay, enough about me. Let's hear a little bit from each of you."

The intense afternoon sun is cutting through the window blinds, creating dramatic lines across Susan's face. CJ grabs the Polaroid camera from the table and snaps a picture.

Ca-jung! A small, square piece of blank film slides out the front of the camera. He grabs the photo and waves it as an image develops.

CJ holds up the picture. "Hi, my name is Charles James, but I go by CJ. I am one of the founders of this club. I want be a professional commercial photographer."

Sophie takes the next opportunity to speak. "Hi, I'm Sophie Alexander. I am interested in art history and being a museum curator. I love artists like Keith Haring and Jean-Michel Basquiat. I drew the club logo, and I am very interested in learning how to make a real film."

"I'm Oscar Garcia. I like movies, and I thought this would be a good way to learn how to make one. I also can help with setting up the props and equipment."

"Hi, I'm Anisha Patel." She initially plans to say something safe but then decides to let the truth come out. "I know I'm going into nursing eventually, since that is what my mom does. But I would actually love to try acting in a movie."

"I'm Matthieu Bernard. My dad works in movies, but I am here because I don't really know anyone at school. Um, except Sophie, that is." Sensing that he is not getting off on the right foot with Mr. Omolo, Matthieu tries to save himself. "I am also a *big* fan of directors such as Stanley Kubrick and Ridley Scott."

Susan is the last one to speak. "Hi, I'm Susan Tran. Since I am into chemistry, I would love to learn about the types of film from a pro. And also I took typing, so I can put our script together."

"Thanks, everyone, for your introductions," Mr. Omolo responds. "Let's gather closer as I demonstrate the equipment."

$$* * * * * *$$

During the next few club meetings, Mr. Omolo teaches them how to use the cameras and gives lectures about important photographers from Dorothea Lange and Man Ray to Malick Sidibé.

Everyone in the club soon becomes close friends, and they meet at lunchtime to work on ideas for their movie.

One afternoon, they are hanging out in their usual spot under a tree. "Susan, do you have any more of those spring rolls?"

Oscar asks as he stares deep into his lunch bag. Hoping it'll sweeten the deal, he adds, "I'll trade you my barbecue chips."

"Here, Oscar," Susan says as she hands him one, "but you can definitely keep those chips."

Oscar bites into the roll and jokes, "Can your mom make extra for me every day?"

"Actually, I made these. Since I became a vegetarian, I have been making my mom's recipes without the meat."

Matthieu pulls a cassette tape out of his bag and places it in Sophie's hands. "Check out this mixtape. I added some songs by The Clash, Talking Heads, and Simple Minds."

Anisha, brushing the grass off her Reebok sneakers, is excited to get their film started. She opens up her notebook to the Cinematics Club notes. "So, what do you think we should make our movie about?"

CJ, reclining on the lawn with his head resting on his backpack, watches the sun filter through the tree's leaves. He starts throwing out ideas. "Mystery, suspense, and *definitely* a good action scene. That would be a cool movie."

"What if we are secret agents on a mission?" Susan suggests, snacking on carrot sticks.

"I think it would be cool to shoot in black and white. Mr. Omolo showed us how dramatic images look with different lighting. We could do cool makeup and clothes just like in old silent movies!" Sophie eagerly responds.

Anisha, looking confused, holds up her sheet of notes. "Wait. Wait a sec…I think we are all over the place."

CJ sits up. "Well, whatever we decide, it *has* to have a cool soundtrack." They laugh—that is one point they all agree on.

"I like the idea of a spy film," Anisha says. "Everyone likes James Bond movies."

Matthieu visualizes the potential. "If we film it in black and white like an old movie, it will look edgy. Think Coppola and *Rumble Fish*."

"I can start writing the script, if everyone gives me ideas. Also, we should take turns filming scenes," Sophie proclaims.

Principal Patterson casually greets students on his walk around the quad. His nonchalant swagger quickly disappears as he spots his usual group of detention students and calls out, "Hey, pick up your trash!"

He dashes up to the quad stage to make an announcement.

"Hello, Noble Knights! This is your commander in chief, Principal Patterson," he says, trying to generate some enthusiasm from the sea of students. "I have been hearing exciting things about the clubs this year. Of course, our football team has made a great start, and it is already leading against last year's winner, Creekwater High. Let's also give some applause to the Noble Knights cheerleaders, our school spirit ambassadors! Our math and science clubs are prepping for their competitions. Our chemistry teacher, Mr. Hart, is also leading the Noble Hikers Club." He peers out across the lawn and calls, "Mr. Hart, come on up and tell us about your hiking trip."

Mr. Hart jogs up to the stage, sporting his Member's Only jacket and Levi's. He opens up his jacket like he is Superman to reveal a Noble Hikers Club T-shirt.

"The Noble Hikers Club is planning a rigorous trek in Yosemite. We are going to camp out and examine the terrain and organisms of the region. We will share photos at our winter assembly! I would say that we are going to be roughing it, but I will be bringing a portable TV." He laughs.

"Fantastic! Thank you, Mr. Hart." Principal Patterson scans his list of clubs and wraps up his announcements. "One last club to mention is our leader in technology, the AV Club. They will be recording all of our exhilarating events, including our upcoming Halloween dance. They will present a collage of highlights in our first-ever Noble High music video, which will premiere at our winter assembly. Thank you!" Principal Patterson sprints off the stage and takes a victory lap before heading back into the administration building.

Sophie turns to the group and says with disappointment, "He did not even mention our club, and we are the only new club this year."

"Don't worry, Sophie." Matthieu wraps his arms around her for comfort. "They don't know what we can do yet. We'll make something original, and it will be something to be proud of."

"We are all in it now," CJ says as he throws his hand into the center. "We are the Cinematics Club!"

They pile their hands on top of each other, pledging their solidarity.

8

Keep Your Eyes on the Road

Saturday mornings hold a new meaning for Sophie now that she has school and a weekend job. They are no longer reserved for waking up at ten and lounging around watching cartoons, like she did when she was in grade school. But there is one holdover she is not willing to give up: waiting for her breakfast cereal to completely dissolve into her bowl of milk.

Sophie sits on her fluffy bedroom carpet with a composition book and begins writing out the script for the movie. Looking over the club's notes, she transcribes a few lines, then goes back to stirring the cereal. The moment arrives when the cereal flakes reach precise sogginess. Pure joy overcomes her as she takes the first bite. A knock on her bedroom door interrupts this euphoria.

"Yes, come in," Sophie mumbles, swallowing the mouthful of cereal.

"Sophie," her mom says as she cracks open the bedroom door, "your dad is out front, and he brought you something from a garage sale."

"Uh, okay," Sophie replies. She wonders why he hasn't come in to tell her himself.

Sophie's mom and dad aren't like the parents on a TV show. They don't sit around and talk about their feelings. What is most important to them is being there for their kids and providing them with a stable home and childhood, something they both lost when they fled Europe during World War II. Sophie's dad is sensible with the family's finances, but for some reason, the sight of a garage sale always lures him in.

Sophie opens the front door and sees her dad in the driveway next to a car she doesn't recognize—a tan wood-paneled four-door Jeep Grand Wagoneer.

"Did you buy mom another car?" Sophie asks.

"No, Sophie. This car is not for Mom. It's for *you*." Simon shakes the car keys.

It takes a few seconds for Sophie to process this information.

"For *me*? Really?" Sophie responds, hoping this is not a dream.

"I was going to pick up some tools at the hardware store last weekend, and I passed this big garage sale. The man was selling everything in his house," Sophie's dad recounts. "He asked me if I was interested in buying this car. I thought of you, since you have your driver's license now. With your job and school, it will be much easier for you if you have your own car."

Sophie, overcome with excitement, lunges to embrace her mom and dad. "Thank you! I can't even believe that this is *my car!*"

She slowly walks around the Jeep, taking it in from all angles, then peers through the driver's side window. Her gaze is drawn to the dashboard—*it even has a cassette deck!*

Simon hands her the keys, and she slides into the driver's seat. Sticking her head out the window, she enthusiastically asks, "Do you want to go for a ride around the block?"

Sophie's mom defers to Simon. "I'll let your father have the first trip. That way he can go over how everything works." She already feels her heart palpitating just thinking about her daughter on the road.

"Dad, let's see how it drives!" Sophie beckons to her father.

Simon gets in. He keeps his eye on the speedometer and gear shift just in case he needs to take over.

Sophie turns on the engine and makes sure every movement is right: *shift into reverse, check the rear-view mirror, look over your shoulder as you back up.*

She slowly drives down their block, and the neighbors wave, taking notice of Sophie at the wheel. At a stop sign, it strikes her how clean the interior is.

"It looks brand new! I wonder why that man was getting rid of everything," Sophie says.

"I was wondering the same thing," her dad answers. "I got to talking with him. He mentioned that he was getting ready to retire and was going to be moving soon. I could tell by his accent that he was French."

"Well, Dad, you were *so* lucky to have come across his sale! I'm sure he was glad to know that his car was going to a good home," Sophie remarks with a big smile.

Sophie feels immediately at ease in the car. She glances over to her dad, resting his arm on the door. She rolls down her window, mirroring him, and puts her elbow on her door. The cool morning wind blows through her hair as she navigates the car down her street.

Sarah hears the car pull back into the driveway and breathes a sigh of relief. Simon is happy to be home too so he can enjoy his usual Saturday morning breakfast and newspaper.

"How did she drive?" Sarah asks Simon, bringing him a cup of coffee and toast.

"She's a good driver, actually. And luckily her school and work are not that far away," Simon reassures Sarah as he gets comfortable at the kitchen table. He puts on his glasses and starts reading the newspaper.

Sophie's mind races as she looks around her bedroom. *What should I wear to work today? Do I have time to call everyone and tell them about my car?*

She looks over at the clock; it is almost eleven a.m. Sophie realizes that she has no time to break the exciting news and puts together an outfit for work. She pulls her hair up into a ponytail, applies some lipstick, and grabs her purse. As she heads out the door, she remembers to bring her camera so that she can start taking pictures at the movie theater.

Her mom hands her a coin purse on her way out.

"Here, Sophie, keep this in your car in case you ever need to use a pay phone in an emergency."

"Thanks, Mom!" Sophie replies gratefully.

"Let me take a picture of you in front of the car." Sophie's mom takes a few pictures and hands the camera back to her daughter.

Sophie confidently opens the car and gets settles in her seat. She stores the coin purse in the glove compartment. Placing her camera in her purse, she notices the mixtape Matthieu gave her and pops it into the tape player. Sophie drives along the boulevard with Simple Minds' "Alive and Kicking" playing, and suddenly the world looks a lot different.

She pulls into the big parking lot behind the movie theater and finds a space next to Robert's Datsun.

Sophie walks around to the Jeep's rear and opens the large back door. She realizes that in her excitement, she forgot to pack a lunch. As she takes in how spacious the trunk is, she spots a metal box. She quickly pushes it out of view and thinks, *This must be something the garage sale man forgot about when he sold the car.*

CJ spots Sophie closing the trunk of the Jeep as he drives his Vespa into the parking lot.

"Is this yours, Sophie?" he asks, pulling up beside her.

"Yes! Can you believe it?" Sophie replies in amazement. "My parents surprised me this morning. I didn't have time to call anyone. As a matter of fact, I better get into the theater. Don't tell Susan! I want to see her reaction. She should be working today."

"Sure." CJ maneuvers his scooter around her and drives off toward Video Vault. He calls out, "I definitely want a ride later!"

Sophie nods and walks around the front of the theater. She looks up at the marquee, which reads INVASION U.S.A. That explains the line of people dressed up like the movie's star, Chuck Norris, in head-to-toe denim.

While Sophie is working, Susan runs up to the little ticket booth and screams at the glass window.

"SOPHIEEEE, CJ told me you got a car!"

Half startled and annoyed, Sophie says, "CJ is supposed to keep it a secret." She screams back, "SURPRISE! It is *so* awesome!"

"I have to get back to the gelato shop, but I couldn't wait to come see you." Susan almost skips away, calling, "Stop by on your break!"

Sophie forgets for a moment what she is doing, then remembers to finish up. She counts the cash, grabs the box, and puts a sign in the window: CLOSED. NEXT SHOWING AT 3 P.M. When she walks through the lobby, she sees Oscar behind the concession stand. It looks like a bomb went off—popcorn is scattered across the counter, and ketchup and mustard have oozed all over the dispensers.

"I think Invasion U.S.A. just happened *here*," Oscar mutters unhappily at the prospect of having to clean up the mess.

Sophie cracks up, then sees that Oscar is not ready to join in on the joke.

"I can help you, Oscar. I am going on my lunch break anyway."

"Thanks, Sophie. But I've got this."

"I'm going to get a sandwich," Sophie says, thinking of a way to cheer him up. "How about I pick one up for you and we can eat them out back? I have a surprise to show you!"

"All right," Oscar says with a sigh, surrendering to the situation. "I'll have this cleaned up by the time you get back." He takes off his jacket and starts wiping down the glass countertop.

Sophie throws her purse over her shoulder and walks out the lobby doors. The afternoon sun streams into her eyes, so she puts on her most recent vintage store find—a pair of cat-eye sunglasses. She walks down the boulevard and glances at the new fall clothes in Chelsea Loft's window. Looking past the mannequins dressed in the latest graphic sweaters, Sophie sees Brittany and Amber from school, carrying armfuls of outfits to try on. Amber whispers something in Brittany's ear. They laugh as they walk into the dressing room.

They look happy together, Sophie thinks.

Sophie arrives at Ciao Gelato and waves to Susan, who is cleaning one of the tables for an eager couple.

"I'm *starving*. Did you take your break yet?" Sophie asks Susan, inhaling the aroma of toasted bread.

"I can meet you in a few minutes," Susan replies as she walks to the counter. "Actually, I want to show you what Francesca, the owner, just brought back from visiting her family in Italy." Susan points to a new prep area with a shiny stainless steel appliance. "Behold, a panini press! We are now serving sandwiches and Italian sodas," Susan proclaims, pointing to the new menu board. "Francesca thought this would be a great addition since no one is making paninis around here. It makes the *best* grilled sandwiches!"

"I thought I smelled something good when I walked in!" Sophie says, reviewing the menu board. "I'll take a cheese panini. Oh, and can I also get one with turkey and cheese? The candy counter got trashed, so I told Oscar I would buy him a sandwich to cheer him up. And can you also include two of those Italian sodas?" Sophie grabs money from her purse to pay.

"Great!" Susan rings up the sale and gets to work crafting the sandwiches. The smell of melting cheese delights everyone in the store. Susan wraps the freshly pressed sandwiches in paper and puts them in a bag with little glass bottles filled with orange soda.

"CJ should be here any minute," Susan tells Sophie. "Why don't you go ahead, and we'll meet you out back on the stairs of the theater."

Sophie cradles the bag as she heads out the door. "Thanks, Susan! Can't wait try your creation!"

Sophie cuts through the alley and sees Oscar on the back stairs of the movie theater. She climbs up and sits down beside

him. This is their favorite hangout spot to catch a few minutes of fresh air on their breaks and watch the action in the
parking lot.

"Did you get the concession stand all cleaned up?" Sophie
asks, handing him a sandwich and soda.

"Thanks for lunch," Oscar responds, still sounding
annoyed. "Yes, I hope the people at the next showing don't trash
it again." He takes a bite, and cheese oozes from the freshly
toasted bread. He asks, "Where did you get this? It's so good!"

"Susan made these!" Sophie exclaims, grabbing a napkin
from the bag. "They are new at Ciao Gelato. Susan and CJ are
coming for their break."

CJ and Susan make their way up the stairs and sit a few
steps below Sophie and Oscar. They dig into their sandwiches.

"Su, these rock," CJ says as he juggles a sandwich in one
hand and the tiny glass soda bottle in the other.

"Thanks!" Susan says, beaming with pride at her new culi-
nary accomplishment.

As they finish up their lunches, Oscar finally says, "Sophie,
you said you had a surprise?"

"Yes, I do! It is in the parking lot. I'll show you!"

They descend the stairs, and Sophie leads them to
her new wagon.

"Sophie, is this *really* yours?" Susan asks in amazement.

"Yes!" Sophie replies excitedly. "My parents surprised me
this morning. I had no time to call anyone."

"This is *the* coolest!" CJ says as he looks inside the car
and grins. "There is *so* much room...you can fit the whole
Cinematics Club in here!"

"It is you, Sophie," Oscar says. "It has your personality."

"Thanks, Oscar." Sophie nods in agreement, then spots the Reel World van pulling into the alley. "I think our break is over—I see Rikki's van. Why don't we plan a trip to Melrose, and everyone can ride in my new car?"

"Okay! Let's plan for next week after we finalize our script with Mr. Omolo," Susan says.

"Let me take a few pictures before we leave," CJ says. He grabs his camera and takes some pictures of them around the wagon. "Sophie, get in the driver's seat. Let me take some shots of you in your sunglasses. I want to get your reflection in the side mirror." CJ crouches down and shoots some quick snaps before they all head back to finish their shifts.

Rikki gets out of the van as Sophie and Oscar walk toward the back of the theater.

"Hey there," Rikki yells out. "I saw that wagon. Nice ride, Sophie."

Sophie dangles the keys in her hand, a proud owner. "Thanks, Rikki!"

Rikki flips his long hair back and picks up his cases. "I'm bringing these reels up to the projection room. By the way, I have another show tonight at the Canoga Fox Club. It's over twenty-one, though. I hope Dylan is gonna show up to this one. I tell him every time we play, and he always flakes."

Sophie and Oscar head into the movie theater through the back door as Rikki carries the cases up the stairs to the projection room. He opens the door and sees Dylan loading a reel onto the projector.

"Here's the delivery. I'll pick these up next week," Rikki says, lowering the metal cases to the floor. He pulls out a flyer from his back pocket and hands it to Dylan. "It is going to be a wild show tonight! We are going to try some *crazy* new stunts."

"Dude, I swear, I am done at six tonight." Dylan grabs the flyer. "I'll be there *for sure!*"

9

A New Look

Mr. Omolo, having finished photographing a City Hall press conference, makes good time as he pulls his 1984 Mazda 626 into the Noble High faculty parking lot. He checks his hair in the mirror, then grabs his leather briefcase along with two cups of java from the Drink 'n' Dunk coffee shop. Dressed in a gray cardigan over a blue patterned button-down shirt, Mr. Omolo walks toward the arts building and hears banging coming from the hallway.

"Hey, didn't I tell you to stop looking at me?" Lee snarls, the wannabe tough boy with a crew cut. He shoves Oscar against the lockers.

Without hesitation, Mr. Omolo drops his briefcase, and the coffee cups splatter against the ground.

"What are you doing?" Mr. Omolo yells, pulling the bully away from Oscar. Seeing that Oscar is shaken up, Mr. Omolo says, "Oscar, go into Ms. Kahn's room and wait for me." Then he turns to Lee, restraining his anger, and says firmly, "Come with me…*now!*"

Oscar picks up his books from the floor and walks quickly to Ms. Kahn's room.

"Oscar, aren't you going to your club meeting?" Ms. Kahn asks, surprised to see him. She turns down the volume on the stereo, which is playing classical music.

"Yes, Ms. Kahn," Oscar replies. He is embarrassed by what just occurred and doesn't tell her any details. "Mr. Omolo saw me in the hall and had something to take care of…" He trails off.

"Oh, I see," Ms. Kahn says cautiously, sensing that he is distracted about something.

Mr. Omolo enters the room with his briefcase and two empty coffee cups. "Hi, Beverly, I took a student making trouble in the hallway to Principal Patterson. It looks like he was late to his usual detention."

Ms. Kahn notices that the coffee cups are empty and laughs. "William, you needed a serious caffeine boost before your club meeting!"

"Uh, no, sorry," he says, disappointed. "I actually picked up one for you on my way here from Drink 'n' Dunk. I accidentally dropped it."

"That's okay," Ms. Kahn replies, smiling as she walks over to her desk. She opens up a paper box. "I picked up these donuts for your club there too. Oscar, why don't you take these with you."

"Thanks, Beverly. I'll make it up to you next week," Mr. Omolo says kindly before leaving with Oscar.

As they walk together down the hall, Mr. Omolo casually confides to Oscar, "The principal is going to expel that jerk. You won't have to worry about him anymore. If you ever have problems and need to talk to someone, you can always talk to me."

Oscar nods, comforted by his sincere words.

Mr. Omolo and Oscar enter the room, which is alive with a cacophony of voices. There are collages of photos and magazine cutouts pinned to poster boards. Sophie, Matthieu, Susan, Anisha, and CJ have already begun reading through the script for their movie.

"Donuts, anyone?" Mr. Omolo announces as Oscar opens the box. "Looks like we have something for everyone…chocolate, plain, sprinkles, and my favorite, which I am claiming—the glazed twist."

"Oscar!" Sophie calls. "Where have you been?"

The group makes a beeline for the donuts, and each one grabs a treat.

Susan, seeing that Oscar is wearing a new T-shirt, exclaims, "Oscar, your Smiths shirt! I love them! I brought copies of the script. Here is one for you. Since you drew the Halloween flyer, can you help us with the storyboards so we can plan the shoot?"

"Sure, Susan," Oscar says, biting into a chocolate donut. As the sugar rush begins, he starts to feel at ease, surrounded by his friends. "I'll get a new sketchbook at the art store."

"Okay, let's get started," Mr. Omolo announces to bring the group back to a structured format. "Take your seats. Before we read the script and review your inspiration imagery, let me take a few minutes to talk about an important photojournalist and street photographer, Henri Cartier-Bresson." As Mr. Omolo turns toward the group and holds up a book of photography, there is a burst of laughter. He doesn't understand why the book would elicit this reaction.

Anisha gestures to the corner of her mouth and says, "Uh, Mr. Omolo, you have a piece of donut hanging there."

Mr. Omolo grabs a napkin and wipes away the sugary donut remnant. With a chuckle, he says, "Thank you, Anisha.

"Henri Cartier-Bresson," he begins, flipping through the large photographs, "is a French street photographer known for capturing one moment in time. It could be a look, an embrace, a laugh. These are what he calls *decisive moments*. So when you are filming your movie, you have a script to work from, but also be open to what happens in the moment."

Mr. Omolo leaves the book open on the table and walks over to the group. "Now, let's go over your script and your ideas for shooting the movie."

Everyone reads from the script in turn, working out their characters. Then they start to brainstorm about locations and wardrobe.

"We can shoot scenes at La Luna. I think the back stairs could be interesting for the lookout scene," Sophie says, and Susan makes a note on the script.

"We can use my house for the agent headquarters. There is always a secret headquarters in any good spy movie," Matthieu adds.

"I can do some cool shots on my scooter," CJ says. He pans around, looking through the movie camera.

Anisha goes over to the boards filled with images. She looks at the pictures of movie stars, both current and classic, and their different fashions: the diaphanous dress Lena Horne wore in *Stormy Weather*; the tailored suits of Bogart and Bacall in *The Big Sleep*; the looks of Jennifer Beals in *Flashdance*, David Bowie, and *Blade Runner*. She turns to the group and asks, "What about the costumes? What are we going to wear? We need a style."

"I think if we mix what we have with some vintage things, it will look great!" Sophie proclaims.

"Are you thinking what I'm thinking?" Susan says, grinning at Sophie. "I think this calls for our Melrose shopping trip."

"I was thinking the same thing!" Sophie agrees. "The theater is closed this weekend for a private event. CJ and Susan, can you take Saturday afternoon off?"

"I can ask Francesca to switch me to later that day," Susan responds.

"Yeah, I can work later in the day too," CJ replies.

"Anisha, Oscar, Matthieu—are you in for Saturday?" Sophie asks excitedly.

Without skipping a beat, they respond in unison, "YES!"

Mr. Omolo wraps up by saying, "Well, this was a very productive meeting. Your script is coming together. By our next meeting, I would like to see storyboards of your scenes, including locations and wardrobe. You can also borrow any of these cameras." Pointing to the equipment, he says, "The Polaroid camera is good for taking quick shots, and you can also use the one-hour Insta-Mat Photo Hut to process a roll of film quickly. Great meeting, everyone!"

Mr. Omolo escorts the group out, and they disperse to their rides: CJ to his scooter, Anisha and Oscar to their moms' cars, and Susan to her brother's. Sophie walks with Matthieu through the student parking lot. It has emptied out except for a few cars remaining from the football practice. The flickering fluorescent streetlights pierce the dark sky.

Sophie opens the door to get into the wagon as Matthieu circles around it for another look.

"This is a great car, Sophie. You're lucky that your dad found that guy who was selling it," Matthieu remarks, making his way back around to her.

"It is *very* lucky. I feel that it was meant to be mine for some reason. Guess what I've been listening to in the car? Your mixtape," Sophie says, starting the engine. She turns up the volume, and Echo & The Bunnymen's "The Killing Moon" plays. She gets out of the car to give Matthieu a hug goodbye. The embrace lingers as they lose themselves into the song.

Sophie speaks softly into his ear and slyly says, "Should we practice for the Halloween dance, because I do not want to be surprised." They start to laugh.

"I better get going," Sophie says hesitantly, pulling away from his embrace. "My parents will start to worry and think I was in an accident."

Sophie gets into the wagon and drives off. Matthieu hears the music slowly drift away with her.

✳ ✳ ✳ ✳ ✳ ✳

"I call shotgun," CJ yells out, driving his Vespa into the parking lot of La Luna. Dressed in a green bomber jacket, cutoff pants, and black Dr. Martens, he jumps off his scooter and darts to the front passenger seat of Sophie's wagon.

"Hey!" Susan calls as she and Anisha race over to the back seats. "We'll each take a turn riding up front. Oscar, you can have the window seat, and I'll squeeze in the middle." Oscar, Susan, and Anisha slide across the burnt-orange leather seats.

Sophie starts the car and turns around. "Okay, does everyone have their seat belts on?" The sound of seat belts clicking closed in unison echoes through the car. "Matthieu is going to meet us down on Melrose. He said we can come back to his house afterward to start filming the movie."

"Cool!" Susan responds, "But Sophie, can we be back here by six? I switched my shift for tonight."

"Same here," CJ says. He starts fiddling with the radio until he comes upon the local music station, KNXS.

"Of course, we'll be back by then. Now, let's hit the road!" Sophie exclaims, navigating the wagon down the boulevard.

The long, wide suburban street lined with familiar stores gives way to the winding canyon road leading into the city. Like a plane descending from the clouds, the car emerges from the green hills onto bustling streets with bumper-to-bumper traffic. Sophie tries to keep her eyes on the road as everyone starts yelling out different things they see out the window.

"Look at her—I love that!" Anisha exclaims, pointing out a girl standing in front of a boutique in a striped jersey dress. She grabs the instamatic camera she borrowed from Mr. Omolo and starts snapping pictures through the open window.

The car turns down Melrose, and a burst of excitement overtakes everyone. A parade of people flows along both sides of the street—punks, new romantics, trendies, and everyone in between.

"Where are we going first?" Oscar asks eagerly, turning back and forth, trying to look at everyone and everything.

"Let's check out X-Ray Specs first," Sophie replies. "It's a vintage store, so we can find some cool retro dresses and blazers."

"Are we going to Mildred's?" Susan asks hesitantly.

"Maybe? It's a trial by fire every time we go there," Sophie answers. She steers her wagon down a residential side street that is lined with cute little white Spanish-style bungalow houses topped with red terra-cotta tile roofs.

"What do you mean?" Anisha asks.

"Well," Sophie elaborates, "it's a used clothing store owned by this woman named Mildred. It's a train wreck inside with clothing racks jammed everywhere, so you really have to dig to find anything."

"And there are *no* price tags," Susan adds, "so Mildred just yells out a price when you ask her how much something costs. If she is in a good mood, you'll get a steal. But most of the time she's in a cranky mood, so she tries to get more money than the item is worth."

"She used to be an extra in all the movies with Joan Crawford and Bette Davis and will tell you the dirt on old Hollywood," Sophie says.

Susan imitates the way Mildred talks in an exaggerated dramatic voice. "Oooh, honey…that dress was worn by Rita Hayworth." She fakes having a throbbing headache, clutching her forehead, and continues, "I simply can't part with that for less than fifty dollars." Everyone cracks up at Susan's impression.

Sophie spots an empty space and parks. They get out of the car and walk up toward Melrose. CJ has brought a Minolta Super 8 movie camera and films Sophie, Susan, Anisha, and Oscar as they walk ahead of him. He focuses on their shadows moving on the sidewalk.

Susan see CJ filming and asks, "What are you doing?"

"Just capturing some *decisive moments*," CJ answers as he zooms in on Susan's face. "This could be good for the opening sequence."

They merge with the flow of people walking along Melrose, and Sophie leads them to X-Ray Specs. The Art Deco neon sign out front greets them, and the jazzy lettering twinkles. Stepping inside, they are transported back to the 1930s and 1940s with wood-paneled walls lined with built-in shelves and mirrors.

Beautiful glass cases are filled with glittering costume jewelry and gloves. The clothes are elegantly organized around a round red banquette sofa on which to rest between mad dashes to the fitting room. Eclectic period items are placed throughout the shop, including a vintage phone booth and a wooden shoe shine stand.

Sophie looks around the store for Matthieu, but she doesn't see him. She glances at her watch and mentions to Oscar and CJ, "It's noon, and Matthieu said he would meet us here. How about if Susan, Anisha, and I look for our clothes. Then we'll come back and see what you've picked out."

Susan, Sophie, and Anisha dash away to the area marked LADIES' LOUNGE. They eagerly circle the racks, pulling out everything from polka-dot dresses to pencil skirts. They take turns trying on their picks in the fitting rooms and playfully perform their best model walks and turns for each other. Sophie and Susan collapse together on the round red velvet sofa as Anisha throws open the dressing room curtains.

"What do you think about this one?" Anisha asks. She turns around in a cropped, striped French-inspired top. "I think it would be cool to wear it with a sari."

"I love it!" Sophie and Susan exclaim in agreement.

Anisha changes and returns gleefully from the dressing room. Susan spots CJ filming Oscar in the phone booth, and she and Anisha head over to them.

Sophie wanders over to a display case. She scans the assortment of gloves—long and short, lace and silk. The store owner approaches Sophie, who smells the scent of her rose perfume.

"Hi, my name is Angela. Can I help you pick out some gloves?" she asks. She is a glamorous Black woman in her late twenties. Her hair is styled short with finger waves and a sparkling clip on the side. With smoky eyes rimmed in kohl, she looks like a starlet from a silent movie.

"Can I see these?" Sophie is drawn to a pair of wrist-length black gloves.

Angela pulls them out and lays them on top of the glass case. Sophie tries them on.

"Perfect fit," she says, twirling her hands around. "I'll take them!"

"They are *made* for you," Angela remarks. "I can hold these and the skirt you have at the register. Come see me at the front when you're done and I can ring you up!"

"Thanks, Angela," Sophie replies. "I'm with some friends, so I'll come over with them. I'll see where they are."

Sophie looks toward the phone booth, but everyone has disappeared. *Maybe they are trying things on?*

Unbeknownst to her, Susan, Anisha, CJ, Matthieu, and Oscar are hiding behind a stack of old travel trunks by the front register, waiting to jump out at her.

"CJ, give me the camera. I'm going to film Sophie," Matthieu says. He stealthily navigates around the clothing racks to find her. He spots her looking around the phone booth and comes up to her with the camera. "Pretend that you are on a mission and you're talking on the phone," Matthieu directs as Sophie smiles at him. With a serious demeanor, she picks up the phone and starts to talk, looking back and forth like she is being followed.

Dinah Washington's song "Mad About the Boy" starts to play. Sophie steps out of the booth and grabs the camera from Matthieu. She starts to circle around him as he mugs for the lens. He closes the trench coat he is wearing and then slyly opens it to reveal his The Clash T-shirt. Playfully he pulls the coat over his face like Dracula and walks toward Sophie until he can wrap the coat around her like giant bat wings. Everything goes dark through the viewfinder.

"I am sorry," Sophie says in a flirty way, "but I am on to you." She peers out from his embrace and spots Oscar and CJ behind the stack of trunks. "I see your accomplices now."

Matthieu turns around as Susan and Anisha's laughter erupts through the store. Sophie bolts over to the trunks and discovers their hideout.

"Got you!" Sophie exclaims. "Okay, did you find something for our movie?"

"I'm getting this trench coat," Matthieu replies.

"This is cooler than cool," Oscar says, placing a fedora on his head.

10

A Storm Is Coming

Sophie follows Matthieu in his convertible as they drive back up the canyon, and the buzz of the city transitions to the peaceful rustle of the hillside. Her wagon chugs up the steep driveway as his little roadster darts quickly to a stop. Everyone gets out of Sophie's car, in awe of the unique natural setting that is so different from their suburban tract home neighborhoods. Sophie hears the magical sound of wind chimes that greets them as they walk past the carport to Matthieu's home.

Anisha, Susan, CJ, and Oscar react in amazement—the same way Sophie did when she first came over. They settle on the natural stone floor in the living room, where there are clear views of the canyon through the walls of windows. On one side of the living room, a small fire is burning in the cinder block fireplace. Under the high wooden beams of the ceiling, the Cinematics Club looks over their script and maps out the scenes to shoot today.

"Matthieu, are your parents here?" Sophie asks, warming herself by the fireplace.

A sliding glass door opens, and Matthieu's dad and little brother come in. Sophie feels a little nervous to meet his family. *Will they like me?*

Marc Bernard is a sophisticated middle-age man who is focused on his work in the movie industry, but he is adapting to a more casual West Coast life. The Los Angeles summer sun has lightened his brown hair in sandy streaks. Marc is carrying four-year-old Leon piggyback, and when he lowers him down, the child immediately runs over to Matthieu to hug him.

"Everyone, this is Leon, my little brother," Matthieu says, prying Leon's tiny hands away from his waist. He starts to tickle him on his stomach, which causes Leon to run off laughing. Matthieu continues, "This is my dad."

Marc quickly looks over this new group of friends.

"Matthieu told me about this film club he joined at school. I look forward to watching your creation." With his French accent and British schooling, he projects an air of refinement.

Leon runs back to him. "We'll keep him occupied while you work on your film," Marc says, and he follows Leon back into the boy's bedroom.

The sound of the wind chimes gets louder as the wind blows the trees back and forth.

A woman runs up the pathway and comes through the sliding glass door. Her long golden-red hair is tousled from the wind as she slides the door shut. She kicks off her sandals and walks across the stone floor. Sophie is taken by how lightly she walks barefoot, her toenails painted pink. It's like she's a fairy floating in from the forest.

"Hi, everyone! I'm Matthieu's stepmom, Genni," she says, smoothing out her windblown hair. She eagerly walks toward them. "I have been looking forward to meeting you! What are you called again?" She recalls the name. "The Cinematics Club! I am so happy that Matthieu is settling into his new school." Genni walks around to each of them, exuding a naturally welcoming presence. Instead of a typical handshake or wave, she clasps each of their hands like she is feeling their energy. The last one she greets is Sophie, whom she winks at. "I am so glad that Matthieu has really taken to school here."

Marc comes out of Leon's bedroom and says with relief to Genni, "Leon was so tired that he fell asleep instantly. I need to make some calls about the film locations, so I'll be in my office." He walks through the living room, already preoccupied with his own business, and closes the door to his office.

Genni notices the camera they've set up to shoot against the couches by the fireplace. "Why don't I put together a plate of snacks for you. I'll be your caterer this afternoon," she says sweetly, walking into the little open kitchen that looks out over the living room. "By the way, you can use the guest room and bathroom to change into your costumes. They're right down this hallway." She points toward the part of the house where Marc took Leon. Sophie, Susan, and Anisha gather their outfits and hurry in that direction.

Matthieu says to CJ and Oscar, "You can use my room to change if you want." They all grab their clothing and head off to Matthieu's room.

Genni cuts carrot and celery sticks and arranges them on a plate. She pulls a bottle of ranch dressing from the fridge and pours it into a dish, which she places in the center of the plate. She finishes off the snack platter with some crackers and cheese. "Magnifique," she proclaims proudly as she grabs one of the carrot sticks to eat.

She is much happier now that she has her family and enjoys taking care of them in a place that finally feels like a real home. Before she became Genni Bernard, she was Genevieve Gray. When she met Marc in New York on a film shoot, she'd had enough of being a struggling actress. She had moved from California to New York to be a serious stage actress, only to be offered TV parts such as "bubbly secretary" or "psycho girlfriend." She, Marc, and Matthieu all needed a new start—one that they could make together.

Genni gazes out the window and watches the sky darken. She calls out, "You better start shooting—you'll lose the light soon!" She puts on the kettle to make some tea as the ominous storm clouds move in.

Sophie, Anisha, and Susan return to the living room in their costumes. The kettle starts to whistle a high-pitched screech as Genni looks up to see the girls standing together near the fire. She quickly turns the burner off. She is intrigued by their unique looks. Sophie is dressed in a black leotard and a long, sheer ballet skirt over leggings. Her hair is pulled back with a few loose waves that fall from a beret. Susan is wearing a black-and-white polka-dot romper over leggings with a tailored black blazer and Sophie's wrist-length gloves. Anisha stands confidently with her long hair pulled back in a sleek ponytail. She is wearing the striped French crop top and leggings and is draped in a sari.

"You look A-MA-ZING!" Genni exclaims. "I must take pictures of you together."

"That's a great idea," Sophie replies, picking up one of their 35mm cameras. "This one has black-and-white film in it."

Sophie hands the camera to Genni and hurries back to where Anisha and Susan are standing by the fireplace. The three of them strike different poses as Genni snaps pictures. Matthieu, Oscar, and CJ return to the living room.

Susan says impatiently, "Finally, here comes the rest of our cast and crew! What took so long?"

"We were reviewing the storyboards for the getaway shot outside," CJ answers, carrying Oscar's sketchbook. He is wearing a dress shirt with tuxedo-style pants, a black tie, and suspenders. Oscar follows him in a dress shirt, vest, and black fedora. Matthieu is the last one to come in from the backyard. He quickly flips through the script and rereads his lines. He has slicked back his hair and is wearing loose-fitting pants, a dress shirt, and the trench coat.

The club takes a moment to absorb each other's transformations. It's like they're seeing different sides of each other, ones that were always there but needed the right light to become visible. Matthieu takes Sophie's hand, pulling her aside. On the couch, they look over the script and whisper to each other while the rest of the club sets up for the first scene.

Genni announces, "I'm going to check on Leon, but I have left you some snacks and drinks. I made some little cups of hot green tea from the health food store; it will be good for your voices."

Oscar arranges the secret files and a briefcase by the fireplace and sets up the movie camera on a tripod. The club begins the first scene, sometimes saying what is written in the script and sometimes improvising.

Sophie cracks up as she flubs her line. "I hope this is going in a blooper reel. Can we start again?" she asks, then quickly gets back into character.

"Okay, cut! I got it!" CJ yells after they do the scene once more. Looking out the window, he sees the darkening clouds moving quickly across the sky. "Look," he says, pointing. "Something wicked this way comes."

"Do you mean the movie or Ray Bradbury's book or are you just getting all spooky on us?" Susan asks.

"That is *portentous*," Anisha says. "I learned that word in my literature class. It's like a sign—something that foreshadows a future event."

"I liked that movie," Oscar replies, adjusting his fedora.

"I meant Ray Bradbury," CJ says, "but it's also a sign that we better hurry and shoot the escape scene. Let's film now and then finish up outside by the pool."

They work through the agent hideout scene in which their secret headquarters is breached. When their hideout is discovered, they run out into the backyard. The camera is facing the house as they flee outside. Everyone takes their places, and Oscar starts the movie camera. Under a sky full of darkening, racing clouds, they sprint out as the camera rolls.

"Okay, now let's position the camera outside the door, pointing toward the pool," CJ says. "We'll all run past the camera and head out of frame."

Matthieu winks at Sophie. He tosses off his charcoal-gray trench coat, and she removes her beret and black pumps. Oscar starts the camera rolling, and CJ calls, "ACTION!"

Anisha, Susan, CJ, and Oscar race through the open glass door and dash past the camera. Out of frame, Sophie and Matthieu wait inside the house. Matthieu clasps Sophie's hand, and they bound outside. With an unexpected boldness, Matthieu and Sophie take a running jump into the swimming pool and land with a big splash. Illuminated by the pool lighting, they swim up to the surface.

Anisha, Susan, CJ, and Oscar are speechless, expressions of surprise and amazement on their faces. Matthieu and Sophie become encircled by the serpentine steam rising from the heated pool. The sky finally bursts, and a gentle rain begins to fall. While wrapped together in a floating embrace, they share their first on-camera kiss.

"Get the camera!" CJ yells to Oscar, who bolts to save the equipment from the rain. Anisha and Susan snap out of their dreamlike state as the drizzle dampens their clothes. Running inside, Susan calls out to Sophie and Matthieu, "That was so crazy cool!"

Sophie and Matthieu linger in the pool, watching the peaceful raindrops create ripples in the blue-green water. Sophie floats on her back and closes her eyes as the rain mists her face. She feels Matthieu's hands beneath her back as he holds her weightless body. He guides her around, and she extends her arms outward, feeling the warm water through her fingers.

"Sophie, I think we better get out of the pool," Matthieu says as he sees his stepmom peering through the glass.

Sophie slowly opens her eyes and accepts that they need to leave their comfortable oasis. "It's going to be *cold*," Sophie says, swimming toward the pool steps.

They run cautiously across the wet cement in their bare feet. Matthieu shuts the door behind them, and they stand dripping on the stone floor.

"What kind of movie are you making?" Genni teases, handing them a pair of beach towels decorated in palm trees and flamingoes. "Don't you love these? I stole them when we stayed at the Grand Sunset Hotel in Beverly Hills."

Sophie warms herself, wrapping her towel around her shoulders like a shawl, while Matthieu hangs his towel over his head like he just finished a boxing match. Sophie collects her pumps and beret, which she left behind on the floor.

"Sophie, I'll take care of having your clothes cleaned," Genni says. "I was planning on going to the dry cleaner on Monday."

"Thanks, Genni," Sophie replies, briskly walking to the guest bathroom.

As she changes clothes, she feels a bit guilty about acting in such a spontaneous, irrational manner. But that feeling quickly fades as she looks in the mirror. An inner glow of happiness and thrill takes over as she thinks, *I can't believe I did that!* Sophie dries her hair with the towel and collects her wet clothing to bring to Genni.

When she returns to living room, CJ, Oscar, Anisha, and Susan are sitting on the floor devouring the snacks and drinks.

"Sophie," Anisha says, sipping a cup of tea, "no one would believe what you and Matthieu did if it weren't on film!"

"I can't wait to see the film we shot today," Oscar says, grabbing a carrot stick. He looks at the empty dish with an annoyed expression and asks, "Hey, who used up all the ranch dressing?"

Susan and Anisha look over at CJ, who has the evidence of ranch dressing on the corner of his mouth.

"Seriously, CJ," Susan laughs, "you and your uncle are *so* alike!"

CJ dabs at his mouth and feels the ranch dressing on his lips. Wiping the evidence away, he replies, "I can't help it! Whoever invented ranch dressing was a genius!"

They all burst out laughing. The rain clouds quickly move past the windows, and the sky clears to reveal the glimmering crescent moon. Matthieu rejoins the group, having changed back into jeans and his The Clash T-shirt.

All of a sudden, Leon races into the living room gripping a centaur action figure. He runs to Matthieu, wanting to play.

"Hey, Leon," Matthieu says as Leon dangles the toy in front of him. "I'll play with you in a sec."

Anisha looks at her watch and yells, "It is five thirty! We better go!"

They scramble to clean up the props, equipment, and wardrobe and pack everything into Sophie's wagon. Sophie searches for her beret to cover her hair, which is still damp and scented with chlorine. She makes a mad dash back toward Matthieu's house just as Genni comes outside holding her beret.

"I found this in the bathroom—I hoped you hadn't taken off yet," Genni says, handing the hat to Sophie.

"Thank you for everything and for having us at your house today," Sophie says as Genni gives her a big hug.

Sophie gets into the wagon and twists her hair up under the beret.

"Oscar, it's your turn to ride shotgun," Susan says, getting comfortable in the back seat between CJ and Anisha.

Matthieu closes up the wagon's trunk and walks over to Sophie's open window. He looks at everyone inside.

"We did good today," he says, feeling proud of their work.

"Thanks, Matthieu," CJ says, extending his hand out the window. "See you on Monday."

Sophie turns on the headlights, and the wagon rumbles down the hill. She sees Matthieu shrinking in her rear-view mirror. She drives down Ventura, where people are streaming up and down the sidewalks, starting their Saturday night. Sophie's attention is divided between the road and the clock. *Five forty-five—almost there.*

They pass the Wise Owl coffee shop, an old diner built in the Googie style popular in the 1950s. With its sweeping roofline and large sign decorated with an owl, the restaurant is busy all day seven days a week. On weekend nights, it's the go-to spot for high school and college students looking for a cheap place to eat and hang out.

"I'm starving," CJ says longingly as they pass the diner. "I want a grilled cheese and a shake."

Susan laughs. "Remember the last time we were there and you ordered the Hooty Owl pancakes? And instead of bringing you the regular-size ones, the waitress brought you, like, fifty silver-dollar pancakes?"

"This traffic is terrible!" Sophie fumes. "I am going to take side streets, and then maybe we'll make it back in time!"

Sophie turns off the main boulevard and cuts through residential neighborhoods. She navigates back onto the main drag just in time to drive past La Luna. Two large spotlights are positioned out front, shining their bright white lights into the night sky. The terrazzo tile is covered with a brilliant red carpet and velvet ropes.

"Wow, I wonder what private party is going on tonight?" Anisha says as she tries to get a glimpse.

Sophie drives around the back of the theater and pulls her wagon up next to CJ's scooter.

"Five minutes to spare," Sophie announces, relieved that she got everyone back by six.

"Sophie, thanks so much for driving! Today was such an awesome day!" Susan says, quickly grabbing her bag. "Sorry, but I gotta run to my shift. Bye, see everyone on Monday!"

"Sophie, can we leave the equipment in your car till Monday?" Sophie nods, and CJ bolts from the Jeep, hurrying to catch up with Susan.

They get out of the wagon and Anisha looks around for her mom's car. She sees the gold Mercedes Benz 300D drive into the parking lot.

"I had a great time. Today was so much fun!" Anisha says, giving Sophie and Oscar a group hug. "I better get going."

Anisha walks briskly to her mom, who is still dressed in her white nursing uniform, having just finished her shift at Valley View Medical Center. Anisha waves at Sophie and Oscar as the Mercedes drives off.

Sophie and Oscar walk toward the back of the theater. "Did Robert tell you what the private event is?" Sophie says to Oscar.

"No, but he must be inside. I'm going to see if I can find out." Oscar walks around to the front of the theater.

Sophie is cold and tired from the long day. *I have to get home and take a shower*. She's about to walk back to her car when she suddenly hears someone yell, "Hey, Moonlight!"

Dylan rushes down the back stairs of the theater. He is dressed like he's going to his own movie premiere in navy dress pants, a blazer, and a skinny tie. He runs up to Sophie and starts jabbering. "Quick! Can you help me out? I just need you to clear away some film reels from the projection booth." Dylan bends over to catch his breath and continues, "Robert is out front, and my school is having its film review tonight. I am showing my movie, and all these famous directors are coming, and they may come up to look at the projection room. It's a mess up there. Please, Sophie, I just need your help for a few minutes!"

"Dylan, I'll help you for a *few* minutes. But then I really need to get home. I am so beat."

Sophie follows Dylan up the back stairs and into the projection booth. There are film canisters scattered all over the place.

"What happened in here?" Sophie says in horror.

"Here are all the student films for tonight's screening," Dylan tells Sophie. "These ones over here are from Rikki's delivery. Can you please take these other reels over to the storage room?" Dylan hands her a set of keys. "Just remember to lock up and bring the keys back to me."

Sophie picks up an armful of film reels and locks them up as Dylan instructed. When she hands the keys back to him, he is engrossed in a phone call.

"Robert, I've got everything under control up here," Dylan says, trying to unwind himself from the phone cord. "I have all the films in order. We've done print inspections, and all systems are go!"

Dylan hangs up the phone and notices that Sophie has even straightened up all the cases.

"Thanks, Moonlight." Dylan clasps his hands together in prayer. "I owe you one!"

"Dylan, good luck on your screening. I know it'll be great!" Sophie says, closing the door to the projection booth. She hears the clicking of the projector revving up as she heads down the hall and out the back door. She finally reaches her car and maneuvers out of the parking lot. On her drive home, she listens to the clanking of the camera equipment in the back of her wagon.

******

Sophie has a sinking feeling as she parks her wagon behind her dad's car. She is already late, and it's a given that her parents are already in worry mode.

She goes inside the house and sees that the kitchen light is on. Her hair is still damp, and she is anxious to take a shower. She walks into the kitchen and smells baked chicken and mashed potatoes. Sarah is arranging dishes on the counter.

"Sophie, I *knew* you were probably going to be late," she says reassuringly. "Your dad and I had dinner already, but I can make you a plate."

"Sorry I'm late," Sophie says. "I meant to be here around six. After I got back to the theater and dropped off my friends, I was asked to help out with their special screening tonight."

Simon puts down the newspaper and peers through his reading glasses. "Sophie, come and have some dinner. It's still warm."

Sophie sits down at the round kitchen table, and Sarah brings her a plate of chicken, creamy mashed potatoes, and a fluffy dinner roll. She enjoys the homey comfort food. Her dad is always content to see Sophie safe at home and eating. He resumes scanning through the newspaper and lets out a burst of frustration.

"Aargh! What a shyster! Every day another crook runs around in this world."

This is the usual routine for Sophie's dad. The family subscribes to several daily newspapers. It is a love-hate relationship for Simon, who is an avid reader. Every day, he reads the papers, only to become aggravated by one or more stories.

Sophie finishes her last spoonful of potatoes. Her dad pours steaming coffee into his olive-green glass mug and settles back down at the table. Sarah brings over a box of pastries for dessert before she goes to the bedroom to relax.

"How are your classes going?" Simon asks, biting into a raspberry Danish.

"Good, Dad. I am doing well in my classes," Sophie replies, reaching for a bear claw. "I even helped found a new afterschool club. It's about photography and filmmaking, and we're learning about different cameras. We even started filming our own movie today!"

Simon, who works at a TV station in their advertising department, knows the reality of that world. He understands the industry politics and how hard it is to find a steady job, especially for women. He only wants to protect his daughter, but his delivery is always direct.

"Sophie, you need to focus on your schoolwork first. You have a job on the weekends now, so I don't want you to put too much time into this movie club. College is your priority."

"I know, Dad," Sophie says, clearing away her dishes. "I'll be home tomorrow so I can do my homework. I'm going to get ready for bed now. Good night."

Sophie says good night to her mom, who is relaxing in the bedroom with the *TV Guide*. After taking a shower and changing into a long T-shirt, Sophie collapses into bed. She glances at the stack of textbooks on her desk—*I know what my plans are for Sunday*. Sophie turns on the radio to a barely audible level. Eurythmics' "Here Comes the Rain Again" lulls her to sleep.

11

The Perfect Kiss

The stark rays of the morning sun bounce off the white stone buildings of the LA Art Museum. The students of Ms. Kahn's modern art history class are gathered in the courtyard surrounding a Rodin bronze sculpture. Their heads jerk up and down as they alternate between observing and sketching in their notebooks. There is an air of freedom about them—they have been released from the confines of campus for Noble High's Field Trip Friday.

Ms. Kahn walks confidently out of the building's main entrance toward her students. She has a sophisticated new bob haircut and is smartly dressed in a linen chemise with a cowl neck and wedge-heeled pumps. One could speculate that her fashionable transformation was in preparation for this day at the museum, but it is more likely because of the recent attention of Mr. William Omolo.

"I hope everyone has observed all these *dramatic* angles created by Auguste Rodin, who is known as the father of modern sculpture," Ms. Kahn says with intensity, circling around the massive bronze. "Everything is ready for our tour of the modern art collection. Please gather all of your belongings, and we will move inside the lobby."

Matthieu leans over Sophie's shoulder, peeking at her sketch. She frowns at her drawing. "I wish I had charcoal. You can't really see the anguish in the face."

Matthieu closes his pocket sketchbook.

"Let me see *your* drawing," Sophie says, nudging him.

Matthieu hesitates for a moment and then hands her his sketchbook. Sophie flips to the last drawing. It is not of the massive sculpture that stands in front of them but a sketch of her profile. She takes a moment to absorb the way Matthieu sees her—a series of graphite lines that move freely across the page.

Sophie tries to find the right words to express what she feels. "This is…really *me*. No one has ever drawn me before except at the county fair, and that was a caricature. The guy drew my head super big with a huge bow in my hair."

They both crack up, hurrying to catch up with the rest of the class, which has gathered inside the museum lobby. Sophie is dressed for the day in a lavender jersey dress accented with several ropes of costume pearls and a long cardigan.

"Here are maps of the museum," Ms. Kahn announces as she passes out the pamphlets to the students. A tall man wearing glasses and a tweed suit with suede elbow patches walks over to the group. "Students, this is Mr. Everett, the head curator of the modern art collection. I have arranged for him to lead our tour. We will have this special opportunity for only thirty minutes, so please take extensive notes. You will be expected to turn in a report next week."

The group follows Mr. Everett through the large halls of the museum, clustering around him as he talks about the brushwork of the Impressionist painters. Then he leads them to a more intimate room filled with Japanese woodblock prints and stops in front of a particular one.

"Now, I want to point out this magnificent color print by the artist Takahashi Hiroaki entitled *Thunderstorm at Tateishi*. It dates to around 1925." His finger draws a zigzag through the air. "Look at how these graphic lines tear across the dark, stormy sky. You can just feel the electricity, can't you?"

The students take notes as they follow him through the museum halls. Mr. Everett glances at his wristwatch as he brings them to the entrance of another exhibition room.

"I hate to end our tour so soon, but I will leave you at our current exhibition featuring local artists from Los Angeles." They stand in front of a large canvas depicting a woman in a long black dress. The figure looks out a window at a red view.

"*La Tormenta* was painted by the Chicano artist Gronk. She represents an American mythological character, and her form symbolizes all things hidden or in shadow."

Ms. Kahn shakes Mr. Everett's hand and announces, "Let's give a thank-you to Mr. Everett for his wonderful tour. You can view any of the exhibitions for another hour, and we will all meet back in the lobby at noon."

The students clap for Mr. Everett and then disperse into the museum. Sophie and Matthieu stay behind with Ms. Kahn and Mr. Everett.

"Thank you again for the tour," Ms. Kahn says. "This is Sophie and Matthieu. Sophie Alexander is one of my top students and has expressed her interest in pursuing a degree in museum studies. I wanted to introduce you before you leave us."

"That is very good to know," Mr. Everett replies, retrieving a business card from his blazer pocket. "Sophie, here is my card. We have an internship program starting in the summer. I encourage you to contact me if you would like to apply."

Sophie takes the card, hardly able to hold back her excitement. "Thank you, Mr. Everett. I will contact you."

Mr. Everett nods and walks hastily away.

"Thank you for the introduction, Ms. Kahn. This is such a big deal!" Sophie says, her heart still pounding. She secures his business card in her sketchbook.

"You are welcome. I know how important this internship would be for your college applications," Ms. Kahn says. "I am going to the educational archives downstairs, but I will see you back in the lobby at noon."

Ms. Kahn descends a spiral staircase, leaving Sophie and Matthieu to themselves.

"Which way should we go?" Sophie asks, watching their classmates dart in and out of various galleries.

Matthieu adjusts his camera, which hangs from a strap across his chest. He has taken to wearing the trench coat from their film. Looking over the museum map, he says, "Well, let's start in the early twentieth century."

Sophie and Matthieu roam the halls and come upon the room marked ART NOUVEAU. Walking past framed drawings, they see a guard standing by a doorway under a sign that says GUSTAV KLIMT: THE KISS.

Sophie stares at the sign. *Is this for real? Maybe it's a sketch.* She grabs Matthieu's coat and leads him over to the guard.

"Excuse me, is this the *real* Klimt painting?" she asks. "I have never seen one in person."

"This is a special loan that is ending today," the security guard replies, serious and direct. "Only two people at a time, and no flash photography."

Sophie walks toward the painting while Matthieu remains at the back of the room. It pulls at her like a powerful force, and she observes all of its brilliance, the intensity of the gold and the geometric patterns that wrap around the embracing figures. She knows that feeling; it's like the moment she and Matthieu kissed as the rain fell upon them in the pool.

The clicking sound of a camera breaks the silence and pulls Sophie back to the room. She turns around to see that Matthieu is snapping pictures.

"Let's take a photo together," Matthieu says, pulling his camera from around his neck. Standing beside Sophie, he holds the camera in one hand, pointed at them. "I'm not sure if this is going to work, but let's try it." He clicks the button as they embrace in front of the painting.

Suddenly the security guard comes into the room and announces impatiently, "We have other visitors waiting to view this painting. Thank you."

Sophie and Matthieu leave the room and rush past a line of people that has formed.

"It's almost noon. We better meet up with Ms. Kahn," Sophie says, checking the museum map.

Walking toward the front lobby, they pass the doors to the museum's theater. A glass case displays a poster for the silent movie *Metropolis*, illustrated with Art Deco–style buildings and a female robot.

"That is *such* a cool film. Have you seen it?" Matthieu says, snapping a picture of the poster.

"I only saw it on TV," Sophie admits. "I wish I could see it on a big screen. I love the look of it and how expressive the actors are without talking. They show their emotions just with their eyes."

Sophie and Matthieu rejoin their class in the museum lobby. Ms. Kahn takes a head count, making sure that every student has returned.

"Okay, we are officially done for today, and I hope everyone is inspired by the art!" Ms. Kahn expresses her exhilaration. "You can join me in the cafeteria for lunch, or you are welcome to leave and get a head start on your reports." Ms. Kahn swings open the museum doors, and the cool breeze greets her. Most of the students follow her as she struts across the courtyard toward the cafeteria. A few students hurry away to start their weekends. Sophie and Matthieu walk back over to the Rodin sculpture.

"Do you want to see *Metropolis* tonight? I can drive," Matthieu offers.

"I wish," Sophie sighs. "I have to work tonight."

"Another time. We have *our* movie to work on. I am getting together with CJ and Oscar over the weekend. CJ wants to film from my car, so we can do the driving shots."

"Susan and Anisha are coming over on Saturday, and we'll plan out how to shoot the next few scenes. I think I'll go home now and start on this report." She flips through her notes from their tour, then asks Matthieu, "I just saw you taking pictures. Did you take any notes?"

Matthieu pulls his pocket sketchbook from his trench coat and hands it to Sophie. She flips past the sketch he drew of her to the next page. The only words written are, "*The Kiss* by Gustav Klimt. Vienna. 1908."

Sophie laughs, "That's it? Well, I'll add this." She pulls out her red lipstick and applies it. She kisses the paper under the words, closes the sketchbook, and hands it back to him.

Sophie walks to her wagon, excited by the prospect of shooting more of their movie. Flipping through her sketchbook, she glances at Mr. Everett's business card and imagines doing a summer internship at the museum.

12

Out of Sequence

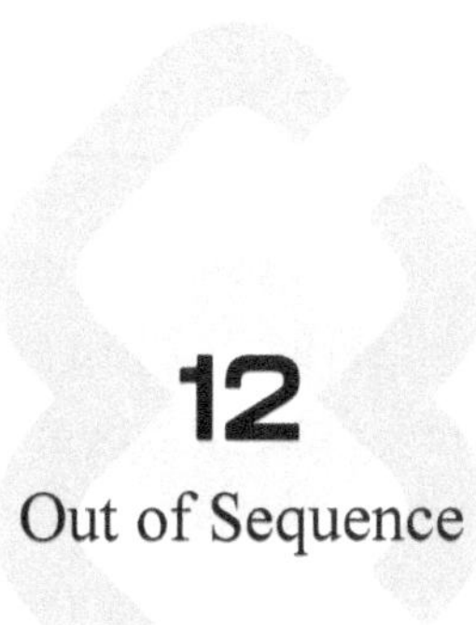

"Do you have any broken Karob bars?" Sophie asks, hovering over the glass concession counter at La Luna.

Oscar is crouched down as he unpacks the boxes of candy. He extends his arm above the case, drops a candy bar on the counter, and then disappears below.

"Oscar, you're a lifesaver!" Sophie clutches the candy. "How's the Halloween dance committee? What are you planning?"

"Sorry, Sophie. We are sworn to keep it a secret. The principal said he is going to make an announcement next week." Oscar's voice is muffled by the sound of crumpling boxes.

Sophie tears open the silver wrapper and takes a bite of the creamy chocolate bar just as Dylan walks into the lobby like he is strutting across the red carpet at the Academy Awards. His hair is swept back, and he is wearing his Ray-Ban sunglasses.

"No autographs, please." Dylan mugs at Sophie, posing for a crowd of invisible paparazzi.

Oscar finishes stocking the candy counter and stands up. "Robert said your movie is really good. What's it called?"

Dylan pushes his sunglasses back on top of his hair and says proudly, "It is called *RoboCruisers*. I filmed it all around downtown in the industrial areas. It's *my* vision of the future. *Blade Runner* is set in 2019, so I just one-upped it to 2020. It is about an elite crime-fighting group. Their state-of-the-art stealth car drives by itself."

"Sounds like the TV show *Knight Rider*," Oscar says matter-of-factly.

"*Knight Rider?* Not even!" Dylan tries to maintain his cool. "My car has a female voice, and her name is Sherrie."

"Like 'Oh Sherrie,' the Steve Perry song?" Oscar shoots back.

"I'll have you know that James Cameron, director of *The Terminator*, was at the student film screening, and he personally gave *me* a thumbs-up."

"Congratulations, Dylan! I hope we can see it." Sophie says eagerly. "Oscar and I are in a film club at school, and we are making our own film."

Dylan, still peeved by the mention of *Knight Rider*, changes the subject. "Oh, by the way, Rikki had a bad accident last night at his Searing Magmä concert. He was doing a flying leap with his guitar and missed the stage. He has a broken arm and leg and is totally bummed out."

"Seriously?" Oscar replies, starting up the popcorn machine.

"Hey, Moonlight, can you help me with the film reels you put in the storage room? Everything got so mixed up on the student screening night, I haven't had a chance to sort them out."

Sophie, swallowing the last bite of the Karob bar, manages to respond, "Sure, I have some time before I have to open the box office."

Sophie washes up in the restroom and heads upstairs to the storage room. It's chilly in there, and she wraps her cardigan sweater tightly around her. Dylan, busily looking through the stack of film canisters, pulls out one metal container.

"Huh, I don't know where this one came from," he says, puzzled, looking for any labels or markings. "Rikki must have gotten the deliveries mixed up." He puts on a pair of white cotton gloves and opens the round metal canister. A smaller reel is stored inside.

"Why would that be here?" Sophie asks.

"I haven't a clue. This looks old," Dylan comments, inspecting the reel. "This is not even the right format. It's eight millimeter."

"I can take it down to Robert's office." Sophie offers.

"Thanks, Moonlight, but I'll call Rikki first." Dylan puts the small reel back into the canister and places it on a shelf. He and Sophie organize the remaining reels.

Sophie checks her watch. "Dylan, I have to get down to the box office. Let me know what you find out about the film."

She goes down into the lobby and immediately feels warmer. She smells the buttered popcorn and sees the hot dogs turning on the roller grill.

"Thanks for the sugar rush, Oscar! I'll be in the box office," Sophie says, passing by the candy counter.

"Sure, Sophie! There's a crazy-long line out there."

The door marked MANAGER swings open and Robert walks out.

"Hi, Robert. I was just going to the box office," Sophie says.

"Sophie, Oscar—great news!" Robert says, elated. "I've been planning a special screening for the Saturday before Halloween. You are not going to believe which film I'm getting!" Before Oscar and Sophie can guess, he blurts out, "*The Rocky Horror Picture Show*!"

Robert shows them a flyer from the Majestic Theater announcing a presentation of *A Nightmare on Elm Street*. "I am booking two back-to-back screenings that night—one at ten o'clock and one at midnight. That will show the Majestic which is the better theater!"

Oscar's excitement fades fast—his uncle never pays attention to anything he does outside the theater. "Our school dance is that night, and I'm part of the group planning the whole thing."

"Oye, mijo, *Rocky Horror* is a midnight movie, and I wasn't going to schedule you or Sophie for that Saturday anyway."

"Thanks, Robert. I can't believe it's only a month away!"

Sophie hurries out to the box office and gets the tickets ready. She scans the line of people waiting, one long blur of acid-washed jeans and permed hair. When all the tickets are sold, Sophie closes up the box office and walks into the theater.

"Bye! I'll catch up with you on Monday," Sophie calls out to Oscar, who is busy behind the concession stand. Exiting through the back door, she pulls her car keys from her purse. CJ slows down beside her on his scooter.

"You outta here?" he says, pulling his headphones down around his neck. Sophie hears the music of Fine Young Cannibals' "Johnny Come Home" playing from them.

"Yes! I'm done. This was the longest day *ever*!" Sophie is so tired she can hardly get the words out. "I was at the museum for my art history field trip. Where did you go?"

"I went with my Spanish class to see a play about Don Quixote." CJ stops his Walkman. "I didn't see Susan working tonight."

"Susan went with Mr. Hart's Chemistry Club to that super-futuristic company, EnBioTek. It was an all-day trip, so she took tonight off. She and Anisha are coming over my house tomorrow to work on our script." Sophie can't hide her big yawn. "Sorry, CJ, I better go…I'm falling asleep."

CJ slowly rides up alongside her, making sure she gets into her car safely. Sophie waves to him as she drives off. He puts his headphones back on, hits play on his Walkman, and zips up his green bomber jacket.

The song starts again, and Roland Gift sings in his soulful, haunting voice. CJ takes in the night lights as he navigates his scooter through the bumper-to-bumper Friday night traffic.

13

In and Out of Focus

"What would your friends like for lunch? Sandwiches or pizza?" Sophie's mom asks as she folds laundry.

"We can order from Napoli's. Susan is a vegetarian now, so we should just stick with a cheese pizza and salad."

"Let's order two pizzas since your dad will want some as soon as he smells it. Better call it in now and he can pick it up. He is leaving for the hardware store soon."

Sophie phones in the pizza order and starts cleaning her room. *Paper—check. Pens—check. Music and magazines—check.*

A red Toyota Supra pulls up in front of Sophie's house. Susan and Anisha get out of the car and head toward the front door. They say hello to Simon, who is fixing the sprinklers.

Steven Tran walks over to Simon dressed in his freshly pressed white tennis outfit. "Hello, Mr. Alexander. Do you need any help?"

"Hello, Steven. No thank you." Simon is surrounded by tools scattered on the ground. "Are you on your way to play tennis?"

"Yes, I have an eleven a.m. court reservation. Is Martin coming to visit soon?"

"He'll be here for Thanksgiving," Simon responds, brushing the dirt from his hands.

"Great. I'll talk to him about DynaRocket. I can set up some interviews for him if he is interested in working there once he graduates. I better get going to the Racquet Centre. Bye, Mr. Alexander." Steven revs his engine and speeds away down the block.

✳✳✳✳✳✳

"Hey!!!" Susan and Anisha come into Sophie's bedroom and close the door. They put down their bags and sprawl out on the floor.

Susan, who's wearing a graphic-print sweater over leggings, pulls out some papers and hands them to Anisha and Sophie. "Here are the next scenes of the script that I typed up. We'll shoot the first one behind the theater, and we can film the other one next weekend at Matthieu's."

Anisha, who's wearing a pink sweatshirt and jeans, pulls a record from her bag. "I brought the new Simply Red album. Can we play it?"

"Cool!" Sophie says, looking at the *Picture Book* album cover. "We ordered pizza and salad for lunch." She pulls the vinyl from the sleeve and places it on her record player.

They read over the script and make notes about changes.

"I'm glad you used my idea to destroy the documents in the fire," Anisha says. "When I saw the fireplace at Matthieu's house, it seemed really cool to add that in."

"Let me take your notes, and I'll type up new copies for Monday." Susan gathers the scripts from Sophie and Anisha and files them away in her backpack. "I think that is *enough* about the film!"

Sophie starts the turntable and moves the arm to the edge of the record. The needle drops and the music begins to play. "I tried to get some info from Oscar about what they're planning for the Halloween dance. He was not helpful at all! He said it's a secret and that the principal is going to make some big announcement next week."

"Seriously?" Susan says, annoyed. "What is the big secret?"

"What are you going as?" Anisha asks as Mick Hucknall's voice pulses from the speakers.

"Matthieu thinks it's dumb to dress up," Sophie replies with disappointment. "But I'm going as Rachael from *Blade Runner* anyway."

"CJ said he wants to go as Mad Max." Susan grabs one of Sophie's fashion magazine's to flip through. "It would be fun to go as Tina Turner in that silver dress." She continues reluctantly, "As soon as I told my mom there was a school dance, she called her friend and asked if her son, Tai, would be my date."

"But did CJ already ask you?" Sophie wonders.

"Well…" Susan trails off. "He didn't ask me directly. He just mentioned that he was going as Mad Max and said it would be cool if I wanted to be someone else from the movie."

Sophie grabs the record sleeve and scans the track names. She drops the needle on another song. "I heard this one on the radio—'Holding Back the Years.'"

"Anisha, what are you going to be? Did Naveen already ask you?" Susan leans back against Sophie's bed.

"Yeah, Naveen asked me to go with him as soon as it was announced. He wants us to dress up in costumes from *Indiana Jones and the Temple of Doom*. His cousin drives a limo, and he has arranged for him to take us to the dance."

"Are you maybe starting to like him?" Susan asks.

Not knowing exactly how she feels about Naveen's nice but constant attention, Anisha replies, "Maybe?"

Sophie hears her dad's car pulling into the driveway. "My dad's back. Lunch is here!"

✶ ✶ ✶ ✶ ✶ ✶

Some say it's magical to sit in a darkened theater watching a movie with strangers. The magic reaches out to you from the moving images that can make you laugh out loud one moment and bring you to tears the next.

Robert's rivalry with the Majestic Theater has moved him to up his game. He has decided to show past hit movies every Saturday afternoon leading up to the big Halloween screenings of *The Rocky Horror Picture Show*. After finishing her Saturday shift, Sophie decides to catch the end of *Purple Rain*. She slides into the far back corner of the theater and starts munching on a slice of cold leftover pizza. Bathed in violet lights and smoke, Prince starts to sing "Purple Rain." Backed by the dramatic drums and guitar, he walks over to his guitarist, Wendy, and gives her a kiss on the cheek. Sophie feels emotion well up in her throat, and she can't help it when her tears begin to fall.

"Psst. Hey, Moonlight." Dylan is peering into the back row, trying to get Sophie's attention. She quickly wipes away the tears on her cheeks.

He spies her pizza and blurts out, "Hey, is that from Napoli's?"

"Shush!" an irritated couple fires back at Dylan. "We're trying to watch the movie!"

He signals to Sophie to come out of the theater. She brushes the pizza crumbs off her flower-print vintage dress and slides out of the row of seats. Dylan walks out into the lobby with her.

"Dylan, what is so important?" Sophie wonders.

"You know that small eight-millimeter reel that I found inside a canister?"

"Did you find out where it came from?" Sophie thinks back on Mr. Omolo's lectures and says, "We are learning about different films in the Cinematics Club at school."

"I called Rikki, and he swore that canister was part of the delivery," Dylan says. "He won't be back for a while—he'll be in casts for six weeks."

"Well, did you look at what's on the reel?" Sophie asks, trying to put an end to the mystery.

"That's what I'm trying to tell you," Dylan explains. "I borrowed an eight-millimeter film projector and set it up. The reel is not very long. It's only a few minutes. It's really strange. Come take a look."

Sophie follows Dylan upstairs, where he has set up the film projector. He flips the switch on the back, and the hum of the motor starts up. With the press of a few more buttons, the light begins to shine through the turning film reel and onto the scuffed white wall.

"There's no sound, but I think the movie was shot in secret." Dylan turns a knob, and the tiny black-and-white picture comes into focus, flickering against the wall.

Sophie starts describing what she sees. "It looks like a street in Europe, since there are cobblestones. Look—there's a shop sign that says 'patisserie.' Maybe France?"

The camera, which seems to be positioned inside a vehicle, pans around to capture a group of people being marched down the street. There are families of all different ages huddled together—men, women, and children. They are wearing stars on their clothing and look frightened and sad.

Sophie feels a chill run up her spine as a scowling man appears in the frame. He is dressed in a dark uniform and shiny cap that has a skull on the top. He appears to be shouting. Suddenly a figure runs from the group and lunges toward the menacing officer. The shiny cap is knocked off, revealing a large scar across his forehead.

The clicking of the projector stops as the movie fades to white. Dylan turns off the projector and flicks the light switch on.

Sophie's brain spins with questions. "Who was that man with the scar? What was he yelling at those people?"

Dylan feeds the film onto the top cassette to rewind the reel. "Based on the clothing, it must be from World War II. The film hasn't disintegrated, so it must have been protected for all these years. But as for who that officer is, who shot the film, and why it came to us…I don't have a clue."

"It's weird that it came here out of nowhere. I wonder if we'll ever find the answers?" Sophie grabs her purse.

She closes the door behind her and makes her way out of the theater. Driving home, she thinks about the club's film. She thinks back over the scenes they have filmed and wonders what CJ, Oscar, and Matthieu captured on their shoot this weekend. *Hope we can see what the film looks like so far at Monday's meeting.*

Sophie's mind drifts back to the mystery movie. She can't shake the image of that officer and the fear she saw on the faces of those families. She wonders if this is what her parents lived through as kids during the Holocaust before they fled Germany. It is a part of her history that remains just as enigmatic as that film reel, since her mother and father never discuss what they went through during the war. When she was a child, Sophie couldn't understand why her family was different from a typical family with grandparents and lots of other relatives. She thinks about her own family photos; one would think the Alexander family began with Sophie and her brother. Well, that's all in the past now.

14

All Dressed Up and Nowhere to Go

Monday is normally the most dreaded day of the week—a "pull the covers over your head and don't get out of bed" kind of day. Except on this particular Monday, everyone in the Cinematics Club is seated and anxious to start their meeting. Today Mr. Omolo is bringing in the first developed reel of their movie to review.

"Dude, stop shaking the table!" CJ calls to Oscar, who has been nervously knocking his feet against the legs. "Just chill. We all want to see what we shot."

Mr. Omolo finally arrives, juggling his briefcase and a cardboard box filled with camera equipment.

"I have the developed film," he announces, unpacking a camera and a long lens. Not a moment passes before they all race up to him at the front of the classroom. "Hey, wait a second! You can all sit back down right now." He waves his hands to direct them back to their chairs. "I know you're all excited to see what you shot so far, but I want to do a little camera demonstration before I set up the movie projector."

There's a collective sigh of disappointment as the Cinematics trudge back to their seats.

"This is my thirty-five millimeter Nikon." William holds up the camera and unscrews the lens. "I am swapping out the typical fifty-millimeter lens for this longer two-hundred-milli-meter telephoto lens. This is useful for sports or shooting por-traits from a distance. It's best to use a tripod, which will keep the camera from shaking."

He demonstrates the camera, snapping pictures of each of them. After finishing his shots, he puts the camera down and pulls out papers to distribute.

"Please take one of these sheets with you to read. It lists the properties of the different lenses and also a few notable street photographers who captured everyday life, such as Henri Cartier-Bresson and Garry Winogrand." He catches the stu-dents fidgeting in their seats. "I can tell the suspense is killing you, so I'll set up the projector now. I also brought another telephoto lens for you to borrow and try out."

CJ walks over to the front table and picks up the camera with the telephoto lens. "William, can you take us with you to your job?"

William wheels a cart to the middle of the room and loads the film onto the Bauer Super 8 projector. "I would love to take you out in the field, but sometimes it gets dangerous. You always have to be prepared for the unexpected. Then again, that's when you usually get the best photographs." He switches on the projector, and the reels start turning, making a con-stant clicking sound. He runs over to the light switch, and the room goes dark.

A white frame appears, and then the movie slowly comes to life. The club is gripped by the flickering images, sometimes expressing awe and amazement and sometimes cringing in embarrassment. Anisha's eyes widen and a smile spreads across her face as she watches herself act for the first time. Oscar is impressed with himself dressed up in the black fedora. Since she has retyped the script numerous times, Susan silently mouths the dialogue as the movie plays. CJ leans back in his chair and studies the camera angles.

Sophie is pulled back into that moment with Matthieu—two bodies swirling together in the water as the rain fell. It was their own version of *La Dolce Vita*.

Matthieu, who's sitting next to Sophie, slides his left hand over her leg and places a piece of paper in her right palm. She opens the tiny piece of torn paper, illuminated by the flickering light, and reads,

We are not imaginary. We are real now.

When the moving images fade to white light, William shuts off the projector, and the classroom is silent. Instead of flipping on the overhead fluorescents, he turns on a round metal work lamp, casting harsh shadows across his face. He clears his throat and begins his critique with the enthusiasm of a team coach.

"This is the first time we are seeing the start of your film. Your story is solid—mysterious and suspenseful. You have really put serious effort into the script, wardrobe, and locations. I even see that you have worked to capture the decisive moment with that pool scene. It is very unexpected, so you deserve high marks for that."

His voice shifts to a serious tone as he continues, "Now, what I want to push you on is your lighting. You specifically chose to use black-and-white film to look like an old movie and evoke a sense of mystery. You put references on your board to Bogie, Bacall, Lena Horne in *Stormy Weather*. Where is the dramatic lighting on faces and buildings? You would be amazed how incredible the light of a neon sign is. I suggest that you think about how to create dramatic lighting and focus more on capturing close-ups of faces. You can check out some books from the library on the photographers I have mentioned or watch some old black-and-white noir movies, like *The Maltese Falcon*. Even today's movies are inspired by them."

William grabs the metal lamp by the clamp and holds it to one side of his head to demonstrate dramatic lighting. As he moves the light around, different shadows fall across his face and the classroom wall. He grabs the slatted window blinds and projects the light through them, creating horizontal lines. Then he shuts the lamp off and starts to rewind the film on the projector. "Great work on your movie. Let's call it a day. Remember to think about the lighting on your next shoot, and I'll see you next Monday."

$$* * * * * *$$

The school bell rings in a loud, jarring *brinnnng*. The day has finally arrived for Principal Patterson's big reveal about the Noble High Halloween dance. It's an extended lunchtime, and everyone is crowded on the grassy quad, even those who usually sneak off campus.

Sophie peers through the telephoto lens, seeing how the scenery and people look close up. She pans around the quad, focusing in and out, looking at different people from afar—the cheerleaders gossiping by the stage, the skaters hanging out by the snack shack, and crews practicing the latest hip-hop moves by the auditorium. She focuses the camera on the stage and zooms in on Oscar, who is placing a poster of his Halloween dance drawing on an easel. She clicks the shutter, capturing him beaming with the rest of the dance planning committee. CJ and Matthieu walk into her frame as they approach her and Susan.

"Today's menu: burger and fries from the cafeteria!" CJ says happily, munching on the crinkle fries, which almost tip out of the paper holder. He sits down beside Susan, who is too buried in the script to catch any of their chatter.

"I snagged some extra fries if you want some." Matthieu hands the red-and-white checkered container to Sophie.

"Thanks, Matthieu." Sophie places the container between her and Susan.

"I think that cafeteria lady has the hots for Matthieu," CJ razzes him while squirting bright red ketchup from a packet onto his fries. "She passes him all sorts of extra things—first a pudding cup, and now fries. And, you know, winking at him." He mimics the expression.

"Yeah, right." Matthieu brushes off the embarrassing attention. "Thanks, CJ. You just ruined my lunch."

"Okay, I added your new lighting notes to the script. I'll have everything ready for Saturday's shoot." Susan files the script away in her Pee-Chee folder and pulls out her lunch box. "I'm starving! When is the big announcement? And where is Anisha?" Susan asks, grabbing some of the fries.

Anisha comes racing over and finds a spot on the lawn by Sophie. She throws off her gym bag and catches her breath. "Did I miss anything? Ms. Hollister kept us late in volleyball. This girl Missy on the other team was freaking out about losing. She takes it *way* too seriously!"

"You didn't miss anything. We're still waiting for the principal." Sophie gives Anisha a big hug and points to the stage.

"Oscar is up there by his poster. He drew that cool skeleton. I saw this big smile on his face through the camera."

Looking around at her friends, Sophie feels like they have a bubble around them—not to keep others out, but a bond that has formed between them since they started the Cinematics Club. A connection that runs on a separate yet parallel wavelength to her family.

"Susan, that looks so good!" Sophie eyes her noodle salad and compares it to her own soggy tuna sandwich. "You should open a restaurant."

"Oh, yeah," Susan replies sarcastically, "my parents would love the idea of me being a chef instead of going into chemistry. Anyway, everyone wants burgers. How many people would be knocking down the door for vegetarian Vietnamese food?"

"About the night of the dance—Oscar and I won't be working. Robert is going to screen *The Rocky Horror Picture Show*," Sophie says.

"What? Really?" CJ says. "La Luna is going to be mobbed!"

Sophie looks over to Matthieu, who is listening to music on his headphones. She knows he is put off by the Halloween dance. *Everyone is going to dress up for fun. Why is he being so stubborn about a stupid dance? Forget about it—don't let it ruin your fun.*

A boy from the AV Club with short feathered hair runs up to the stage to check the microphone mounted on the wooden lectern. He starts the audio system, and Whodini's "Freaks Come Out at Night" blasts from the speakers. The crowd erupts in howls and cheers.

Principal Patterson walks up to the stage with his usual swagger. He shoots a look at the AV Club student, who fumbles with the stereo equipment. The song abruptly stops, and Ray Parker Jr.'s "Ghostbusters" theme plays.

"Hello, Noble Knights!" the principal announces, pushing his black shades down the bridge of his nose. "You may have thought Sonny Crockett from *Miami Vice* just walked onto campus. I assure you, I get mistaken for him all the time," he says half jokingly, gesturing to his white linen suit and teal T-shirt. The crowd of students stares at him blankly. The principal flashes a smile to keep the energy going.

"You have all been patiently waiting to hear more about the Halloween dance. First I would like to thank our planning committee, which has been working night and day to make this happen. They're standing right behind me—please give them a big round of applause!"

A dozen students, including Oscar, take a few steps forward as everyone claps, then proceed to assemble by the side of the stage. Matthieu takes off his headphones and starts paying attention. He flashes Oscar a thumbs-up to show his support.

Principal Patterson pulls a sheet of paper from his inside jacket pocket and reads over his notes.

"The Noble High Halloween dance will be held on Saturday, October 26 from six to eleven p.m. Sven Synth from KNXS will be our DJ for the night, spinning all the hits!" Whistles and cheers erupt across the quad.

"There will be a bake sale during the dance. Don't be tricked and grab some delicious cupcakes, cookies, and brownies baked by our students and our cafeteria. All the proceeds will go toward funding next year's event."

Feeling that he has the audience in his hands, the principal pulls the microphone from its stand and starts to walk around the stage like a rock star.

"Let's talk about the next exciting part of the dance—our Halloween costume contest! This is your chance to express yourselves, teachers and staff included." Principal Patterson looks over the next section of his notes and seems impressed by what he sees on the paper. "We have some exciting prizes this year, thanks to generous donations from our local businesses. Let's start with third prize: a pair of tickets to Wizards and Water Slides, the ultimate arcade and water park located in beautiful Canoga Meadows. Our second-prize winner will receive a gift certificate from A Taste of Class Tux Rentals. The lucky gentleman or lady can attend their prom or a sophisticated party in evening attire from their Dynasty Collection. And saving the best for last…our first-prize winner, thanks to Lyle's Ticket Broker, will receive a pair of tickets to see the Cure perform live!"

A loud roar erupts from the students. Susan starts to choke on her noodle salad. "Did he say the Cure?"

CJ, seeing her struggling, thrusts his soda into her hands. He wraps his arms around her from behind, ready to perform the Heimlich maneuver if necessary. Susan downs the soda and clears her throat.

"Thanks, CJ!" Susan lets out a big breath and feels the air flow through her. She notices that CJ's arms are still locked around her in a bear hug. "Uh, CJ, I'm okay now…you can let go."

CJ releases his grip. "I just wanted to make sure you were okay." He innocently sits back down on the lawn.

"That was scary, Susan. You looked like you were going to turn blue," Sophie says.

"I took a CPR class, so I was ready," Anisha says, pulsing with adrenaline.

"I am sorry, but I was so surprised about the Cure tickets. You know how much I love them!" Susan replies, in disbelief about both the concert and almost choking in front of the whole school.

Principal Patterson walks back to the lectern and returns the microphone to its stand. "There is one last little detail. In addition to the DJ, we will have a live band performing." He smiles at the students and holds them in suspense. "But you know, I think I will save that surprise for the night of the dance. I'll see everyone at the biggest Halloween party ever!" He puts his shades back on and saunters off the stage as the bell signals the end of the long lunch.

"I can walk you to English just to make sure you're okay," CJ offers as Susan gathers her bag.

"I'm good, CJ. Some fresh air is all I need. Thanks again for the soda." Susan clutches the drink as she and Anisha walk away.

"See you later," CJ says, leaving Sophie and Matthieu in the quad.

The silence feels uncomfortable as Sophie and Matthieu walk toward their art history class. *Something is obviously bothering him...just come out and ask him already.*

"Matthieu, what's wrong? You haven't said anything all through lunch."

"I'm just not into the whole dance or the gotta-show-your-school-spirit BS." Matthieu's words fall out his mouth with little care or concern. "Oscar is cool, but I don't have to put on some act like the rest of them."

"Got it," Sophie replies just as abruptly. "You know, Matthieu, the world is not against you."

That finally gets his attention. Her words break through and bring a spark of light back into his blue eyes. They walk together into Ms. Kahn's art history classroom, which is already pitch black except for the glow of the slide projector.

"Welcome, Sophie and Matthieu. Please take your seats." Ms. Kahn stands by the projector. "Today we will begin with the 1930s. This was a turbulent time when Surrealism and Abstraction were major art movements. Surrealists like Salvador Dalí were inspired by dreams and the subconscious."

A painting of stark black, gray, and white forms fills the projector screen. "This was painted by Pablo Picasso in 1937. The title is *Guernica*, a town in his home country of Spain. It was a powerful antiwar statement as Fascism raged across Europe."

Sophie looks up from taking notes and is struck by the painting. Her eyes race back and forth across it, taking in the figures' anguished faces—the same expressions she remembers from the mysterious film reel.

15

Ready for the Close-Up

"If I'm shooting with this long lens, how far away should I go?" Sophie yells, climbing up the back stairs of La Luna. Susan keeps waving until Sophie gets halfway up the metal stairs.

"Does this look good?" Susan poses underneath the theater signage, the neon glow shining on her face. She leans against the brick wall wearing gray checkered high-waisted pants with suspenders.

Sophie adjusts the focus and the aperture and props the camera against the railing to steady it. She clicks the shutter and advances the film.

"Great, Su! Now turn your body and look over your shoulder." *Click...click...click...* Sophie snaps a few more shots. "Okay, let's get some more with the hat."

Susan puts on Oscar's black fedora and tilts it back on her head. She twirls and strikes a few more poses.

"Wow, now I know how hard it is to be a supermodel!" Susan laughs.

The back door of the theater swings open, and Oscar walks out into the alley. Dressed in his costume, he looks over a page of the script as Susan hands him back his hat.

"The sun is going to be setting soon." Sophie sits down on the cold metal stairs and peers down the alley. "Where are CJ and Matthieu?"

"They're probably still at Video Vault. I'll run over and get them." Oscar darts down the alleyway, intercepting CJ and Matthieu.

"I've got a thirty-minute break, so we better get this shot," CJ announces, carrying the movie camera.

Sophie descends the stairs to meet Matthieu. She pulls him closer by his trench coat collar and takes a black eyeliner pencil from her pocket.

"This is going to make you look like you stepped out of *Metropolis*. Just stay still and look up," Sophie says, applying the kohl liner. Matthieu's blue eyes look even more intense as he stares into hers, like the "stranger" she first encountered at the box office.

"I'll set up the tripod at the bottom of the stairs." CJ secures the movie camera to the stand.

"CJ, Oscar, and I will run down the stairs, and we'll end up right underneath the sign," Matthieu says.

"Finally it's my turn to film! I haven't even tried the movie camera yet." Sophie familiarizes herself with the equipment.

Susan reviews the script and checks their wardrobe. "Oscar, take off your name tag. CJ, your suspenders look cool hanging down, but better pull them back up."

"I like this look." CJ pulls his suspenders back over his shoulders and tucks in his dress shirt.

"We better film now! We're losing the light," Sophie calls out, positioning herself behind the camera.

Matthieu, Oscar, and CJ run up to the top of the stairs and wait for their cue.

"And…action!" Susan yells from below.

As dusk arrives, CJ, Oscar, and Matthieu race down the stairs, ending up at the brick wall. The neon sign pulses on and off, casting flickering shadows. Sophie takes the camera off the tripod and comes in for a close-up on their faces. The clicking sounds of the camera stop.

"CUT! We've got the shot!" Susan throws the script pages into the air.

"Sophie? How did it look?" CJ asks impatiently, collecting the camera equipment.

Sophie appears stone-faced until she breaks into a big smile. "It looked…amazing! It was just as exciting to be behind the camera."

Oscar lets out a big huff. "That's a relief. You got the shot!" He puts his name tag back on his vest and walks to the back door of the theater. "Robert is going to be looking for us. We better get back inside."

"Yeah, I have to get back to Video Vault." CJ pushes his suspenders down.

"I've got another hour at Ciao Gelato." Susan tugs on CJ's loose suspenders. "Stop by and I'll sneak you a scoop before my shift ends."

"Wait, CJ, I'm coming with you. You were going to loan me a copy of *Repo Man*." Matthieu joins CJ and Susan as they walk down the alley.

Sophie waves goodbye to them and lugs her 35mm camera with the telephoto lens up the back stairs. She takes pictures of the neon sign, the view, and the sunset. *What a great way to end the day.*

Sophie is still looking through the lens when the Reel World Ltd. van drives up. A man steps out of the van, and she snaps a few pictures. It is not Rikki but an older man whose face is obscured by his flat cap. Sophie is startled when Dylan steps out the door behind her.

"Hey, Moonlight, I was looking for you." Dylan hands Sophie a videotape. "I transferred that old film reel onto VHS. I haven't figured it out, but see if you can crack the mystery movie."

"Oh…okay." Sophie is taken by surprise. "Hey, the film delivery van just arrived. It's some new guy." She points at the truck. "I'm going to the box office now. Thanks for the videotape."

Sophie grabs the door and heads inside as Dylan runs down the back stairs to the waiting van.

******

"Is that you, Sophie?" Sarah's voice comes from the kitchen.

Sophie closes the front door, carrying her bag and her camera. She walks into the kitchen to find her mom fixing a bowl of spaghetti with tomato sauce.

"Hi, Mom, that smells so good!"

"How was your day? You must be hungry. Your father and I already ate. I'll leave this pasta on the table for you."

"Thanks, Mom. The day was good. I got A's on my art history and chemistry exams. And I filmed a scene in our movie for the first time. I'll just put my stuff away and come back for dinner."

Sophie unloads her bag and camera in her bedroom. She changes out of her clothes and into a comfy long gray sweat-shirt with a cut-off neck. After putting her hair up in a butterfly clip, she settles at the kitchen table with the bowl of spaghetti. She reaches for the can of Parmesan cheese and sprinkles a plentiful amount on top of the pasta. Sitting crossed-legged on the chair, she winds the pasta around her fork. After finishing her dinner and clearing the table, she makes her way back to her bedroom.

Looking inside her bag, Sophie notices the VHS tape Dylan gave her. She places it on the shelf with her other videocas-settes. Sophie turns off the light and climbs into bed. When she removes her hair clip, her curls fall freely over her pillow. She turns on her teal digital clock radio, which flashes ten thirty p.m., to listen to music. Sophie closes her eyes, and memo-ries replay in her mind—the neon of La Luna's sign, Oscar's fedora, Matthieu's dark-rimmed eyes, and the film delivery van. The images swirl around as the Psychedelic Furs' "The Ghost in You" lulls her restless mind to sleep.

✳ ✳ ✳ ✳ ✳ ✳

Sophie finishes typing the last line of her art history report on Surrealism. She gathers the books and notes that are scattered around her bedroom floor and tidies them on her desk beside her typewriter. *Finally done!*

The house is silent, since her mom and dad are doing their usual Saturday shopping. The phone rings, and she picks up the receiver.

"Hello?"

"Hi…Sophie?" Matthieu asks.

"Yeah, it's me. I just finished typing my paper on Surrealism. What are you doing?"

"I'm working on my paper on the Bauhaus, the German art school," Matthieu says. "I'll see you at the movie theater later today."

"Great! I'll see you later!"

Sophie hangs up the phone and spots the videotape from Dylan. She pulls it from her bookshelf and walks into the living room. She sits down on the beige plush carpeting, turns on the large TV, pops the tape into the VCR, and presses play.

Watching the black-and-white movie again, Sophie feels the same chills as before. She runs to her room and comes back with a notepad and pen. She plays and rewinds the tape a few times, pausing on certain frames to jot down notes.

- *juillet 1942 (street poster)*
- *Pâtisserie du Jardin*
- *broken windows on shops*
- *families in a line (men, women, children)*
- *officer (cap, a large scar across forehead)*

Sophie suddenly hears her dad's Peugeot sedan pulling into the garage. She quickly hits eject on the VCR. She grabs the videotape, turns off the TV, and dashes to her bedroom. Sophie shoves the notepad and tape onto her bookshelf and turns on her clock radio. She closes her bedroom door and changes into her clothes for work—black pants and a white dress shirt.

After applying eye shadow and lip gloss, she grabs her purse and heads toward the kitchen, where she hears her mom and dad.

"I'm leaving for work," Sophie says, searching her purse for her car keys.

Sophie's parents have piled shopping bags on the kitchen counter.

"Did you finish your homework?" Simon asks, pulling a pair of navy men's pants from one of the bags.

"Yes, Dad. I have everything ready for Monday. I'll be home by seven tonight."

"We'll have dinner together, then," Sarah says as Sophie dashes out the front door to her wagon.

✶ ✶ ✶ ✶ ✶ ✶

"Company meeting in the lobby in five minutes!" Robert announces as he fast-walks past Oscar and Sophie.

They stare at each other in confusion.

"Company meeting? When have we ever had a company meeting?" Oscar says.

Sophie shrugs.

Robert returns to the lobby with Dylan, and everyone assembles by the candy counter. The lobby is decorated with Halloween-themed posters and life-size figures of movie monsters.

"This is the first weekend of October, which marks the beginning of the countdown to our big screenings of *The Rocky Horror Picture Show*. In addition to the Majestic Theater, we are also competing against the new Valley View Multiplex, which is putting on their own scary movie marathon." Robert points to a stand-up sign on the counter. "I have placed a notice here and one in the box office window. People can now buy their passes for our screenings. Sophie and Oscar, please point this out to every customer."

"Okay, Robert," Oscar and Sophie reply.

"Dylan, is the film ready for our screening of *The Hunger* this afternoon?"

"All systems are go!" Dylan, who's wearing a Midnight Oil T-shirt and jeans, gives the thumbs-up. He takes a sip from his cup and vents, "Robert, there's a weird delivery guy working for Reel World now. He has no clue about film."

Robert adjusts his tie. "I was just on the phone with the owner, Monty. He said that guy came into Reel World looking for a job, and it worked out since he needed someone to fill in for Rikki for a few weeks. Well, that's a wrap on our company meeting. Oscar and Sophie, let's make this the best Halloween ever for La Luna!"

Robert makes some final adjustments to the life-size Halloween decorations scattered around the lobby as Dylan leaves for the projection booth. Sophie waves to Oscar, who is arranging candy corn in the concession case.

There's a long line of people outside the theater. A mix of dyed ice-white and black hair alternates down the line like the squares on a chess board. Sophie walks out to the box office and turns the sign on the window from CLOSED to OPEN. She opens the speaker and says, "Welcome to La Luna, how many tickets for *The Hunger*?" Pointing to Robert's sign, she adds, "You can also buy passes for our Halloween screenings, including *The Rocky Horror Picture Show*."

As soon as Sophie gets through the whole line, she sees Matthieu through the glass. He walks up to the window dressed in army surplus cargo pants and a sweater that is starting to fray at the edges. She slides a red ticket to him. "I get free passes, so it's on the house. I am going on my break soon. I'll find you inside."

"Thanks. I'll get the treats." Matthieu goes into the lobby while Sophie completes her routine of closing the box office.

The previews are finishing as Sophie opens the door to the theater. The curtains in front of the screen close, and the light from the projector fades to darkness. Standing in the back, Sophie looks around the dim theater, searching for Matthieu. Slowly, the blue velvet curtains part again, and a beam from the projector lights up the theater.

Sophie walks down the aisle until she spots Matthieu. She slides down the row past a couple wearing black outfits, sunglasses, and blue lipstick and sits in the empty seat.

Matthieu hands Sophie a clear bag of colorful candy. "Oscar said that they were out of licorice, so he got these from Popsicle."

"Jelly beans!" Sophie can't resist and pours some into the palm of her hand. When she bites into one of the pink capsule-size candies, her mouth fills with the flavor of cotton candy. She lays her head on Matthieu's shoulder as the chilling music of Bauhaus's "Bela Lugosi's Dead" plays under the opening of *The Hunger*. She looks around at the audience, many of them dressed like they stepped out of the movie, faces painted chalky white and hair sculpted into spikes.

Matthieu whispers into Sophie's ear, "Do you think anyone here is a real vampire?" She nearly lets out a laugh, but Matthieu muffles her with a cinnamon-flavored kiss.

✳ ✳ ✳ ✳ ✳ ✳

Sophie still tastes the spicy cinnamon as she pulls her wagon up to the Insta-Mat Photo Hut.

"Hey, Sophie," says a teenager with a sandy-blond mullet and a Rush T-shirt. He leans out the window of the drive-through photo developing kiosk.

"Hi, Chris," Sophie says, shutting off her motor. "I dropped off a roll of black-and-white film to be developed. I'm here to pick up my eight-by-ten prints."

"Okay, give me a sec." Chris searches for her order in the tiny orange building capped with a red roof. He opens up a large envelope and checks the contents. "I have your black-and-white negatives and twenty-four enlarged prints." He pulls out a receipt pad and adds up the order on his Casio calculator watch.

"Your total is fourteen fifty." Chris leans out of the window, handing Sophie the envelope.

Sophie searches through her purse and hands him the cash. "Thanks, Chris."

"Hey…" Chris's voice cracks with nerves. "Are you going to the Halloween dance?"

"I'll be there." Sophie starts up her engine, and it sputters. She turns the key again, and the engine makes a loud grinding sound. "Sorry, Chris, I better get home while the car is running!"

Sophie guns the accelerator, and her wagon clangs out of the parking lot. She knows that Chris was just a few breaths away from asking her to the dance, and she feels panicked at the thought of telling him a stupid excuse, since they grew up in the same neighborhood.

Sitting at her bedroom desk, Sophie turns on her periwinkle desk lamp and opens up the large Insta-Mat envelope. She pulls out the enlarged black-and-white prints, which still smell of developer. She examines each print closely: Susan against the alley wall; Su aglow in the neon lighting; Su posing in the fedora; the sunset from the top of the stairs; the Reel World van in the alleyway.

Sophie looks at the last prints in the stack. She remembers shooting a few random pictures of the new delivery man to finish the roll.

An old man coming out of the van, wearing a cap.

The man dropping a film reel.

The cap falling off his head.

The scar.

The scar across his forehead.

Sophie's heart beats fast as the prints fall from her hands. Her mind races for a logical explanation.

Lots of people have cuts. He's an elderly man—he could have fallen. He just happens to have a scar that looks the same as that young Nazi officer's.

Sophie grabs the photo of the man, her notepad, and the VHS tape from her shelf. She opens her bedroom door and walks calmly to the living room. Sophie's dad walks by just as she pops the tape into the player.

"Sophie, did you rent anything good?" Simon asks.

"Oh, it's a new science fiction movie that just came out," Sophie says, hoping to avoid his attention. "You would find it *really* boring, since you hate this type of movie."

Sophie's dad yawns, ready to fall asleep. "Well, it better not be too scary. Just don't stay up late."

"I won't, Dad. Good night."

Sophie hears her parents' bedroom door close, and she turns on the TV. She presses play on the VCR. As soon as the young officer comes onto the screen, she hits pause. The officer freezes in place, as Sophie compares the face on the TV to the one on the photo.

Same scar.

Looks like the same face.

Sophie turns off the TV, hits eject on the VCR, and grabs the videotape. She hurries back to her room and buries the unmarked tape and notepad on her bookshelf. She turns off her desk lamp and lies down on her bed as raindrops streak down her window. She tries to make sense of things.

Who is this delivery man?

How could he possibly be the same person?

16
Stop and Go

The smell of wood and paper hits Sophie as she opens the large door of her neighborhood public library. The one-story brick building sits on a quiet residential street across from a small sliver of green space called Laurel Dell Park. The library is especially quiet on Sunday mornings, and the lighting is subdued except for the beams of sun shining through the clerestory windows. A few patrons are in their usual seats at the long oak reading tables.

Sophie stops at the card catalog. Pulling open one of the long thin drawers, she searches through the cards for the photographer Henri Cartier-Bresson. She reaches for a piece of scrap paper and a tiny pencil, which sit on top of the card catalog, and jots down the name of a book and the call number.

Walking down the aisle of art-themed books, Sophie scans the numbers on the spines until she spots the one for Henri Cartier-Bresson. She pulls the large book from the shelf, cradles it in her arms, and walks toward the checkout desk. She has one more thing to find—one she can't erase from her curious mind.

"Hello, I'd like to check out this book." Sophie slides her laminated library card toward the librarian. "I'm also looking to find out about an event during World War II. Can you help me?"

The librarian, an older man in a gray sweater vest over a crisp button-down shirt, takes the book and points across the room at a petite woman sitting at a desk. "You'll need to speak with our head librarian, Mrs. Ushiyama. I can hold this book for you until you leave."

"Thank you," Sophie says, and walks toward the librarian. She pulls a notepad from her tote bag and asks in a hushed tone, "Excuse me, I'm looking for information on France in 1942."

Mrs. Ushiyama, outfitted in a two-piece rose skirt suit with shoulder pads and a white blouse with a bow, lifts her gaze from the book on her desk. "Yes, I can help you. France in 1942— that would be during World War II, after they surrendered to the German forces and collaborated with the Nazi regime."

Sophie points to her notepad. "How can I find out what happened in *jewlet* of 1942?"

"Ahh—you mean *zhweeyah*. Juillet means July in French." Mrs. Ushiyama rests her hand on her chin, her mind reaching back into her vast knowledge of subjects. She gets up from her sturdy desk chair. "Wait here. I'll be right back."

A few minutes pass, and then the librarian guides Sophie to the microfiche reader, which sits in a private wooden cubicle at the back of the library.

"Please have a seat. I found a newspaper article dated July 24, 1942." Mrs. Ushiyama points to the large illuminated screen. "On July sixteenth and seventeenth, the largest roundup of Jews in Paris was ordered for deportation to concentration camps. This is known as the Vél d'Hiv roundup because the Vélodrome d'Hiver, an indoor sporting arena, was used as a detention center. See if this is what you're looking for. If you have any other questions, I'll be at my desk."

Sophie sits down and leans toward the screen. "Thank you for helping me. I am searching for an officer who has a big scar on his forehead."

Mrs. Ushiyama walks back to her desk as Sophie reads the article. She pulls out her notepad and writes:

- *France invaded by Nazi Germany, 1940*

- *Régime de Vichy, French State*

- *Vel d'hiv sports arena*

- *Drancy transit camp, France*

Sophie stops writing and wonders, *What does any of this have to do with an old man in a delivery van?*

She puts away the notepad in her tote bag and gets up just as Mrs. Ushiyama rushes toward her.

"Miss, wait! I found another article from 1946 that might be of interest." The librarian pulls the transparent film sheet out of the large box reader and replaces it with another microfiche card. "This news article reports on the capture and trials of the officers responsible for the Vél d'Hiv roundup. One of the Nazi officers, who was not captured, is referred to as Balafre." The librarian points to a small picture at the bottom of the article. "Here—this is the only known photo of this officer. He was called Balafre—which means scar in French—because of the large slash across his forehead. To this day, no one knows where he escaped to or whether he is dead or alive."

Sophie stares at the tiny grainy picture of a man—the same man she saw in the old eight-millimeter film Dylan found at the theater. *What if this is the same man from the delivery van? Why would he appear here—and now—delivering films? The reel! Could he be looking for the reel?*

Sophie realizes that Mrs. Ushiyama is still standing right beside her. "Can I make a printout of this article?" she asks.

The librarian sets the microfiche machine to print, and a copy spits out the bottom. Sophie takes the printout and slides it into her notepad. "Thank you for your help!" She checks out the photography book at the front desk and pushes the heavy door open, leaving the library. She walks down the Jacaranda-lined path to the parking lot and gets into her wagon.

Sophie looks out her windshield at Laurel Dell Park, where families are lying on the grass and kids are playing. She tries to make sense of the information she has just learned but can't come to any logical conclusion. *This is just me jumping to some crazy idea. My dad always says I watch way too many movies.* She switches to thinking about Monday's Cinematics Club meeting and drives away, listening to Tears for Fears's "Mad World."

✳ ✳ ✳ ✳ ✳ ✳

The usual big high school milestones are homecoming, prom, and graduation. But for Noble High, the Halloween dance has been elevated to that level, thanks to Principal Patterson. This isn't your ordinary spike-the-punch, nobody-on-the-dance-floor kind of party. This is the hottest event that every LA high schooler tries to gain access to. Last year, a group of students from Cherimoya High tried to sneak in through the gym's ventilation system. They were found stuck in the air ducts the following day but still bragged that they'd been at the dance.

Now that October has arrived, the administration building is transformed with black-and-orange paper streamers cascading down the walls. Posters are on display of the 1984 costume contest winners, all of them legends dressed as characters from *Purple Rain*, *Ghostbusters*, and *The Karate Kid*. A portrait of Principal Patterson dressed as Mozart hangs above the winners' pictures to remind everyone he is the maestro.

Sophie walks through the administration building clutching the Henri Cartier-Bresson book, and Matthieu carries the 35mm camera with the telephoto lens. The school day is over, and students and teachers are whizzing along the corridor. They walk past a big calendar that marks the days until the Halloween dance—twenty-one days to go!

Sophie and Matthieu walk though the quad under a pastel blue sky. There is a vacant quietness except for the rhythmic "Ha! Ha!" of the Karate Club students practicing their moves.

"It's kinda eerie," Sophie says, looking around at the empty campus.

"I like it better this way," Matthieu says as CJ and Susan run up behind them.

"Hey, we were trying to catch up with you guys!" Susan says, securing her backpack over her Esprit jumpsuit and sweater.

Sophie, Matthieu, CJ, and Susan pick up their pace and enter the Cinematics Club classroom. Mr. Omolo is demonstrating how to operate the film projector while Oscar and Anisha huddle close by and watch. Mr. Omolo tilts his head at the sight of the latecomers.

"Glad you could join us," Mr. Omolo remarks, clearly not amused by their tardiness, even if it's only a few minutes. "I set up your latest reel. Anisha and Oscar learned how to operate this film projector."

The club members settle into their seats, and Mr. Omolo walks to the front of the classroom, where he is framed by the white projector screen. He notices the crummy mood he is in and takes a breath. "I want to take a moment before we view your latest reel to make an announcement. You have all put in an incredible amount of work. And positively, you *do* listen to my critiques. Unfortunately, I need to cancel our Monday meetings for a while. I have been assigned a very important news story and will not be here for the next few weeks. Today will be our last meeting until November."

Everyone is stunned by the news. Anisha, wearing a Sade T-shirt and white jeans, offers a diplomatic and sincere response.

"Mr. Omolo, I want you to know how much I have learned from this club. I am proud of what we have done, and we will finish this movie!"

Oscar and Susan both light up and smile at each other.

"That's all right, Mr. Omolo. Not that I don't love this club, but the Halloween dance is only a few weeks away. I'm on the planning committee, and it's like the mob. Once you're in, there's no escaping," Oscar says matter-of-factly.

"Mr. Hart nominated me to represent the Chemistry Club at the assembly, and I will be giving a presentation at our display table," Susan says, relieved to have one fewer responsibility in her long list of commitments.

"That is so awesome, Su!" Sophie exclaims as everyone claps.

Mr. Omolo pulls out a copy of their script. "I see that you have one more scene to film this weekend. As soon as you are done with that reel, CJ will deliver it to me, and I can get it processed for you. I want to assure you that your film will be edited in time for your school assembly."

"I'm also working on the soundtrack," CJ says, holding up a mixtape.

"We are going to film the last scene at my house," Matthieu says, flipping through the pages of the Henri Cartier-Bresson book.

"This movie is in good hands, Mr. Omolo!" Sophie reassures him. She hands him the 35mm camera and pulls out the enlarged black-and-white prints. "I shot these photos with the telephoto lens. What do you think of the lighting?"

Mr. Omolo takes the prints and pins them up on the wall. He walks slowly past the photographs, inspecting each one. "Sophie, these are very well framed, and you made good use of the natural lighting." He points to one of Susan by the neon sign. "Very well composed. It is a bit blurry. Just be aware of the camera shake, but in this case it actually adds a bit of mystery to the portrait. Nice work."

Sophie smiles. "Thank you, Mr. Omolo. It was my turn behind the movie camera, so I'm looking forward to seeing the new scene."

"That's right—I almost forgot. Let's get the show on the road!" Mr. Omolo signals to Oscar. "Lights, please."

******

Sitting inside a tiny ticket booth feels like looking out of a fish tank, seeing the swirl of people and life pass by. There are the common tiffs between couples and the meltdowns when children don't get to buy candy at Popsicle. Sophie can spot the usual suspects as they walk past her little fishbowl. She has a growing desire to break out of this bubble. Maybe this feeling started with meeting Matthieu or making the movie with the

Cinematics Club. Right now, all Sophie can think about is telling Dylan what she found out at the library.

After selling the last ticket, Sophie races up to the projection booth. She knocks on the door and slowly peers into the room. Dylan is loading a film reel onto a projector while cradling the phone with his shoulder.

"Robert, I am *still* waiting on that delivery," Dylan barks into the phone. "I'll let you know as soon as I get it. I have to set up the next movie for the eight o'clock showing. Bye."

Dylan hastily hangs the phone back up on the wall.

"Sorry, Moonlight, I don't have time right now." His attention is focused on the movie projector. "I have to get this film loaded for the next showing, and Robert is on my case about a delivery. He just added the Mexican supernatural movie *Macario* for Day of the Dead."

"Hey, you know that old film reel we watched?" Sophie tries to form a sensible explanation, "Well…I went to the library and found this article about a roundup of Jews in France in July of 1942. The article had this little photo of an officer called Balafre, which means scar in French." Sophie holds out the library article and points. "Look, he has the same slash across his forehead as the officer in the film."

"Okay," Dylan replies, unimpressed, still occupied with the projector. "Well, great detective work."

"You don't get it!" Sophie feels frustrated, since Dylan originally told her to find out about the movie. "This officer is responsible for the murder of Jews, and he has *never* been caught…until now." She pulls out her enlarged print. "I took this photo of that new delivery man. He was wearing a cap, but I just happened to catch him as it fell off. Look, he has the same gash across his forehead."

Dylan stops and stares closely at Sophie's picture. There is a pause, and Sophie senses she has gotten through to him. That is, until Dylan lets out a belly laugh.

"Let me get this straight—this old guy who can barely get out of the van is the Nazi from the mystery reel? Okay, I know how we'll get him. We'll take the Staff of Ra replica in the lobby, and we'll melt his face off with the beam of light, just like at the end of *Raiders of the Lost Ark*. Sorry, Moonlight, but they held the Nuremberg trials for the head Nazis. You should be learning about that in school." Dylan turns his attention back to the projector.

Sophie closes the projection room door behind her without another word. She wants to climb back into the bubble of her ticket booth. *I don't understand why he acted like that. He was interested in the old film before, and now he couldn't care less.* Despite Dylan's sour reaction to her theory, she can't just bury what she's learned.

Sophie finishes her Friday shift, and the sky is pitch black at seven thirty. She swings the back door open and walks toward her car, where someone has traced WASH ME on her dusty rear window.

Sophie, unfazed by the silly graffiti, gets into the driver's seat.

"Wait, Sophie!" CJ yells out as he and Susan run up to her wagon. Out of breath, he gasps, "My scooter is out of gas. Can you give us a ride home?"

"Sure. Get in!" Sophie says, comforted by their friendly faces.

"Thanks, Sophie! I was going to get a ride with CJ." Susan catches her breath and gets into the front seat. She holds up a video box. "Look, I rented *Electric Dreams*. Want to come over?"

"I didn't realize the Vespa was on empty. I'll leave it here and get it tomorrow." CJ balances a gigantic Drink 'n' Dunk cup as he slides into the back seat. "Did you see what I wrote on your window?"

"Oh, that was *you*. Thanks a lot," Sophie says, unsurprised.

The Reel World Ltd. van pulls into the alley, and Sophie's attention is immediately drawn to it. She watches the delivery man slowly get out of the van as Dylan comes out to meet him. They speak to each other, but she can't make out what they are saying. *I better just tell them.*

"I know this is going to sound *crazy*, but…you see that old guy with Dylan?" Sophie takes a deep breath. "I've discovered that he is a Nazi. I accidentally took this photo of him the same day we were shooting. He has the same scar across his forehead as one of the head Nazis who was never caught."

She pulls out the article and the photo from her notebook. Grabbing the emergency flashlight her dad put in the glove compartment, Sophie shines the light across her evidence.

CJ and Susan lean in and compare the pictures.

"It does look like the same scar," Susan agrees.

CJ takes a big slurp from his drink and grits his teeth. "I hate Nazis."

"Rikki always said that La Luna was his last stop of the day. I wonder where this guy will go after this," Sophie says.

"Well, let's follow him and see," CJ proposes, thirsty for adventure.

"We shouldn't chase him all over the city. Why not show CJ's uncle and let him help?" Susan says, obviously hoping to avoid a wild-goose chase. "I want to get home and watch my movie. It's so awesome when the computer falls in love with the girl and then gets jealous."

"The computer gets *jealous*? Tron is so much better!" CJ replies.

Sophie, disregarding their banter, is determined to follow the van. As the delivery man and Dylan are busy handling the film reels, Sophie puts her key into the ignition.

Crannnng.

The wagon makes a loud grinding sound. She turns the engine off and then on again.

Crannnng.

Sophie bangs her hands against the wheel in frustration. "I've had this problem before. I knew I should have told my dad! Now my car won't start and we are going to lose the delivery guy!"

"I'll just run back to Ciao Gelato and call home. I'm sure someone can come and get us." Susan gets out of the Jeep and immediately spots her brother's glowing red Toyota Supra driving into the parking lot. "Steven!" She waves her hands above her head, jumping into the path of the car's headlights.

Steven slams on the brakes and yells, "Are you crazy? I could have killed you! What are you doing?"

Susan races over to his window and sees a pretty woman sitting next to him. "Oh, hi, I'm Susan, Steven's younger sister." Dismissing the fact that this is his date's first impression of her, Susan quickly gets her brother up to speed. "CJ's scooter is out of gas, and Sophie was going to drive us home, but now her car won't start."

"Oh," Steven says. "Well, this is Aimee. She works at the Racquet Centre."

"We have dinner reservations at Chez Louis at eight thirty. Steven, I think we have plenty of time to give them a ride home." Aimee keeps a smile on her face in spite of this unexpected interruption. This is her first date with Steven, and she has made a special effort to get dressed up in a fashionable red bubble dress accented with a big bow and pumps.

"Hi, Aimee." Susan gives a sigh of relief. "Thanks, Steven! I'll go get them!"

Susan races up to Sophie's car. "Steven is going to take us home. Come on!"

"Cool!" CJ grabs his backpack and drink and gets out of the car.

Sophie locks up her wagon, her eyes still glued to the van. *It hasn't left yet. There's still time.*

Steven steps out of the car in a Pierre Cardin navy suit, and Susan, Sophie, and CJ pile into the hatchback's back seat. The overpowering smells of woodsy Drakkar Noir cologne and floral Beautiful perfume hit them all at once.

Sophie doesn't waste a breath. Leaning forward between the two front seats, she points ahead. "Steven, do you see that delivery van? Please follow it!"

"Sophie, what are you saying?" Steven is completely confused by her outburst. "I'm taking you home."

"The man driving the van is a wanted Nazi criminal. I have proof. I just need to see where he is going."

"Are you pulling my leg?" Steven says, not amused.

Sophie rattles off the CliffsNotes version of the story as Steven and Aimee look out into the alleyway. "We don't have much time," she pleads. "He's getting into the van!"

"I'll follow him for a few minutes, but then I am taking you home. Aimee and I are not going to miss our fondue dinner.

Everyone buckle up!" Steven punches the cassette tape into the player, and Gary Numan's "Cars" plays.

"Awesome!" CJ exclaims, slurping up the last of his thirty-two-ounce drink.

The Supra idles until the van starts to drive away. Then Steven shifts into gear, and the car takes off like a rocket into the bustling Ventura Boulevard traffic. The car immediately stops again as they land right behind a traffic jam.

"I am going to take a back alley. We'll meet up with the van farther down the road." Steven takes a right turn, and everyone gets tossed to the left as the car swerves around trash cans and some skateboarders.

"Steven!" Aimee screams, digging her freshly painted red fingernails into the black dashboard. "Slow down!"

The car barrels down the alleyway, and then Steven makes a sharp left back onto the boulevard.

Sophie scans the sea of cars. "I don't see the van anywhere."

Susan looks out the hatchback window. "I don't see it behind us." She turns to CJ, who is leaning against the window, and notices his sickly appearance. "CJ, are you okay? I think he is hyperventilating!"

Sophie looks over to CJ, who is breathing heavily. "I think he's carsick. Steven, can you open the sunroof?"

Steven presses the button, and the sunroof slides open. Peering at CJ in his rear-view mirror, he says, "You *better* not throw up in my car."

"Did you just drink all thirty-two ounces of that pop?" Susan asks, looking scared as CJ grasps his chest.

"It was iced coffee." CJ gasps the words out between deep breaths. He leaps up through the sunroof, feeling better as the cool night air rushes against his face. As the caffeine overload subsides, he enjoys the perch from the sunroof. CJ takes in the lights, people, and music blasting from cars as they stream by him.

Steven checks the time and announces, "It's getting late. I better just drop you at home. Sorry, Sophie, but we've lost the van."

"No, *I'm* sorry that I dragged everyone on this chase. I don't want you to miss your dinner. Susan, let's check out the view on the way home."

Sophie and Susan squeeze up through the sunroof as CJ takes a rest in the back seat. "The Valley looks so cool from up here!" Susan says, the wind blowing through her hair.

Sophie smiles for the first time tonight as she takes in the thrilling view with her best friend. When the car stops at a red light, Sophie spots the Reel World Ltd. van.

"Look!" she calls to Susan. "The van!" Sophie ducks down and points it out to Steven. "There it is!"

The van wobbles and pulls to the side of the road—it looks like one of the tires is blown out. Steven drives up right behind it and shuts off his headlights. Susan drops back down inside the car. Everyone holds their breath as the van's door slowly opens. Aimee pulls a tiny bottle from her LeSportsac handbag and holds it up like a weapon.

Steven looks over at her, puzzled, and whispers, "What's that?"

"It's a personal protection device called the Screamer. It makes a loud screeching noise if any creep gets near me."

A man slowly gets out of the van to inspect the flat tire.

"He is *really* slow. We can take him! Su, hand me my tennis racquet." Steven cracks his knuckles and prepares for action.

Sophie strains to make out the man's face and reports, "It's *so* dark. I can't see him from here." Her heart beats fast as she readies her automatic camera.

Susan reaches over the back seat and grabs a racquet from the trunk. She hands it to her brother. "Be careful."

Out of the dark, a voice yells out in anger, "Not again! Monty is gonna kill me!" The man stands up and walks with a slow limp toward Steven's car.

Steven panics and flashes his headlights on. Holding his hand up to shield his eyes from the blinding light, the delivery man limps closer.

Sophie, snapping pictures with her camera, sees that the man has black hair. She calls out, "Rikki? Is that *you*?"

"Sophie?" Rikki recognizes her voice.

Confused and embarrassed, Sophie tells everyone in the car, "That's Rikki—he's the guy who usually delivers films to the theater. He's not the Nazi I thought we were following." She leans out the window and asks, "Do you know anything about the delivery guy who is filling in for you? He is an old man who wears a cap."

Rikki scratches his head; he has a newly cut shoulder-length mullet. "I dunno. I told Monty I needed to get back to work, and I picked up this van tonight to give it a test drive. I was supposed to be out for weeks, but I guess my bones are bionic or something. See ya—I gotta get this tire fixed." Rikki limps over to the sidewalk and makes a call at the pay phone.

"I don't understand," Sophie says, puzzled. "That other guy exists. I have pictures of him."

"Sophie, we believe you," Susan says.

"We've got your back," CJ reassures her. "Next time he crosses your path, we'll be there."

Steven starts the car and turns the headlights on, and the Supra roars away. "Well, all I know for sure is that we are dropping everyone at home now." He takes Aimee's hand. "There is a bubbling fondue pot waiting for us at Chez Louis."

* * * * * *

Sophie wakes in the middle of the night and finds herself tangled in her comforter. Burning up, she throws off her sweatshirt and lies back in bed in her tank top. Her mind is racing. *There must be a way to end this chase.*

She walks to her bedroom window. As the white drapes fall around her, she looks out at the peaceful sky filled with stars.

She settles back into bed and tries to sleep before the sun comes up.

17

Crash and Burn

Sunday: No work. Movie shoot at Matthieu's house (noon).

Sophie grabs her magenta marker and checks off the day on her Picasso wall calendar. October features the artist's self-portrait bathed in blues. It is of special significance in marking his birthday.

Self-Portrait in Blue Period, Paris, 1901

Sophie pulls a duffel bag out of her closet and lays out things to take to the shoot—vintage gloves, belts, and scarves. She reads through the day's script before zipping it up in the bag. Glancing in her dresser mirror, she looks over her outfit for the shoot and makes sure it looks the same as before—a black leotard with a sheer ballet skirt over leggings. She affixes her beret on her head, grabs the duffel bag, and heads down the hallway to the kitchen.

Simon is immersed in the Sunday newspaper. It's spread out across the table as Sarah brings him a cup of coffee in his green mug. He takes a sip and makes a puckered expression just as Sophie peeks in.

"What is this?" Simon asks Sarah.

"It's decaf. You know the doctor said you need to watch your diet and caffeine." Sarah notices Sophie's outfit. "Are you off to finish your big movie?"

"Yeah. I'll be home for dinner. Everyone is meeting at Matthieu's house. Anisha said she could pick me up."

"I…I already got your car fixed." Simon tries to get the words out in spite of the bitter aftertaste in his mouth. "I took it over to Gene's Auto Body this morning. It was the starter. You shouldn't have any problems now."

Sophie gives her dad a big hug, "Thank you! I better call Anisha." She goes over to the white wall phone in the kitchen nook and quickly dials.

"Hi, Ani. It's Sophie. I'm so glad you didn't leave yet! You don't need to pick me up. My dad got my car fixed. I'll see you at Matthieu's!"

Sophie is so excited about the shoot that she runs straight to the front door.

"Sophie!" Sarah calls out, spotting the duffel bag on the linoleum floor. "Don't forget your bag!"

Sophie runs back to retrieve the bag. "Thanks, Mom!"

"Don't rush on your drive," Sarah says. "It might rain later, so call us and let us know you're all right."

******

Sophie drives toward the canyon road and sees a blanket of gray clouds moving in. Her wagon chugs up the steep road until she reaches the top of Matthieu's driveway. She parks her car beside his silver Fiat Spider and grabs the duffel bag from the trunk. Walking by Matthieu's car, she spots letters written across his dirty windshield—WASH ME. Sophie spies the culprit arriving and flashes a grin. CJ speeds up on his Vespa with Susan clutching his waist for dear life.

The scooter comes to a stop. Keeping her eyes clamped shut, Susan asks, "Are we here?"

"We have landed." CJ smiles, parking the scooter.

Susan slowly opens her eyes and breathes a sigh of relief. She pulls off the mod-style Lambretta helmet and looks around at the lush green surroundings. "Welcome to the Ewok forest."

CJ, Susan, and Sophie walk through the courtyard as the breeze blows through the wind chimes. The door is left open as a welcoming sign. Anisha and Oscar are already rehearsing their lines on the living room couch.

"You beat us here," CJ says, relaxing on the couch by Oscar.

"My mom just dropped us off," Anisha says, her hair slicked back into a sleek braided ponytail. Proudly pointing to her gold hoop earrings, she says, "She let me borrow these."

"Very Sade!" Susan inspects Anisha's look as she smoothes out her helmet hair. "I better get changed. My hair must be a mess! Oscar, can I borrow your fedora?"

"Yeah, but I'll need it later for my scenes," Oscar says, handing Susan his hat.

Susan hides her hair beneath the fedora and makes a beeline to the bathroom with her backpack.

"Um, is Matthieu around?" Sophie asks.

"Yeah, he went to help his dad with something," Oscar replies, putting down his script. "He already set up the camera equipment by the fireplace."

Genni, wearing a Sonia Rykiel black jersey dress and draped suede-heeled boots, walks into the house with Leon racing in front of her. She unloads large paper bags onto the kitchen countertop as he climbs onto one of the bamboo barstools.

"Hi, guys!" Genni calls out, pulling out containers of take-out food. Leon grabs at one of the bags. "No, Leon, these are for our guests. We are going to get burgers and fries with Grandma."

Matthieu and his dad walk into the living room. Marc gives Matthieu's friends a short hello and a wave as he leans into the kitchen. "Genni, I finished my call with the director. Things are still a mess, but I'll get everything on track. It's good for Matthieu to listen in and hear how much work goes into making a studio film." He looks with interest at the takeout food and then finishes his train of thought. "I'm ready to go visit your mom. I'll wait for you in the car with Leon." He looks over at Leon. "How about I race you?"

Leon jumps off the stool and bolts toward the door as Marc jogs behind him.

Genni wraps her scarf around her neck and waves to the club, who are sprawled out on the couch. "We're leaving now for my mom's house in Santa Monica. I got you sushi and teriyaki for lunch. We won't be back until late, so have a great shoot!" Genni looks at Matthieu. "You can call us at Grandma Penny's house if you need us. Please don't destroy the house or end up drenched in the pool." She winks and closes the door behind her.

✳✳✳✳✳✳

Now that Matthieu's family is gone, the house is now the private hangout for the Cinematics Club. Everyone is sprawled in the living room on the Moroccan carpets of ochre and blue.

Oscar struggles with the wooden chopsticks, trying to lift pieces of chicken teriyaki to his mouth. Frustrated, he finally he gives up. "Forget this, I'm using a fork."

Susan lifts her chopsticks to demonstrate. "Oscar, hold them like this." She places his fingers in the correct positions. "Now try."

Oscar pivots his fingers on the chopsticks and finally gets a morsel of chicken into his mouth. "Thanks, Su, but I'll stick with forks." He grabs one and digs into his pile of chicken glazed with tangy golden teriyaki sauce.

Susan feasts on her plate of vegetable rolls as CJ moves his California rolls around like they're backgammon checkers.

"CJ, what are you doing?" Matthieu asks as he shifts the sushi back and forth across the plate.

"I'm working out my scooter scene. I think the camera should be handheld." CJ stares strategically at his sushi rolls.

"We don't even have to add any props. Your house has so many interesting things," Sophie says, admiring the vases and sculptures that decorate the room.

Matthieu rolls the sleeves of his white dress shirt above his elbows and unbuttons his black vest. "My dad brought all those back when he worked in Europe and North Africa."

"Did you ever go with him?" Sophie asks, taking the empty plates to the kitchen.

"Sometimes—I was little." Matthieu moves his hand across the carpet. "My dad got this rug in Morocco." His eyes drift to the large window. "He bought it with my mom."

The phone rings and jolts Matthieu from his memories. He answers it in the kitchen. "Hello. Yes, this is the home of Matthieu Bernard." He listens to the caller, then says, "Okay, thank you. I'll let my parents know."

Matthieu hangs up the receiver, and not a second passes before the phone rings again. "Hello. Uh, yes, this is Matthieu… oh, hi, Sarah. Yes, everyone is here and Sophie is okay. Do you want to talk to her?" He listens to Sophie's mom, then responds, "Yes, the school just called my house. Terrible news. I'll let everyone know, and we won't be filming too late. Bye." Matthieu hangs up the phone.

"Shoot! I forgot to call my mom," Sophie exclaims. "What's going on?"

Matthieu becomes very serious as he breaks the news. "Well, the school just called. There's a gas leak at Noble." His solemn expression quickly turns to happiness. "School will be closed for the whole week!"

Everyone erupts into cheers. "Woo! Yeah!"

"I hope the Halloween decorations don't explode," Oscar says with concern.

"How about some dessert to celebrate?" Susan suggests.

"Good idea! Then can we finally start the shoot!" CJ says.

"Check the freezer," Matthieu says, sitting back down by Sophie. Shifting uneasily, he asks, "Can you help me with my eyes again?"

Sophie pulls the black eyeliner pencil from her bag and applies it. Out of the corner of her eye, she spots a furry animal. Surprised, she asks, "Is that a cat?"

A gray striped feline with large droopy eyes stands in the doorway of Marc's office. Matthieu explains, "Yeah, he always stays in my dad's office. His name is Buster. My dad loves those old Buster Keaton movies, and the cat has the same big eyes."

"Oh, he's cute." Sophie smiles and puts the pencil away. She looks into Matthieu's dark smudged eyes and confirms, "You're ready."

Anisha and Oscar join Susan in the kitchen, searching for treats in the freezer.

"There's Frusen Glädjé ice cream, chocolate and vanilla," Susan says, passing the pint containers to Anisha and Oscar. "Let's scoop these into bowls."

Anisha and Oscar carry the bowls into the living room as everyone gets comfortable on the floor again.

"How awesome to have a week off!" CJ says, scooping up ice cream from his bowl. He notices how silent the room has become as everyone slips into a food coma. He senses the need for inspiration to get them in the mood for the shoot. "It's too quiet in here…where's the music?"

Matthieu turns on the stereo and adjusts the knobs until sounds play from the large speakers.

"This is Sven Synth broadcasting live from LA's *cutting-edge* radio station, KNXS. Better turn this one up—Depeche Mode with 'Shake the Disease.'"

Sophie can't help but get caught up in the emotion of the music. "Come on!" She pulls up Susan and Anisha, who join her in dancing and singing along with the song.

Sophie mouths the lyrics as she make eye contact with Matthieu, who reflects back the same intensity, like there is an invisible wire sending electric currents between them.

Anisha, Susan, and Sophie dance together and then take a bow when the song ends.

CJ, getting comfortable lying on the Moroccan rug, props his head on an embroidered throw pillow. Not satisfied with the song selection, he points to The Clash album by the record player. "Matthieu, that's what I'm talking about! Play me something from *Combat Rock*."

Matthieu reaches for the album and pulls out the vinyl. He drops the needle, and Joe Strummer begins to howl "Straight to Hell." The Cinematics Club lies on their backs as the music echoes off the walls and ceiling beams. Like paper doll cutouts, they grab each other's hands to form an unbroken chain.

The song fades into distorted noise when the needle hits the inner groove of the record. CJ, finally feeling a jolt of inspiration, springs up with a burst of energy. "Let's finish this movie!"

******

The Cinematics Club assembles at the top of the asphalt driveway and stares down the steep slope. They examine the logistics of the scene under a sky streaked with dark grays.

Susan buttons up her black blazer over her polka-dot romper and steps under the carport to review the script pages. Oscar says, "I'm in this scene. Can I have my hat back?"

"Oh, sure!" Susan says, taking off the fedora. Oscar props the hat on his head and waits for his acting cue.

CJ blocks out the scene using his hands as a frame and announces the direction.

"Matthieu, Sophie, Anisha, Oscar—stand together in that order. I want to do a close-up shot of your faces. Matthieu, you should have your head turned away and then look right into the camera when I get to you." CJ scans the script again. "You will be revealed as the double agent who is looking to escape. You'll get into your car and drive off down the hill. Now, everyone get into place!"

CJ grabs the Minolta Super 8 movie camera and starts filming. He slowly walks from right to left until he reaches

Matthieu, who delivers his sinister look directly into the lens. Matthieu then breaks away from the line and jumps into his convertible. The motor revs, and he disappears down the hill.

"Cut!" CJ yells, and stops filming. He walks to the edge of the driveway and sees Matthieu at the bottom of the road.

Matthieu shifts the car into gear, turns around, and accelerates back up the driveway. He asks CJ, "Did you get it? Are we good?"

"Oh yeah, we're good!" CJ calls out with satisfaction.

Matthieu, finished with his scene, slicks his tousled hair back into place as CJ passes him the movie camera.

Sophie's sheer ballet skirt and Anisha's sari start to billow as the wind surges through the canyon. CJ grabs his helmet and gets onto his Vespa. Matthieu prepares the camera and sits down at the top of the driveway.

"I'm ready," Matthieu says, looking through the viewfinder.

CJ secures his helmet, pushes the kick-starter, and revs up the Vespa.

Matthieu starts filming and calls, "Action!"

Whizzing by Matthieu, CJ swerves and crashes into the brush at the bottom of the hill.

BRSSHHHHH.

Uncertain what he just witnessed, Matthieu races down the hill, Susan, Sophie, and Anisha behind him. Oscar follows, holding his fedora in place.

CJ sits up in the leafy shrubs that cushioned his fall. He slowly removes his helmet and looks at his scooter lying beside him.

"*What happened?*" Matthieu asks, propping the scooter upright.

"Are you okay?" Susan looks CJ over for cuts and bruises.

"Your pupils look normal," Anisha says, examining his eyes. "No head trauma, so your brain is still good."

"You must have nine lives," Oscar proclaims. "I thought you went flying!"

CJ scans his surroundings and spots the cause of his crash. Pointing through the trees, he explains, "Look, over there! That deer jumped in front of me, and I didn't want to hit it."

Sophie hears the rustle of leaves on the ground. She catches sight of the beautiful brown deer as flashes of light filter across its form. *It's so beautiful.* Then, quick as a flash, the deer vanishes into the trees.

Matthieu grabs CJ's hand and helps him to his feet. CJ brushes the remaining leaves from his clothing and walks to his Vespa. Circling the scooter, he declares, "It's all in the reflexes—not a scratch!" He puts his helmet on and whizzes back up the driveway as the club runs after him.

"I know I got the shot," Matthieu says. He retrieves the movie camera and hands it over to CJ.

"Let's finish up with Oscar and Anisha," Susan says, turning to the last page of the script. "CJ, do you want to film this?"

"Yes, let's do this." CJ props his helmet on his scooter and prepares the movie camera.

Anisha and Oscar act out the last lines of the script, and then CJ calls, "CUT! THAT'S A WRAP!"

Instead of laughs and hollers, the club is eerily silent. They look at each other, all experiencing the same feeling. They have come to the end of their project, and this journey they have experienced together is done.

"I can't believe we're finished, that it's really over," Sophie says with sadness.

"Well, there is still the editing and music. I'll hand the reels over to my uncle," CJ says. "Matthieu, can I leave the gear in your room tonight, and I'll swing by tomorrow to get it?"

"Sure. I also want to give you a tape to check out. There are some cool Bowie tracks." Matthieu walks with CJ into the house.

"Our movie is going to be the *coolest* thing at the school assembly," Oscar declares. Then he remembers, "I can't believe we won't be at school together for a whole week."

"We can always meet up at the library," Anisha says. "I better change before my mom gets here. She would freak if she found out I'm in a movie."

"Wait…what?" Susan replies, surprised. "Your mom doesn't know *anything* about our movie?"

"Well…not exactly," Anisha says reluctantly. "She wants me to be a nurse and focus on my math and science classes. I always just tell her we're getting together to study. If I told her I was acting in a movie, she would *never* let me come. I can hear her voice in my head: *Don't waste your time on such nonsense. This is not going to get you into a top university.*" She grabs her backpack and continues, "It's weird, 'cause my mom used to sing and dance with me all the time when I was small. But when I started pointing to the TV and saying I wanted to do that, she stopped, just like that."

"You are *really* good in our movie." Sophie hugs Anisha, giving her a vote of confidence.

There's the sound of a car engine and a burst of headlights as a gold Mercedes pulls up the driveway.

"Oh no, it's my mom!" Anisha shrieks, panicking.

Raya Patel steps out of the car in her white nursing uniform. Her black hair is pulled back in a bun, and there is a look of exhaustion on her face from a long day at the hospital. Raya sees Anisha in her striped crop top and sari and is confused by her daughter's outfit, since Anisha was dressed in leggings and a sweater when she dropped her off earlier.

"Anisha, what are you wearing?" Raya says.

"Hi, Mom," Anisha quietly replies. She decides to come clean. "Um…we were filming a movie that will be shown at the school assembly. We are learning all about photographers and making a very professional film."

Raya rubs her temples and lets out a sigh. "We'll talk about this later. Let's just go home." Opening the car door, she asks, "Oscar, do you need a ride?"

"Thanks, Mrs. Patel." Oscar grabs his bag and gets into the back seat. Anisha sits silently in the front seat by her mom.

As the Mercedes drives away, Anisha sees Sophie and Susan waving to her in the side-view mirror.

"I hope Ani doesn't get in trouble," Susan says, throwing her backpack over her shoulders.

"I'll call her. She'll be okay." Sophie gives Susan a goodbye hug.

"Come on! You've got to use this Bowie song," Matthieu says as he and CJ walk back outside toward Sophie and Susan.

"Anisha and Oscar just left," Sophie tells them, not mentioning the quarrel between Anisha and her mom.

"We better get going too." CJ hands Susan her helmet as he sits on his Vespa.

"Are you sure you're okay? Not dizzy or anything?" Susan asks with concern.

"Nine lives—that's what Oscar said," CJ replies assuredly, starting up the scooter.

Susan puts the helmet on and wraps her arms around CJ's waist. The sputtering scooter disappears from view.

* * * * * *

The night falls upon Sophie and Matthieu finding warmth in each other's arms. A thin blanket of fog rises up the canyon. She feels the gentlest rain against her cheek.

"I don't want to go, but I know my mom is going to worry," Sophie says, gazing up at Matthieu.

"Then stay. Just stay," he implores, not wanting their time together to end. He grasps her hand and leads her inside the house. His intense dark-lined eyes pierce hers. "Come for a swim."

Before Sophie can say anything, he picks her up and carries her toward the pool.

"Wait, Matthieu!" Sophie, swept up in the impulsive moment, wraps her arms around his neck. "I'm not going in like this again. I've got my leotard on. Let me take off my hat and skirt."

"Okay, fine." He releases Sophie to the floor. "But I'm jumping in now." Matthieu runs out to the pool.

Sophie shakes her head and laughs, hearing the splash. She walks over to the glass door and catches glimpses of Matthieu swimming in the dark pool, illuminated only when he appears above the surface. She catches sight of his shirt, vest, and tuxedo pants discarded by the side. Walking back to the couch, she zips opens her duffel bag and checks to make sure she has a change of clothing.

Sophie's mind races between the thrill of the night swim and the knowledge that her mom is going to worry about her driving home. *At least I can call and let her know I'm alive.* She walks to the kitchen and dials home on the wall phone.

"Hi, Mom. I just wanted to let you know I'm fine. We finished filming." Sophie listens to her mom as she watches water droplets misting the window. "Yeah, it started to drizzle." She glances at the black cat wall clock as its eyes and tail sway back and forth. It says six o'clock. "I'll be leaving soon. Yes, I will be home for dinner at seven."

Feeling a sense of relief, she hangs up the phone and takes off her beret, letting the waves of her hair fall free.

SCREEEEECH.

Sophie is startled by the piercing sound of a cat's scream. She steps quietly toward Marc's office and slowly peers through the door, which has been left ajar. The room, with its wood-paneled walls and built-in bookshelves, is lit only by a metal 1950s Stilnovo Italian desk lamp. Sophie gasps as she sees a tiny mouse race out from underneath the desk.

"Buster? Was that you screeching?" Sophie asks as the large droopy eyes of the gray cat come into view.

Extending her hand in a gesture of friendship, Sophie steps slowly around the desk. Buster brushes against her hand and retreats to a cubby in the bookshelf. She looks at the picture frames displayed on the shelves—color photos of Genni, Matthieu, and Leon and faded family photos from long ago. Sophie notices a folder full of papers strewn on the floor. *The cat must have knocked these over when he was chasing the mouse.*

Sophie hurries to pick up the papers. She puts them back into the folder and places them neatly on the desk by the phone. Noticing one sheet that has slipped under the desk, she kneels down on the floor to reach it. When she turns over the paper, the air leaves her chest.

THIS CAN'T BE! THIS CAN'T BE! Sophie's mind surges as she stares at a black-and-white photograph of Balafre, the officer with the scar across his forehead from the old film reel. Her heart beats fast as she clutches the picture.

Looking toward the doorway, she sees a shadow approaching. Her gaze pans upward from the wet feet to the soaked black pants, bare chest, and dripping dark hair until she meets blue eyes smudged with eyeliner. Sophie can't seem to speak; Matthieu's look is pained, like she has ripped open a scab.

"What are doing in here?" he quizzes her.

"Uh…I was calling my mom, and then I heard this loud screech. I followed the noise in here and saw that it was Buster scaring a mouse away. He must have pushed these papers off the desk." Sophie, still gripping the photograph, feels her arm tremble as she holds it up. "This man…who is he?"

Matthieu walks slowly toward Sophie and takes the picture. With wounded eyes, he hesitates a moment and then answers, "It's someone from my dad's past. It doesn't matter now." He puts the photo into the folder and grabs her hand, leading her back toward the pool. "I thought you were coming for a swim."

Sophie stops before they make it outside. Not knowing exactly how to phrase it, she probes, "Matthieu, is that man… is he part of your family?"

"What?" Matthieu's sadness turns to anger, and he lets her hand go. "That Nazi killed my dad's family. He has been looking for Balafre, not knowing if he is alive or dead. That's why he keeps a file on him. Now you know. Happy?"

Sophie tries to understand what she's just heard, wanting to rewind and play the conversation back. Then everything becomes crystal clear in her mind, and she nearly explodes with the news. She clutches Matthieu by his bare shoulders, knowing that she has the answer.

"Matthieu, you don't understand! I've found Balafre! He's alive here in LA." She paces back and forth, sharing her detective work. "I know it sounds crazy, but I took pictures of him that day we were shooting behind La Luna, and it's the *same scar*!" Sophie beams, knowing she has solved this mystery. She waits for Matthieu to hug and kiss her, but he stands there motionless.

Matthieu leaves Sophie standing by the office and walks back to the pool to retrieve the rest of his clothes. He throws his shirt and vest on loosely and walks back to her, ready to close the door on the skeleton that she has dragged out of the closet. His initial urge to flee changes into fight mode.

"You know *nothing* about my family. All you know are fairy tales and sunshine. Do you know what we've gone through—losing my mom, and how many schools I've been to? And now you want to ruin it even more. I'm not telling my dad *anything* about this." Matthieu's fiery emotion turns cold. "Sophie, you should go home now."

Stunned by his hurt-fueled reaction, Sophie grabs her duffel bag and runs out to her car. She doesn't look back as she drives away through the canyon. Her throat tightens until tears flood down her cheeks.

What happened? I thought Matthieu would be so happy and that this would help his dad."

✶ ✶ ✶ ✶ ✶

The murky fog has fallen, and Sophie steers slowly through the barely visible Valley. Her emotions race, making her feel disoriented. She remembers the time she was pulled under by a rip current while swimming in the ocean. She didn't know what had happened until she finally came up for air, finding herself thrown farther from the shore. Her head throbs like she was just pounded by that same violent wave.

The sight of her home brings comfort as she pulls into the driveway. She wipes the tears away and checks her face in the rear-view mirror.

Sophie carries her bag into the house and smells the aroma of hamburgers. She walks into the kitchen and finds her dad flipping patties in a frying pan as her mom takes baked potatoes out of the oven.

"Sophie, just in time for dinner!" Sarah says, slowly unwrapping the foil around the potatoes. She notices Sophie's flushed face and walks over to feel her forehead and cheek. "You feel a little warm. We should check your temperature."

Sophie holds in her emotions and replies, "We did a lot of filming today. I think I am just going to rest in bed now."

"It's good that you will be home all week, since school is closed. I can make you some soup or scrambled eggs," Sarah says.

"Thanks, Mom, maybe later. Also, if Matthieu calls, tell him I'm busy."

Sarah asks, "Sophie, did anything *bad* happen today?"

Not wanting to reveal what she has discovered, Sophie reassures her mom, "Oh, no. He didn't do anything *bad* to me. The movie…it's done, so I'll spend this week concentrating on my homework and reports."

Simon smiles. "That is the right thing to do. You need to concentrate on your studies. It's good to have friends, but your studies come first. You will be applying to colleges next year. You can't let having fun distract you from your future. We will definitely let Matthieu know that you are *not* available."

Sophie drags herself to her bedroom and pulls the white curtains closed. She collapses onto her bed and falls asleep until the next morning.

18
Hide-and-Seek

This Monday morning feels different—no alarm clock beeping, no rushing out the door to make it to school before the bell. Sophie opens her eyes to see the sun shining through the curtains. Sitting up in bed, she realizes she is still wearing the leotard and ballet skirt from the day before. Grabbing a sweatshirt and knit skirt, she heads toward the shower to start the day.

Changed into fresh clothes, Sophie pulls her wet hair back with a butterfly clip. After a typical morning bowl of cereal, she closes herself in her bedroom. Working through subject after subject, Sophie tries to stop her thoughts from drifting to Matthieu.

There's a knock on her bedroom door, and Sophie opens it.

"Susan and Anisha are here," Sarah announces. "You should take a break. It's already one o'clock, and you haven't had lunch or been outside today."

Sophie glances over at her clock radio. She hadn't realized it was already afternoon. She closes her art history book and puts on her black ankle boots. Taking out the butterfly clip, she wraps a vintage polka-dot scarf around her hair like a headband.

Susan and Anisha are waiting in the kitchen.

"My sister just dropped us off," Susan says. "Want to do my favorite type of exercise? Let's walk to the mall."

"Did you already eat?" Sophie asks, feeling her stomach rumble.

"Yeah, I had a sandwich," Anisha replies.

"I'm good," Susan says. "I had my salad."

"I'll make a sandwich to take with me." Sophie piles some cheese onto bread, grabs a drink, and puts everything into a paper bag. "Grab and go!"

Sophie, Anisha, and Susan walk past the mowed green lawns of the quiet suburban neighborhood.

"Ani, what did your mom say when you got home?" Sophie asks, biting into her sandwich.

"She was too tired to talk much. She'd had a bad day at the hospital. But she did say that the hoop earrings looked good on me," Anisha says, putting on a pair of neon-pink sunglasses.

"That's a relief," Susan says. "She looked pissed! I was worried that you were going to be grounded or something." She pulls off her cable-knit sweater, revealing a Siouxsie and the Banshees T-shirt. She ties the sweater around her high-waisted pants.

"You looked good on the back of CJ's scooter. Did he ask you to the Halloween dance?" Anisha wonders.

"It's stupid, but I haven't told him about my mom setting me up on a date." Susan searches for the right words. "I don't want to ruin our friendship."

"It's obvious he likes you. He just doesn't know how to tell you," Sophie says.

"Speaking of liking…" Susan changes the subject. "What did you and Matthieu do after everyone left?"

The night flashes back through Sophie's mind. "He wanted to go for a swim," she answers.

"Ooh…that sounds good!" Anisha says.

"And then it turned into a nightmare," Sophies admits.

"Wait! What happened? *Did he attack you?*" Susan holds up her hand, stopping Sophie from walking.

"*No!* That's what my mom thought too," Sophie explains. "It was because of the Nazi."

Confusion crosses Anisha's and Susan's faces as they look at each other.

"Matthieu was in the pool waiting for me. I was excited and nervous at the same time! I went to change and heard Buster the cat screeching, so I went into his dad's office to see what was happening." Sophie takes a sip from her drink and continues, "The cat had knocked some papers off the desk, so I went to pick them up. One of them was a photo of that same Nazi, the one with the scar on his forehead. Just as I was putting the papers back on the desk, Matthieu came into the office. I asked him about the picture. He told me that his dad has been searching for that officer because Balafre killed his family."

"Are you *serious?*" Susan can't believe what she is hearing. "So he must have freaked out when you told him what you've discovered. Did he take you in his arms and kiss you?"

"Not exactly." Sophie swallows the last bite of her sandwich. In a tone that reveals her raw heartbreak, she says, "I thought he would…I thought he would see how much this could help his dad. But not only is Matthieu not going to tell him, he told me to leave."

Heat rises to Susan's temples, and she wastes no time saying exactly what she thinks. "What a jerk! You're the best thing that's ever happened to his mopey self. I say he is officially kicked out of the Cinematics Club!"

"It's good that we don't have to be at school this week. It would be *totally awkward* to see him today," Anisha says in a more diplomatic way.

"Now I get it! I thought it was strange when your mom called and asked us to come over," Susan tells Sophie. "I guess she wanted us to cheer you up."

As they leave the neighborhood for the busy main street, Sophie spots Matthieu driving his silver Spider. She pulls Susan and Anisha behind a hedge to hide.

"Look! It's Matthieu," Sophie whispers to them.

They peek out to watch him.

"He *must* be going to your house," Anisha says. "See, I bet he's already sorry."

"Yeah, already sorry that he messed with the *wrong girl*," Susan says, still fired up.

"I think the coast is clear." Sophie steps out from behind the hedge and signals to Susan and Anisha. "Let's check out the mall."

Anisha turns to Susan and says matter-of-factly, "For a vegetarian, you sure are ready to fight."

******

Shopping is always a good distraction. The Fashion Runway is the more refined mall in the neighborhood compared to the huge Promenade. This is the mall parents love to go to, since there are no video game arcades or food courts that are magnets for teenagers.

Sophie, Susan, and Anisha meander from store window to store window through the park-like outdoor mall. They stand in front of Henri, a shop filled with mannequins posed like they're at a glitzy soirée. Sophie is mesmerized by the plastic figures dressed in the latest fashions from Paris, from little black dresses to wrap coats. She peers through the window, imagining the exciting world of late-night New York art gallery parties and fashion shows like the ones she reads about in *Interview* magazine.

"Look at how cool that zippered jacket is!" Sophie points to the Azzedine Alaïa with zippers crisscrossing the front.

"It must be, like, a thousand dollars!" Susan exclaims. She digs into her purse and counts her money. "Too rich for me. I can buy something at Snax."

"Me too!" Anisha agrees.

Susan, Anisha, and Sophie buy treats at Snax, the dessert shop in the center of the mall. They take their goodies and sit down on a stone bench to people watch.

Anisha breaks off a piece of her oversize chocolate chip cookie. "It's still gooey from the oven!"

"Anyone want to try some of my brownie?" Susan asks, offering the dark rich cake topped with fudge.

"Sure!" Sophie takes a piece of Susan's brownie and hands her a chunk of her salt-covered pretzel.

A man and a woman stroll out of the Royal Buccaneer restaurant carrying shopping bags.

"Is that Ms. Kahn and Mr. Omolo?" Sophie's eyes widen.

"So this must be his *special assignment!*" Susan shakes her head. "I love the Royal Buccaneer. I miss their French dip sandwiches *a-joooo*."

"I don't think they saw us," Anisha says, wrapping the rest of her cookie in its paper bag. "Do you want to head back now? We can work on our chemistry homework."

"That sounds good, Ani." Susan gets up and feels the brownie sugar rush. "I'm ready for our walk back. This is the best PE class. If only we could do this every day!"

"We would get automatic A's if this was our exercise!" Sophie smiles as they walk past the stylish store workers and customers.

******

The week drags on as Sophie busies herself with school assignments. Her mom acts as her screener when the phone rings. She takes notice when cars drive past her bedroom window, just in case one of them is Matthieu's.

When Friday lunchtime finally arrives, Sophie finishes her art history report on Frida Kahlo. She spreads thick layers of peanut butter and jelly across rye bread and gets comfortable sitting cross-legged on the fluffy living room carpet. Putting her plate on the coffee table, Sophie grabs the remote control and flips through the TV channels. She stops when she sees Laurence Olivier's Heathcliff crying out to Merle Oberon's Cathy, "Be with me always."

Wuthering Heights. *I love this movie.*

Sophie feels tears welling up in her eyes since this is one of her favorite romantic flicks. She imagines Matthieu wandering the dusty canyon fire roads like they're the English moors. She's lost in the movie when she hears her mom's voice.

"Sophie, you better finish your lunch. Don't you have work this afternoon?"

"Of course, Mom." Sophie eats the last crust of the sandwich. She turns off the TV and brings her dishes into the kitchen. Before she gets ready for work, she asks her mom, "Matthieu…uh…did he ever call?"

Sarah hesitates and then says, "You haven't said what happened between the two of you, and I hope it's only something silly. He has actually called every day, sometimes twice." Sarah hands Sophie a dry cleaning bag with her black vest. "I don't like having to tell him that you're busy every time. You are going to have to see him when you go back to school next week. So you better find a way to work things out."

"Okay. Thanks, Mom." Sophie takes her black vest and goes to her bedroom.

Matthieu wouldn't be calling like that if he wasn't sorry, right?

✳ ✳ ✳ ✳ ✳ ✳

TWO WEEKS UNTIL ROCKY HORROR! DRESS FOR THE TIME WARP!

The announcement jumps off the marquee of La Luna as Sophie sits beneath it in the box office. CJ, dressed in his green bomber jacket, pulls up to the curb on his Vespa.

"Hey, Sophie!" CJ yells over the loud sputtering motor. "Our last film reels are at the lab! They're getting developed! I'll catch you later!" He zooms away.

Sophie catches only bits of CJ's words—*film reels, developed*—and pieces together the meaning. She tallies up the ticket sales from the eight p.m. showing of the action film *Commando*, locks up the cash and receipts in Robert's office, and heads over to the candy counter.

"What the… Are you supposed to be special forces?" Sophie can't control her laughter.

Oscar, not amused, is dressed in olive military coveralls and streaks of black face paint. "This is *not* how I'm dressing for the Halloween dance! My uncle says this will help sales for our Commando Combo—hot dog, popcorn, and soda for three dollars. It's actually working, 'cause everyone bought the combo."

"Wow! Great job, Oscar!" Sophie pulls the instamatic camera from her purse and snaps a picture of him in his getup. "I saw CJ drive by, and he said our final film is being processed. I have to start on my costume for the dance. I can't wait!"

"There is *so* much to do. I'll be hanging decorations until the doors open that night," Oscar says, cleaning up cardboard trays from the candy counter.

"I'm going home. See ya later!" Sophie waves to Oscar.

Sophie swings open the back door and can barely see the moon, as a layer of fog has moved in. She spots her wagon in the parking lot.

"Mooooonlight! Wait!!!!" Dylan yells, rushing down the back stairs.

Sophie stops cold in her tracks and turns around. "What now, Dylan? You already had a good laugh at me because of my *crazy* idea about the delivery man."

"That's what I want to talk to you about!" Dylan tries to organize his thoughts. "I was a jerk…sorry." He rolls up the sleeves of his thermal shirt, and then his words fly out rapid-fire. "That reel! *Something's* going down. I just got a call from Max, the theater owner. He *never* calls me, *ever*. Now, out of the blue, I get this call about how I have to keep that reel safe and not let *anyone* touch it. And how there is supposed to be an extra delivery coming on the night of the big *Rocky Horror* screening."

Sophie can't believe what she is hearing. She had finally put the whole discovery behind her, but now she feels validated—her intuition was right all along. "So now you believe me? Even about the delivery guy?"

"Something is definitely going on with that old guy with the scar." Dylan starts to climb back up the stairs as the fog grows thicker. "I don't know what'll happen that night, but it's going to be something *big!*"

Sophie feels like she is on a roller coaster ride, inching up the towering hill, uncertain what she'll encounter once she arrives at the big drop. Her brain can't handle any more uncertainty after this long week, especially knowing she will have to see Matthieu on Monday. Will he pretend they don't even know each other?

✳✳✳✳✳✳

When she arrives home, Sophie gets comfy in her long ribbed sleep tank and looks over magazine cutouts from the movie *Blade Runner*. She runs a glue stick over the backs of the figures and arranges them on a white poster board.

Two weeks till the Halloween dance. Think! Robots, replicants, futuristic Los Angeles.

Sophie gets up from her bedroom floor and opens her closet. She pulls out a black skirt suit her mother found stored in the attic. It's one of the few items Sarah has that belonged to her own mother—an elegant jewel-embellished blazer with shoulder pads and a pencil skirt from the 1940s. Unzipping the plastic garment bag, Sophie inspects the outfit and compares it to the pictures from the magazines.

Trying on the blazer, she stands in front of the mirror to see a perfect fit. She wonders what her grandmother was like. *If this suit could only talk.* Sarah tells stories now and then about how her mom, who was an incredible seamstress, found work making costumes for Hollywood actresses. There were glamorous and not-so-glamourous tales about the studio lots, but for Sarah, growing up in the shadow of the Hollywood sign was like being in the land of Oz.

Sophie hangs the suit back in her closet as the phone rings. Her heart starts beating fast, and she slowly opens her bedroom door.

"Sophieee," her mom calls out. "Pick up the phone. It's Susan."

Sophie is relieved and disappointed at the same time. She picks up the phone in her room and says, "Thanks, Mom. I've got it."

Susan hears the click of Sophie's mom hanging up and blurts out, "Did you talk with Matthieu?"

"I haven't yet, but my mom says he has been calling every day." Sophie feels like it has been an eternity since she saw Matthieu that night at his house.

"Oh, so he *must* be super miserable and mopey by now! He's trying to make up for what happened!"

Sophie realizes it's time to end the cat-and-mouse game. "I'm gonna call him. I'll do it tomorrow for sure!"

"Yeah, that's a good idea. We all have to see each other on Monday anyway when we go back to school. I can *totally* still give him the cold shoulder if you like," Susan says, always ready to back up her best friend. "I want to hear *everything* he says!"

"Thanks, Su. I'll call you tomorrow. Bye."

Sophie hangs up her phone and starts pacing back and forth, rehearsing what she should say to Matthieu.

Act like you haven't even thought about him at all.

"Hi, I heard you called."

"Matthieu, what did you want to talk about?"

No…that's dumb.

Sophie gives up thinking about it for now. She runs her eyes over her bookshelf, searching for inspiration. Her notes on Balafre…the latest *Vogue* magazine…

She grabs a photo album and sits on her bed. Her fingers brush across the front cover, which she painted with the Cinematics Club logo. She slowly unsticks the plastic-covered pages and flips through the album. The happy memories flood back. Sophie looks at the black-and-white pictures from the first shoot at Matthieu's house—everyone looks so cool in their costumes. She makes her way through the rest of the pictures and sees that the album is only half filled. *Our story is not over yet!*

Sophie puts the photo album back on her shelf and pulls aside one of the white curtains. The fog has settled over the neighborhood, and she can barely see anything beyond her bedroom window. She turns on her clock radio for a musical distraction and shuts off the light. Finally climbing into bed, she closes her eyes.

"This is Sven Synth, and you're listening to LA's *cutting-edge* KNXS. It's Friday night, and I am broadcasting *live* from the hottest dance club this side of the 101, the Spotlight. Can't get in? We're not leaving you out on the curb. Just turn up your radio wherever you are! We're starting the party right now with Depeche Mode and 'Shake the Disease.'"

Sophie is instantly transported back to the last day of the film shoot. She remembers everything—the Japanese lunch, dancing to this song in Matthieu's living room, the filming…

Tap-tap…tap-tap.

Hearing the knocking against her bedroom window, Sophie's eyes snap open, but her body remains frozen. She doesn't want to look at what could be making the sound. Her hand slides down the side of her mattress—she has a baseball bat under her bed in case there's ever a burglar.

She hears her name being called in a whisper.

"Sophie…Sophie!"

Slowly creeping out of her bed, she turns the music down. Sophie feels her heart thumping. She carefully pulls the curtains apart…revealing Matthieu standing on the lawn. He is not hiding behind a costume but is simply dressed in a T-shirt and jeans. Sophie has no words as she looks back at him through the glass.

Matthieu, surrounded by the fog, presses his right palm against her window. The word I'M is written on his skin in black marker. He ends the sentence by pressing his left palm to the glass, marked with the word SORRY.

Sophie places her palms against the glass, lined up with his hands. Without needing to say a word, this is her gesture of acceptance. Matthieu slides a paper through an opening in the window. She unfolds the sheet.

Would you go with me for a walk?
Fire road.
Sunday. Noon.

I'll have answers for you.
—Matthieu

Sophie looks up from the letter and sees the remorse in his blue eyes. She smiles and nods. Like a heavy weight he has been carrying for the past week has been lifted, Matthieu smiles before disappearing into the dense fog.

Sophie, feeling like a passing thunderstorm is moving away, closes her curtains. She climbs into the comfort of her bed, still grasping Matthieu's letter.

19
Back to the Beginning

The leaves, changing from green to gold, fan out across Sophie's view as she drives along Windswept Canyon Road. The fog from the past few nights has cleared, and she catches sight of the light blue sky through the canopy of trees. Sophie sings along to Howard Jones's "No One Is to Blame," which is playing on the car radio. Anxious excitement stirs in her belly as she accelerates up the driveway and parks her wagon at the top of the hill.

Adjusting her newsboy hat in the rear-view mirror, Sophie grabs her purse and steps out of the car. She drapes her cross-body bag over her long cardigan sweater and looks around for Matthieu. Like a deer camouflaged in the brush, she catches him waiting for her in the shadows of the leaves. She walks toward him, and he greets her with an outstretched hand.

"Hi, my name is Matthieu. Enchanté." He shakes her hand. "Umm…that guy you saw last time you were here is—how do I say it?—an idiot."

"*Ahn-shan-tay*," Sophie responds to his French greeting. "Nice to meet you, Matthieu. Hmm…so that was your evil twin? I hope I never have to see that…how do you say… *jerk* again."

Matthieu grasps his chest like *you have pierced my heart.* He takes her hand and leads her up to the fire road. From the barren dirt path, they walk past yellow wildflowers and turn onto a trail that leads into a shady forest of oak and walnut trees. They spot a fallen tree to rest upon.

"Is this where you tell me about your dad and why he has a picture of Balafre?" Sophie asks, finding a somewhat comfortable part of the tree to perch on.

Matthieu grabs a twisted branch and starts drawing a map in the dirt. He brushes aside the hair that keeps falling into his eyes. "When I turned sixteen in January, my dad thought it was time I learned about his family, our history."

Sophie wonders about her own family's history. "My mom and dad never talk about what happened to their families in Europe during the war. We just have old photos of family members on the wall. I don't know why they don't want to talk about it."

Matthieu points the stick at some lines he's drawn on the ground. "This is France, where my dad was born and his family lived in an apartment in Paris. His dad, Maurice, was a watchmaker, and his mom, Emile, was an artist. Then the Germans invaded Paris. There was a roundup of Jews in 1942. My dad was about seven years old. Before his mother and father were taken, they arranged for him and his little sister, Sabine, to be looked after by their neighbors, who lived on the top floor of the building. Theo was a French soldier who had been married in secret to a Jewish woman."

Matthieu draws a line between France and another shape. "Theo and his wife smuggled my dad and his sister onto a train, and they finally made it to England. That is where they lived until the end of the war. The last time my dad saw his parents, he was looking out the apartment window at an officer in black. That officer with the scar—Balafre—*he* is the one who took his mom and dad away."

Matthieu stomps away the markings in the dirt with his black combat boots. He tosses the branch back into the shrubs and sits on the downed tree next to Sophie.

Is this destiny? Could something so horrible have brought us together?

Sophie reaches into her bag and reveals a videocassette.

"What's on the tape?" Matthieu asks, noticing the absence of any artwork or label.

"I think you should see this now," Sophie tells him.

✱✱✱✱✱✱

Matthieu and Sophie follow the trail back to the fire road, where the intense sun radiates. As they approach Matthieu's house, BMW and Mercedes-Benz cars are lined up all the way to the edge of the driveway. Sophie and Matthieu crouch down in the shrubbery and watch casually cool people arriving.

"No!" Matthieu exclaims. "I forgot that my dad and Genni are having a party."

He grabs Sophie's hand and leads her around to the side of the house. His bedroom has wraparound windows with white wood paneling and cinder block walls. Matthieu slides open one of the windows and climbs inside. He helps Sophie in and closes the mini blinds over the window. Light projects through the slats as she looks around his room, which is spare except for a low platform bed, a desk, and posters of The Clash and Talking Heads.

Sophie pulls the videotape from her bag, and Matthieu pops it into his VCR.

"There's no sound," Sophie says, sitting on the bed.

Matthieu hits play on the remote control and sits down beside her.

Sophie feels the same chills she did the first time she saw the reel. Matthieu pauses the tape on an image of the officer, which jitters up and down on the TV screen. He walks closer and stares at the scar on the officer's forehead like he's making a photocopy in his memory.

"We can get Balafre!" Sophie insists. "This tape is a copy that Dylan made. He has the film reel that came in a mysterious delivery. There is going to be another film delivery on the *exact night* of the Halloween dance." Sophie catches her breath. "I know that this old Nazi didn't come out of hiding to be a delivery guy. He is looking for *these reels*. I went to the library, and the librarian told me there was only one photograph ever taken of him. Now he is here, and this film proves what he did."

Matthieu ejects the tape. He wants to chuck it across the room but restrains himself when he sees the impassioned light in Sophie's eyes. He knows that he cannot turn his back again—not on her, and not on the courage he needs to face the past.

"I don't want my father to know about this." Matthieu kneels on the floor and hands her back the tape. He hears the music and laughter from the party. "He's happy now. Sophie, we do this together, and we do it alone. This will be our secret mission."

Sophie sits down beside Matthieu on the floor, and they take a break from the intensity of the moment. The sound of

a saxophone drifts into his bedroom from the outdoor speakers—Sade's "Your Love is King." He takes her newsboy hat
off and places it on his head. She sees the faint markings *I'm
sorry* on his palms as he brushes her loose waves away from
her face. They embrace and kiss as the light from the blinds
zigzags across them.

I have to tell him.

"Matthieu," Sophie says, taking a breath for air. "You aren't
exactly the only one I've told about Balafre."

He leans back in to kiss her lips again, entangling his hands
in her floral-scented hair. Then the information sinks in. "Wait!
Who else knows?"

Sophie gathers her hair and puts her cap back on her head,
leaving Matthieu's hair to fall into his eyes. "Well, there's
Susan and CJ—they were helping me when I was trying to
follow Balafre in the delivery van. And my car wouldn't start,
so there was also Steven, Susan's brother, who drove us on that
chase. Oh, and his girlfriend, Aimee."

"You're kidding me. This is your *secret* operation?"
Matthieu shakes his head, finally giving up on the idea of
being in control.

"We are actually *really good spies*, not just in our movie,"
Sophie reassures Matthieu with a smile.

Genni's voice calls from outside his bedroom door. "Matti?
Are you in your room? Your dad is getting ready to make his
announcement about the movie in a few minutes."

"Yeah, okay." Matthieu helps Sophie out his window and
whispers to her, "Don't go. Wait right here!"

Genni slowly opens the bedroom door and peeks her head
in to see Matthieu standing in front of the window with the
blinds closed.

"Matti, what are you *wearing*?" Genni asks, surprised by the sight of his combat boots and ripped pants. "Better change quickly." She hurries away and closes the door.

Matthieu speaks to Sophie through the blinds. "I'll be out in a sec. Wait for me."

Sophie catches a glimpse of Genni breezing out to the party in a forest-green dress. Her long copper hair is permed and gathered on top of her head with a jeweled comb. The blinds shoot back up, and Matthieu jumps out his bedroom window. His hair is loosely gelled back, and he has changed into the white dress shirt and pants from the movie shoot.

"I'd better go. It sounds like the party is starting." Sophie turns to walk back to her car.

"Stay a little bit longer. I know a place where we can hang out." Matthieu grabs her hand and leads her to a hidden terrace above the pool area, surrounded by ferns and palms.

Sophie, sitting on a stone bench, marvels at the view of the party down below. Chinese paper lanterns are strung above the pool, and servers buzz around the guests with silver trays of champagne and cheese. She watches Matthieu as he snakes around the glitzy guests and kneels down beside a white linen–draped table filled with drinks. He reaches up to take a bottle of champagne, but just at that moment a server walks by and places it on her tray. Sophie laughs, watching the slapstick event play out.

Matthieu climbs back up to the secluded spot, clutching a tall glass bottle of sparkling water. "I tried," he says, defeated, passing it to her.

The refreshing bubbles tickle Sophie's throat. She drinks half the bottle and hands it back to him. "I guess I was thirsty."

Matthieu gulps down the rest of the water. "Have you heard from CJ about our film?"

"CJ said the last reels are being developed. Even if Mr. Omolo is gone for the rest of the month, we still should have a meeting after school on Monday," Sophie says.

Her attention is drawn back down to the stylish people laughing and dancing around the pool, a sea of teased hair and shoulder-padded dresses. The DJ plays Les Rita Mitsouko's "Marcia Baïla" as Marc makes his grand entrance. The guests erupt into loud applause and sing along with the song in French.

"It is my pleasure to introduce Monsieur Marc Bernard, the Cinéma du look producer of the film *La Vie en Bleu*!" the DJ announces, the sunlight bouncing off his silver satin duster.

Marc, dressed in a boxy light gray Armani suit, wraps his arm around Genni as he waves to the guests. The DJ passes a microphone to Marc, who looks around the crowd for familiar faces.

"Your dad is going to speak. I think you'd better get down there." Sophie stands up and puts her bag over her shoulder.

Matthieu and Sophie walk hand in hand down the terrace steps, and then she lets go, heading toward the driveway.

"I will see you at school tomorrow," Matthieu calls out. He rushes down to the party.

Sophie lingers long enough to see Matthieu joining his dad as he begins his speech. She retrieves her wagon from the valet and starts the ignition, thinking of all the things she has to do.

Tomorrow, School
Our Film
The Halloween Dance
Capturing a Nazi

Two weeks and counting…

20

A Spark Starts a Flame

There is an unusual electric excitement humming through Noble High on Monday morning. Energized by having a surprise week away from school and the anticipation of the upcoming Halloween dance, the students chatter loudly in the hallways.

Sophie sits alone at her lab table in an empty classroom, the first student to arrive at Mr. Hart's first-period chemistry class. Susan soon slides in next to Sophie on her high-top metal chair, and Anisha joins their huddle as well.

"So? Did Matthieu call? Show up? Get down on his hands and knees?" Susan asks, leading the broken heart investigation.

"Everything's okay now," Sophie reassures them. "He invited me over to his house yesterday, and we went for a walk. Matthieu told me about his dad's life in Paris as a kid. He survived the Holocaust, but his parents were taken away. Matthieu's dad only told him on January eighth, when he turned sixteen."

"Really? That's sad," Anisha says.

"Wow, I understand. My parents barely escaped from Vietnam to come to America," Susan says. "But what about that old delivery guy? Does Matthieu believe you *now* about him and about the film?"

"I brought the video and showed him Balafre. Matthieu wants to help catch him now." Sophie gives them the thumbs-up. "There was a party for his dad going on, so we didn't have time to make a plan. I told him that we should have our film club meeting after school today even though Mr. Omolo won't be there."

"I'm glad he's not out of the Cinematics Club," Anisha says, flipping through a magazine. "Do we need to meet in the photo room? It's always smelly in there from the chemicals."

"I'm glad you two are cool again. It would have been awkward to have to edit him out of our movie," Susan jokes. She opens her notebook and pulls out her homework. "If Mr. Omolo isn't here, we don't have to meet at school at all. Let's go grab some food!"

"How about the Wise Owl?" Sophie suggests.

Anisha looks up from her magazine. "I vote for that!"

"Wise Owl it is! Let's tell the guys." Susan curiously looks over at Anisha. "What's that magazine?"

Anisha holds up the cover. "It's the new issue of *Missy Mode*." She flips to an article. "Look, I knew it! Matthieu was born on January eighth, so that makes him a Capricorn."

"What are you talking about?" Sophie asks, skeptical of horoscopes.

"This article is called *Are You and Your Guy a Match?*" Anisha points to the sea-goat astrological sign. "'A Capricorn guy builds a hard-to-climb wall around him. But once you pierce through his gloomy bad-boy shell, you'll find he is protecting his delicate heart.'"

"Yup, I told you—gloooomy," Susan confirms with a nod.

"Gloomy, huh?" Sophie raises her eyebrow at Susan's Cure T-shirt. Then she rests her arm on Susan's shoulder and sighs like she's sitting in *Casablanca*'s Rick's Café instead of in Mr. Hart's classroom, surrounded by beakers. "Of all the high schools in all the towns in all the world, he walks into mine."

The three friends laugh together as Mr. Hart enters the room, which has filled up with buzzing students.

Anisha gathers her books and catches her lab partner giving her lost puppy-dog eyes. "Naveen is waiting for me." She smiles and hurries over to their table.

As the school bell rings, Mr. Hart leisurely walks to the front of the classroom. He is extremely relaxed as he addresses his hyper students.

"Hello, everyone. If you think it looks like I was away on vacation for a week, you are *absolutely* correct!" Mr. Hart places his briefcase on his desk and gestures to his newly tanned complexion. "I'm glad to see that the school did not explode from the gas leak, and I feel like a *million bucks* after going to Footsteps in the Sand Resort." He shakes his head, and grains from the beach fall from his hair. "I literally just stepped off the plane, but I still remember that you have homework due. Please pass your assignments to Anisha, who will be my TA for today."

Anisha, feeling encouraged by her new responsibility, gathers everyone's papers and leaves them in a neat stack on the teacher's desk. Mr. Hart puts on safety goggles and a white lab coat over his palm tree shirt. He writes on the chalkboard and slides the panel up for the students to see.

BUNSEN BURNER EXPERIMENT
- SAFETY EQUIPMENT

- RAINBOW FLAME EXPERIMENT
  WITH METAL SALTS
- DBDMC

"Today we will learn about using a Bunsen burner. First order of business is making sure that you make it through this semester unharmed, so please put on your safety goggles and lab coats. Second, I will demonstrate the rainbow flame experiment, which you and your lab partner will work on during this class. And lastly, most importantly, DBDMC, which stands for Don't Burn Down My Classroom.

"Let's get this Bunsen *startedddd*!" Mr. Hart calls out like an announcer at a boxing match.

As the students put on safety gear and set up their equipment at their lab tables, Mr. Hart ignites the mood by playing Power Station's "Some Like It Hot." His colorful enthusiasm is contagious as each wooden stick, dipped into a metal salt, turns the burner's flame to a brilliant hue.

"Isn't this amazing? It reminds me of the rainbow I saw while I was windsurfing after a tropical rainstorm. Okay, students, now you and your lab partners will go through each of these metal salts and document the color you see for each one. I'm going to walk around the room and observe your work," Mr. Hart says, turning off his burner.

Anisha and Naveen get busy with the project as Sophie and Susan set up their equipment. Six glass beakers holding the metal salt solutions are lined up across the table, each of them labeled.

"Can you light the Bunsen burner?" Sophie asks. "I'm not good at that part."

Susan picks up the striker and lights the Bunsen burner, adjusting the gas valve at the base. Sophie dips a stick in one of the beakers and fans it over the burner, causing a burst of autumn colors.

"Calcium chloride turns the flame orange," Sophie says, writing down the finding on their worksheet. She tests a few more of the metal salts, and then Susan does the last three.

"Sodium chloride turns the flame a yellow-orange," Susan announces as Mr. Hart circles around their table to examine their work.

Susan pulls the stick from a deep green solution and waves it over the burner. "Ooh, I love copper chloride!"

Sophie watches the flame turn a dreamy blue green. The flowing colors remind her of the magical night of swaying palm trees and swimming with Matthieu.

"The last one is strontium chloride, which is turning the flame a bright red orange." Susan says, waving the stick to reveal the color.

The flash of cadmium red pulses like the neon sign behind La Luna, where Sophie's mind drifts until Susan turns off the Bunsen burner.

After everyone cleans up their tables and scatters to their next classes, Sophie remains focused on their club meeting.

The flame is out now, but the spark has been lit.

✷ ✷ ✷ ✷ ✷

The Wise Owl parking lot is sparsely dotted with sedans and town cars. The diner is deserted except for a handful of customers sitting at the front counter, enjoying their mid-afternoon coffee and pie. Anisha, Susan, and Sophie make a beeline to the back of the restaurant and find the big round red booth where the other members of the Cinematics Club are already sitting. They squeeze onto the vinyl seats and look over the menus as the scents of fried eggs and hash browns permeate the air.

"CJ, quit flipping through the jukebox. I want to hear 'Antmusic.'" Oscar drops his dime into the machine's slot. "Push G-8."

"I'm the one sitting on the taped-up middle seat, so I get to pick the next song." CJ punches the buttons on the tabletop mini jukebox, and the sound of drums bursts from the speakers.

Sophie flips through the menu as Matthieu makes a quick drawing in his sketchbook. She looks over his shoulder to see a sketch of a water glass. "I think you should call this one *This is Not a Glass*, just like Magritte's *This is Not a Pipe*."

Still sketching, Matthieu breaks into a smile. "You're so surreal. I'll dedicate this one to you." He finishes the drawing by writing, *"This is Not a Glass" —Sophie Alexander, 1985*

Sophie's cheeks flush pink, unable to hide her happiness at being here with Matthieu.

A waitress wearing a stiff polyester uniform dress with an owl stitched on the top sashays up to their table. She pulls a pad and pen out of the dress pocket and pats her sprayed bouffant hairdo. Through the smacking of chewing gum, she asks, "Can I take your order?"

"We're going to split the hot fudge brownie." Susan nods at Anisha and Sophie.

"Fries for me, thank you," Matthieu says, then turns his attention back to his sketchbook.

"I'll have the It's a Hoot Burger Combo," Oscar requests.

CJ remains laser-focused on the menu. "Sorry, I can't make up my mind. I'll have the combo too—no tomato, please."

The waitress gathers up the menus and asks, "You're all good with just water?"

Everyone nods, and she walks away, rolling her eyes, already anticipating a measly tip.

"Okay, we have to get down to business now," Sophie announces, breaking through the chitchat. "This is an official club meeting. CJ, have you heard from your uncle? What's happening with our film?"

"I saw him over the weekend, and he showed me the film," CJ says, trying to get comfortable on the squeaky taped-up vinyl seat.

"And??? How does it look?" Oscar rests his black fedora on the back of the banquette.

"How was the acting?" Anisha asks.

All eyes lock on CJ as the sun beams through the large window.

"Okay! Here's the scoop. The film looks....*awesome*!" he announces. "There are some camera shakes, but the final cut will be wicked! This is definitely going to get us an award at the assembly."

Anisha smiles with anticipation.

"What about the music?" Matthieu slides a dime toward Oscar for the jukebox. "And why is your uncle not coming to our club meetings?"

"I gave him the mixtape." CJ leans back against the booth. "His place was a *total mess*, cameras and proof sheets everywhere. He's working on something super secret. He just kept saying it's some big story that is going to make the front page."

"I know what it is!" Oscar blurts out. "I bet he's going to cover our Halloween dance!" He drops the dime into the jukebox.

"You're joking, right?" Matthieu says, still not getting sucked into the Halloween dance frenzy. "CJ, pick a song for Sophie."

"Don't even have to look: C-4."

"Matthieu, if you don't come to the dance, you're going to miss Sven Synth and a chance to win a free tux rental," Susan teases.

Everyone at the table playfully head-bops and moves to the music as The English Beat's "Save it for Later" plays on the jukebox.

The waitress returns, skillfully balancing plates on both of her arms. She passes out the order. "Okay, I've got the fudge brownie for the ladies, Hoot Combo, Hoot Combo hold the tomato." She leaves the check by the edge of the table, signed with her name, Peggy. Before dashing off, she hands the last plate to Matthieu. "And fries for the Capricorn."

Sophie and Susan look at Anisha in amazement.

"What did I say?" Anisha says, unfazed, scooping up a spoonful of fudge.

The club polishes off their meals, and a food coma starts to take hold of the booth. The waitress clears away their dishes and says, "You can pay me when you're ready."

Sophie downs her water; she has one last thing weighing on her mind. "You know that film delivery guy, the secret Nazi with the scar? Well, I think we can catch him." Sophie looks around the booth and sees that she has everyone's attention. "Dylan told me that there is a special delivery coming the night of *Rocky Horror*—the same night as the dance. I think it must be another old eight-millimeter reel like the one he found. This is the evidence Balafre is looking to get rid of."

"How are we actually going to *catch* this guy? This is not our movie. We're not real spies!" Matthieu interjects.

"Is he like the bad guy from *Beverly Hills Cop*? You know, that one with the art gallery?" Anisha asks. "What if he has a gun?"

"We tried to follow him before. Maybe it's better to just call the police now," Susan says, seeing that they're in way over their heads.

"Dylan is going to be at La Luna that night. I can't let this guy get away, knowing the horrible things he has done to hurt so many people." Sophie feels that this is the story of so many Holocaust survivors, including her own family. "Matthieu, this is for justice!"

"I thought bad guy from *Beverly Hills Cop* was a drug dealer." Oscar places his hat back on his head. "Sorry, I can't help you guys with this. I'll be at the dance all night, probably cleaning barf off the floor."

"Sophie, I'm sorry, but Naveen will freak out if we leave before the costume contest. He really wants that tux rental," Anisha says.

"I totally understand. This is *the* big night of the year," Sophie agrees.

"CJ, you've been weirdly silent this whole time," Susan observes. "What's up?"

All eyes turn to CJ, who is reclining in deep contemplation with his hands locked behind his head. Channeling the solemn focus of Robert Shaw from *Jaws*, CJ commands their attention. "I'll catch him for you, but it ain't gonna be easy."

"What's your plan?" Matthieu asks, intrigued.

CJ sits up. "Let's get one thing straight—we're not going to let this Nazi get away. He's going *down*." He arranges the condiment bottles on the table like a director setting up a scene. "Okay, our target, Balafre, is the ketchup bottle. Dylan will be the mustard. Sophie, Matthieu—you're salt and pepper." He looks at the last condiment that hasn't been assigned. "That makes me the sugar. Sweet!"

"Even though we're not going to be there, can Susan, Anisha, and I be the napkin holder?" Oscar requests.

"All right." CJ pushes the silver holder to the side of the table. "You are the napkins, which will stand in for Noble High." He moves the condiments around as he reveals the details. "There will probably be a line of people in front of the movie theater, so we'll attack in the alley. As soon as Rikki arrives to meet Dylan, Sophie and Matthieu, you will block the van in with your cars. When Balafre shows up, there will be no way for him to leave with the reel. I will create a distraction, holding him there for just enough time for the cops to nab him."

"I thought this was going to be difficult. This plan sounds pretty easy," Sophie says, relieved.

"We've got this! What could go wrong?" CJ says, very assured.

Matthieu grabs the ketchup bottle. "For my dad, I want to make sure he's put away *forever*."

The waitress, squinting in the glaring sun, waves for CJ to lower the shade. He turns toward the window. "Sophie, I see some perv looking into the back of your car."

The club huddles together by the window to see a man circling Sophie's Wagoneer.

"Why is that creep looking into my car?" Sophie watches, worried. Then she catches sight of his face. "That's him! That's *Balafre*! Why is he looking at my car? Maybe he knows who I am?" Her heart begins to pound.

"Everyone, *duck*!" CJ lowers the blind quickly, and they all slide down in the booth, hiding from view.

Matthieu peers back through the shade. "I say we take him now!" He grabs a dull knife from the table.

"No, Matthieu!" Sophie exclaims. "He wants the film reel. We have to get him then!"

Matthieu unclenches his fist and puts the knife back on the table.

"He's gone. I don't see him anymore," Oscar says, sneaking a peek through the blinds.

"Do you think he wants to steal your car?" Anisha sounds a bit freaked out.

"Meeting's over now. Let's go. He may come back!" Susan searches her purse for cash.

"I've got this." Matthieu grabs the check, marked fifteen dollars, and throws down a twenty-dollar bill.

"Thanks, Peggy, keep the change," he says to the waitress as she picks up the check, surprising her.

Everyone scrambles out of the booth and bolts through the diner toward the front doors. They race to the parking lot and look around for any sign of Balafre.

"The coast is clear!" Oscar calls out.

"Why was he looking at *my car*?" Sophie says again, checking through the windshield to see if anything is missing.

"He was looking in the back," CJ says, knocking on the rear window.

Sophie inserts her key in the rear door. The back window slides down, and she reaches inside to unlock the tailgate, which thumps open like a giant oven door.

Books, notebook, umbrella…what could he be looking for? She spots the metal box that was left inside the car when her dad picked it up from the garage sale.

"What's in the box?" Matthieu asks.

"I totally forgot this was back here." Sophie pulls the rattling metal case toward the edge of the trunk. She flips the lid open and is baffled by the contents. There is no glowing light emitting from the trunk like in *Repo Man*. Pushing aside the screwdrivers and pliers, she finds passports and tiny black-and-white photos.

Matthieu and CJ look through the passports and pass them around.

"They're all different photos and different names! John, Richard, James…" Matthieu riffles through his handful of passports. "They're *all* Balafre!"

CJ, piecing the mystery together, blurts out, "You're driving the Nazi's car!"

Sophie is jolted by the words. "I…I…I never looked in that box before. My dad had no idea. He would *never* buy a car from a Nazi!" A sinking feeling overcomes her, and she climbs into the back seat. Anger turning to guilt, she says, "My dad paid that monster money just so I could have a stupid car."

Susan and Anisha slide into the back seat to comfort her.

"Your dad didn't know. He just wanted to make you happy," Anisha says, pulling out a tissue as Sophie's eyes well up with tears.

"We'll get him, Sophie," Matthieu assures her. "It's our destiny now."

"*And* that scumbag will cough up the money for the car, no doubt," CJ declares, putting the passports back in the box.

"Better keep that box safe. That's evidence," Susan points out.

The long shadows of the palm trees start to fade as the sun sets. Sophie drives away with Susan and Anisha, leaving Oscar, Matthieu, and CJ standing in the middle of the Wise Owl parking lot. One by one, cars fill in the spaces around them as the dinner hour arrives.

"I'm heading over to Video Vault. Later." CJ speeds off on his scooter.

"Matthieu, can you drop me off back at school? I have another dance committee meeting," Oscar asks.

Matthieu keeps his usual repulsion for the school dance in check. "Sure, Oscar. Let's go."

Under a sky streaked with electric oranges and blues, they drive past the large glowing owl sign. Matthieu takes one last look around the diner for Balafre as they drive away.

21

By the Light of the Moon

Sophie's week flies by like she's watching a movie in fast-forward. The classes, the tests, and the homework all seem to blur together until Saturday arrives. She steps across those familiar turquoise and azure tiles that lead her to La Luna. The front marquee shouts, ONE WEEK UNTIL ROCKY HORROR! She is surprised to see the red letters spelling out METROPOLIS for that night's billing. Sophie spots the soft gleam from the half-lit moon. *That's a good sign.*

As Sophie walks past the haunting life-size vampire and movie monster figures, there is an eerie quietness in the lobby—no popcorn popping, no hot dogs grilling. Sophie opens the manager's office door. "Hi, Robert, where *is* everybody?"

Her voice trails off at the sight of an unfamiliar face. Instead of Robert buried in paperwork, a man sits alone in the corner. He is an older gentleman dressed in a well-worn suit with a neatly folded blue handkerchief tucked into his jacket pocket.

"I'm sorry," Sophie says, "I didn't know that Robert wasn't here. I'll come back later." Embarrassed for barging in, she slowly starts to close the door.

"You are not interrupting anything. Robert will be back soon. Please, come in," the man says warmly, waving for her to enter.

Sophie walks to the metal desk drawer and retrieves her name tag.

The man notes her sparkly tag as she affixes it to her black vest. "Sophie—that's a lovely name. You must be new. How long have you been working here?"

"Thank you," Sophie replies as she notices the moon stitched on his handkerchief. "Just a few months. I started over the summer. I'm working in the box office."

"Well, that is the *best* place to be." He speaks conscientiously, like a sage. "You get to see all the patrons first, all their excitement and anticipation, before they even step inside La Luna. This is where everyone can forget about the world outside and be transported to a magical place. That is why I love it, why I bought this theater so very long ago."

"You…you're the owner?" Sophie is amazed—it's like finally meeting the man behind the emerald-green curtain in *The Wizard of Oz*.

Evoking the wise aura of Yoda and Mr. Miyagi, the man sits introspective and still. His silver hair almost erases the dark strands of his younger days. "Yes, I'm Max Greenfeld. I was lucky to find this place. Or, I should say, La Luna found me. I was in the army during World War II, way before your time. I've seen the darkest of days. I was one of the lucky ones who got to come back home. The movies gave me a way to feel alive again. When I saw that this place was for sale, I bought it with every dime I had saved. That was in 1952."

Sophie is struck by Max's thoughtful and heartfelt words. She imagines that maybe her grandfather might have been like him.

"I *do* like working here," Sophie says, looking around at the framed movie posters. "It must have been so cool how everyone dressed up to go to the movies back then!"

"It was very glamorous," Max reminisces. "Everyone working at the theater would wear costumes for the premieres." He laughs. "You should have seen the merman and mermaid costumes when we had a giant pool put in the lobby. That was for the opening of an Esther Williams swimming movie!"

"There are surprises every time I come here," Sophie says. "Even tonight! I've always wanted to see *Metropolis*."

Max smiles. "It's my personal favorite."

"I can't wait to see it, then." Sophie smiles back.

The office door swings open, and Robert walks in. "Max, we have everything—" Caught off guard by Sophie's presence, he stumbles over his words. "Uh…hi, Sophie. I didn't see you there. This is Max Greenfeld, the owner of La Luna."

"We already had a formal introduction," Max says.

"I better open the box office now." Sophie turns to Max. "It is very nice to meet you."

Sophie closes the door behind her and smells the buttered popcorn. She rushes over to the concession stand, illuminating under the purple glow of ghoulish black lights.

"I was looking for you earlier! I just met Max, the owner," Sophie says to Oscar, radiating an ultra-white smile at him. Her excitement fades fast as Oscar turns to her with a bright red bruised cheek. "What happened?"

"It's nothing," Oscar mutters, continuing to tend to the popcorn machine.

"What do you mean, *nothing*?" Sophie goes behind the candy counter and scoops up some ice from the drinks machine. Folding the ice cubes into a white napkin, she presses the freezing-cold bundle against his bruise. "My mom always says that ice helps with swelling. Oscar, who did this to you?"

"It was that racist jerk from school, Lee. I was out back and saw him trying to bust into your car. When I asked him what he was doing, he punched me," Oscar says, keeping secret that this wasn't the first run-in with Lee.

"Thanks for helping, but *not* if it means getting hurt." Sophie sighs, removing the compress. No one wants to be in Lee's crosshairs—when he chooses to pick on someone, he makes their life hell. Whenever she sees Lee at school—his tall, lanky frame and sneering scowl—she takes another route. "We should tell Robert. Is that creep still in the parking lot?"

Oscar feels his frozen cheek. "No, not anymore, thanks to him." He throws a candy bar into the air, and CJ catches it.

"Hey! Did you sneak in the back?" Sophie sighs.

"Dylan let me in." CJ unwraps the chocolate bar and takes a bite. Unfazed, he continues, "Seriously, there's only one thing I hate more than a Nazi…and that's a frickin' Nazi with pimples."

"You should have seen it! CJ came riding up and rolled his scooter right over Lee's foot," Oscar tells her, enjoying this part of the story.

"Yeah, it definitely left a tire mark on his boot." CJ flashes a satisfied grin. "Well, my good deed is done for the day. I'm going to Video Vault. All the horror films are flying off the shelves." Dancing in a skank style, CJ sings the Selecter's "Too Much Pressure" with a British accent as he exits the theater.

"Look at the line out there." Sophie hands the makeshift ice pack back to Oscar and walks out to the little gold ticket booth. She sets up the box office and turns the sign to OPEN.

Dylan, looking polished in a dress shirt and skinny tie, leans toward the speaker. "Hey, Moonlight, these are teachers and students from my film school. I told them about the *Metropolis* screening." The eager patrons shuffle past the ticket window as Dylan greets them one by one.

Sophie keeps up a smile throughout the endless line of avant-garde moviegoers dressed in black. After selling the last ticket, she exhales a deep breath and happily closes the box office window and speaker. From her little fishbowl, she watches Robert and Dylan escort Max out of the theater. They're engrossed in conversation, but she can't make out what they are talking about. They shake Max's hand before he goes on his way.

Turning to step out the tiny back door, Sophie hears a knock on the box office glass. She spins around to find nobody there. Suddenly a head slowly rises up—the dark hair, the blue eyes, and finally the mischievous grin.

"Matthieu!" Sophie utters in a whisper. Under the brilliant light of the marquee, she quickly locks up the golden ticket booth as Susan rushes up to them.

"CJ told me what happened!" Susan exclaims, balancing a cup filled with creamy chocolate gelato and a tiny fluorescent-green spoon. "I brought Oscar a scoop to cheer him up."

"He called me too. I wanted to see if Lee was still making trouble," Matthieu says, scoping out the Saturday night crowd passing by the theater. "CJ also told me that *Metropolis* was playing."

Sophie understands the way Matthieu says *Metropolis* like a secret code. This will be the night that makes up for missing the screening at the museum.

"Follow me. I'll let you in." Sophie opens the front door. "I have to lock up the cash box in the office. Oscar should be finished with work too. I'll bring you some tickets."

She disappears briefly inside Robert's office and brings out the red paper tickets. Sophie walks over to Susan, Oscar, and Matthieu, who are reclining on the gold velvet couch.

"The movie is going to start soon. I hope we can find seats together," Sophie says, passing out the tickets.

Matthieu lifts his camera and snaps pictures of Sophie standing next to a tall monstrous creature.

"Thanks, Su." Oscar scoops up the last drop of gelato.

"Lee is a major slime bag." Susan relaxes against the cushion in her polka-dot romper and black blazer. "He obviously doesn't have anything better to do. Wasn't he expelled?"

"I haven't seen him around school," Matthieu says, advancing the film in his camera.

Oscar touches his puffy cheek. "He better not show up at the dance."

******

They walk into the partially dimmed theater and look for a block of empty seats.

"Cinematics! Over here!" CJ calls from the back corner of the theater. He has taken over a row by tossing various articles of his clothing across the seats—a jacket here, a hat there.

Susan, Oscar, Sophie, and Matthieu squeeze down the sticky-floored aisle to claim their seats.

"I see this is our VIP section," Sophie laughs. She picks up CJ's green bomber jacket off her seat and passes it back to him.

"Here are your smelly socks." Oscar tosses them over Susan's head to CJ.

"I'll keep this one," Susan says, happy with her seat. She puts on the black trilby-style hat.

"Hey, these are primo seats. Only the best for our club." CJ puts back his outfit and gets comfortable. "Can't wait to see *our* film on the big screen," he says, looking toward the velvet curtains.

"I'm gonna be, like, ten feet tall!" Oscar smiles with pride.

"We're all gonna be larger than life," CJ says. He looks over at Susan. "Can I stop by on Sunday to pick up the stuff for my Halloween costume?"

"Sophie, Anisha, and I are going to Melrose tomorrow. We'll be looking for stuff for our costumes." Susan props the hat back on CJ's head, and her black hair falls diagonally across her face. "Can I bring you the fabric on Monday?"

"Oh…okay…sure." CJ shrugs, staying cool and pretending not to be disappointed.

"Do you realize this is the last time we'll be here together before the big night?" Sophie says with a bittersweet feeling. She turns to Matthieu, and their eyes meet.

"It will be a night we will *never* forget," Matthieu focuses on their plan.

A spotlight picks up Robert against the blue velvet curtains as he strides out in front of the eager cinephiles. He taps on the microphone, and a boom echoes through the speakers.

"One, two, three…testing. Hello, I'm Robert Garcia, manager of La Luna. We are proud to welcome you to our screening of *Metropolis*. This 1927 silent movie by German director Fritz Lang will be accompanied tonight by a live pianist. Thank you for coming to La Luna."

Overjoyed by the success of the night, Robert concludes his introduction and walks to the side of the theater.

The spotlight and house lights fade away as the velvet blue curtains part. A loud roar of applause erupts as the title appears on the big screen. Sophie rests her head on Matthieu's shoulder as he holds her hand on the armrest. The movie and music transport everyone in the theater to another place and time.

* * * * * *

Sophie stares into her bedroom mirror, looking at her face and hair. She doesn't want to disappear, exactly—it's a feeling that she wants to transform into something else the way a superhero puts on a costume to posses incredible powers and strength. In a gray sweater dress and black ankle boots, she sneaks into her brother's bedroom. Untouched since he went back to college, posters of Rush and Minutemen still hang on the wall. She grabs a big jar of hair gel from his desk and closes his bedroom door quietly.

Returning to her mirror, she scoops up a handful of the clear gel and runs it through her damp waves. Sophie slicks back her hair, creating a deep part on the left. She applies dark purple lipstick from a Halloween makeup kit. Looking at her reflection, she sees a new stronger side of herself bubbling to the surface.

"Mom!" Sophie calls out before she reaches the front door. "I'm going now."

"Did you finish all your homework for tomorrow? So—" Sarah is taken aback by her daughter's new look.

"I finished my homework. Anisha, Susan, and I are going shopping on Melrose. This is just for fun," Sophie explains.

"Okay, just be back for dinner. Your dad is helping Arnold down the street with his lawn mower. You better take off that makeup when you get back. He just doesn't understand these new fashions," Sarah says, ever the peaceful negotiator.

"Thanks, Mom. I will. Bye." Sophie rushes out the door.

22
The Perfect Disguise

The Valley canyon road is peaceful early on this Sunday afternoon. The sky is dotted with tiny gray clouds that tease a future rainstorm. Sophie's wagon comes to a stop at a red light. She fumbles in her purse, searching for gum.

"I can't wait to get to Melrose! How do I look?" Anisha sweeps a fluorescent-purple shadow across her eyelids.

"Super cool!" Susan shouts out from the back seat. She pulls out her eye shadow palette and applies a bright orange shade. "This is practice for my costume."

"Did you find a dress yet?" Anisha asks, turning back to Susan.

"I didn't. I *have* to find everything today," Susan says, determined to complete the task.

Sophie finally finds the pack of gum stuck to a plastic cassette tape case. "Anyone want some gum?" She passes the pack to Anisha, then reads the words scribbled on the tape case: SONGS FOR SOPHIE. "Look, Matthieu must have slipped this into my purse. He's always making me mixtapes."

"Naveen likes Prince, but he's more into movies than music," Anisha says. "I think he wants to be Indiana Jones for real. He's memorized every line from *Temple of Doom*." She takes a piece of gum and passes the pack to Susan.

The light turns green, and Sophie pops the tape into her dashboard player. She cranks up the volume as Tones on Tail's "Go!" blasts from the car speakers. Sophie and Susan sing along to the song as Anisha extends her arm out the window and surfs the air. The car sails down the canyon into the waking city.

Sophie turns the volume down on the stereo. "What time are you and Naveen going to the dance?"

"He said he'll be over at five." Anisha's distracted by the street scene. "He wants to take pictures with my family and be there *right* when the doors open."

Susan's bubble gum pops loudly. "He is super hard-core about this dance!"

"I think that's sweet." Sophie smiles at Anisha. "I hope you win a prize at the costume contest."

"Sophie, you better not get yourself into trouble at La Luna," Susan advises, misting hairspray across the side of her hair. "Look at everything you've already done to find out about that Nazi guy. Matthieu could at least go to the dance with you."

"Su, I'm not going to be in danger," Sophie says, reassuring her best friend like she's talking to her mom. "CJ, Dylan, and Matthieu will be there. I'll just be in my car."

Sophie turns onto Melrose, which is like a fashion runway—punk guys in ragged sleeveless flannel shirts decorated with music pins and girls in miniskirts, studded belts, and pumps. She squeezes the wagon into a space between two beat-up clunkers. As they walk up the street, they come across a wall tagged with colorful graffiti lettering.

"Wait a sec. Let me take some photos!" Sophie pulls out her instamatic camera. "I have some film left on this roll."

Anisha smoothes the wrinkles from her white stirrup pants and crewneck sweater. Susan, dressed in charcoal-gray pants and a men's button-up shirt, runs up to Anisha and gives her a big hug for the photo.

"Let's do a shoe shot together," Sophie calls out from behind the camera lens.

Susan extends her black boot as Anisha points forward her purple shoe with buckles. Sophie puts her ankle boot into the shot and clicks the shutter. "Got it!" She advances the film.

✶ ✶ ✶ ✶ ✶ ✶

This time of year, the witching hour takes over Melrose with a parade of stylish ghouls and smoke machines puffing out a haze of fog from the shop doors. The window of X-Ray Specs comes alive with mannequins attending a fantasy masquerade ball. Sophie, Anisha, and Susan marvel at the masks, gowns, and jewelry that adorn the plastic partygoers.

"I hope they have my silver dress and wig." Susan grabs their hands and tugs them into the store.

They dash to the dress section, and each takes a rack to scour.

"How about this one?" Anisha asks, pulling out a six-ties-style minidress covered in mirrored sequins.

Susan's eyes widen, and she shouts, "I love it!" But when she grabs the tag and sees the price, her excitement dies out fast. "Not for thirty dollars!" Anisha hangs the dress back on the rack.

Sophie finds a 1940s silver lamé evening gown with puffy sleeves. She holds it out to Susan. "How about this one?"

"It's perfect, but I don't want to get my hopes up." Susan reaches for the tag, then starts jumping up and down like she won the fashion lottery. "It's only fifteen dollars!" She rushes into the dressing room and returns with a triumphant smile. Channeling her inner Tina Turner from *Mad Max Beyond Thunderdome*, Susan holds up the dress in front of her and proclaims, "I must win those tickets."

Anisha and Sophie clap at her performance.

Susan gulps and proclaims with pursed lips, "I just swallowed my gum." Looking around the store, she asks, "What about a blond wig? Do you see one anywhere?"

"I need to find a black wig for my costume," Sophie says, rummaging through a basket of vintage silk scarves.

"Let's look around." Anisha leads the search team.

Screamin' Jay Hawkins's "I Put a Spell on You" boils out from the speakers as a mysterious woman slinks around the racks wearing a feathered Venetian carnival mask.

"What can I help you with, my lovelies?" the woman purrs as her smoky eyes shift back and forth.

Sophie recognizes the scent of roses. "Angela?"

The woman, dressed in a leather skirt and lace camisole, breaks into a wicked grin. "Good guess!" Angela spies the silver dress draped over Susan's arm. "Looks like you've discovered one of our treasures. Can I help you find something to go with it?"

"Um…I'm dressing up as Aunty Entity from *Mad Max*. Do you have blond wigs?" Susan asks.

"I need a black wig," Sophie chimes in. "I'm going to be Rachael from *Blade Runner*."

"Those are both great costumes." Angela is impressed. "Unfortunately, we don't sell wigs here. Try Jeepers Creepers down the street."

"Thanks, we'll check it out!" Sophie says, excited to finish the costume hunt.

Susan pays Angela for her dress as Anisha looks at the jewelry displayed next to the cash register. Sophie reaches into her bag and pulls out a flyer.

"Angela," she says, placing the paper on the counter, "the movie theater where I work will be showing *The Rocky Horror Picture Show* this Saturday. Um…do you think you could post this in your window?"

"*Rocky Horror*." Angela glances over the flyer. "A ten o'clock showing—it's unusual to see it before midnight. I don't know how many people will drive out to the Valley, but I'll post it for *you*."

"Thank you!" Sophie says, feeling good about helping the theater.

Sophie, Susan, and Anisha head out the door and make their way down the block. A crowd lines the sidewalk as a shiny hearse slowly cruises by. A skinny pale rocker with spiky ink-black hair waves from behind the wheel.

"Is that who I think it is?" Susan stands on her tiptoes, trying to catch a glimpse.

"Who is it?" Anisha asks, bewildered.

"It's Sven Synth!" Sophie shouts. Excited by the sighting, she snaps some pictures.

"That's what he looks like?" Anisha asks, disappointed. "I thought he was going to be some blond Swedish guy."

The hearse rumbles away as the crowd watches the parade of classic cars decorated for Halloween.

"Don't you remember his song?" Susan sings, "*Boom! You smashed my heart. Boom…boom….boom…boom!*"

"It was on the radio *all the time* in junior high. Brittany and I even made up our own dance to it," Sophie remembers. "He did have blond hair in the video."

$$* * * * * *$$

"I can't see anything. Is the store really there?" Anisha hesitates, staring into a gap between two buildings.

Fake smoke billows out of a long, narrow pathway lit only by a neon arrow flashing from the side of a building.

"Yeah, Ani, Jeepers Creepers is just down here." Sophie grabs her hand.

They form a human chain as they pass through the thick corridor of fog. Once they emerge from the white haze, Sophie, Susan, and Anisha enter a retro wonderland filled with metal lunch boxes, packaged gags, and kitschy decor.

"Fake blood, vampire fangs, trick gum!" Sophie calls out whatever catches her eye.

They wander up and down the aisles until they find an entire wall lined with wigs—a rainbow of colors, from short bobs to floor-length locks.

All three girls try on different styles, racing back and forth to the row of fun house mirrors. Susan, wearing a long, spiky blond wig, poses in front of one mirror that stretches her tall and skinny. Anisha chooses a purple witch wig to match her bright eye shadow and steps in front of the next mirror, which makes her look short and wide. They crack each other up, making funny faces at their psychedelic reflections as The Three O'Clock's "Her Head's Revolving" plays.

"I'm going to get this one!" Susan says, shoving her loose black strands underneath the blond wig.

Sophie walks up to a regular mirror, looking at herself in a jet-black pinup-style wig with curled bangs.

My costume, my disguise. Am I still me, or am I becoming something else?

"Sophie, or should I call you *replicant*?" Susan looks over her shoulder at the new reflection. "You're really going to fool everyone. No one is going to recognize you!"

Susan and Anisha wander to the front of the store, leaving Sophie by the mirror. As she twirls around, Sophie catches sight of a figure in the mirror. *Oh no...not him!*

She bolts from the wall of mirrors down one of the aisles filled with retro toys and dolls. Sophie slowly peeks around the shelves and watches Lee trying on rubber monster masks. Her heart racing, she dashes to the front register trying to avoid running into him.

"I'll take this one. I'm in a hurry, please." Sophie pulls off the black wig, and the surprised cashier rings it up quickly.

Susan and Anisha, carrying Jeepers Creepers bags, are surrounded by plush toy dogs barking at their feet.

"We've gotta go—now!" Sophie implores, grabbing their hands. "It's Lee. He's here."

Sophie, Susan, and Anisha jump over the invading toy dogs and race out the door through the smoke. They keep running until they reach the end of the block.

"Stop, I need to catch my breath!" Susan gasps, panting. "I don't think he followed us."

"Why are we running?" Anisha asks, looking down the street.

"That bully from school, Lee—he was going to break into my car at the theater. He punched Oscar in the face when he confronted him."

"I didn't know he did that to Oscar," Anisha says, feeling bad.

"Oscar didn't want anyone to know," Sophie confides.

The palms trees provide a safe roadmap back to the wagon. Sophie, Susan, and Anisha pile in with their packages and take a rest in the car. The bright afternoon sunrays shine through the windshield.

Sophie puts on her cat-eye sunglasses and starts the car. The adrenaline rush from their flight drains away, replaced by self-doubt. She grips the steering wheel, mad at herself for being afraid and running away.

How am I going to be strong on Saturday?

"Sophie? Everything okay?" Susan asks, seeing her friend's hands clenched around the steering wheel.

"I'm sorry I ruined the day. We were having such a great time." Sophie's voice is heavy with disappointment.

"Are you kidding?" Susan lounges across the back seat. "This was an awesome day! I got my costume, and we missed running into super jerk, thanks to you."

Anisha pulls out bracelets from her bag and dangles them in the air. "I got these charm bracelets for us." She gives one to Sophie and one to Susan. "They each have a C for the Cinematics Club. They'll bring us good luck on Saturday."

Sophie slips on the silver bracelet, and the charm catches the sunlight. "Thanks, Ani. It's awesome."

Susan leans forward and extends her hand, her bracelet dangling around her wrist. "Here's to the Cinematics Club. We're going to make Saturday the best night!"

Sophie and Anisha place their palms on top of Susan's, setting their future hopes in motion.

✳ ✳ ✳ ✳ ✳ ✳

The night always comes too soon. The clouds have drifted back in, illuminated by the last fiery glow of the sunlight. After dropping off Susan and Anisha, Sophie sees the pink-and-yellow sky dim to darkness. Driving through her neighborhood, she passes houses decorated with orange lights, carved pumpkins, and cloth ghosts swaying from trees. She catches sight of her deep purple lipstick in the rear-view mirror and quickly pulls to the side of the street. *Dad is going to flip out!*

Sophie reaches into the back seat for the tissue box, one of the items her mom packed for "emergency" situations. She pulls out a tissue and wipes away all traces of lipstick before driving the rest of the way to her house.

As Sophie walks up the driveway, she sees the garage door open, lit by a hanging utility lamp. Her dad is hunched over the engine of his car. His dad radar is not muffled by the staticky news broadcasting from his pocket radio, and he looks up at the sound of her footsteps.

"Hi, Dad," Sophie says, hiding her shopping bag behind her back. She senses that her disappearing bag trick isn't working.

"Did you go shopping?" her dad questions, plunging back under the hood with a wrench in his hand.

"Uhh…yeah, but it's just for the Halloween dance on Saturday," Sophie explains.

"Dance…hmmm." Her father grabs an old rag to wipe the grease from his hands and shuts the car hood. "Watch out for the tools. By the way, your mom is making meatloaf for dinner."

"Sounds good, Dad. I'm starving." Sophie steps around her father's rusty metal toolbox on the floor. She notices a wooden clock on the worktable. "What's that? Did you get it at a garage sale?"

"Oh, that. It's your mother's cuckoo clock. She was going through some old boxes and found it." Simon picks up a tiny painted wooden bird. "I am going to get it working for her."

"Did it ever work?" Sophie asks, intrigued by the quaint carved birdhouse.

"It used to. It was in the nursery when you and Martin were little. It was one of the few things your mother was able to bring with her when she came to this country." Simon inspects the clock's gears through a magnifying glass.

"It'll be nice to hear it again," Sophie says, tracing her finger along the chipped edges of the wooden bird. Her eyes wander across the worktable, scattered with paintbrushes, rulers, and T squares, until she sees an old torn sepia-toned photograph of a young man. "Is this you?"

Simon barely moves his head to look and answers shortly, "Yes."

"I've never seen this one." Sophie nudges her dad for an answer consisting of more than one word. "When was this taken?"

"Oh, Sophie, it was a long time ago," Simon answers vaguely, buried in the mechanics of the clock. "It was taken right before I came to this country."

"Where is that tower in the background?" Sophie asks, probing further.

Simon thinks back. "I stayed in Italy for a short time after the war ended before I could come to America."

Sophie feels like she is trying to turn the knob of a door that will open only a crack, revealing a world her father doesn't want her to know about. She thinks about her own secret. *If only he knew about Balafre and our big plan for Saturday.*

"Well, maybe *one day* you'll tell me about it. I'm going inside to let Mom know I'm home." Sophie leaves her dad as he picks up his faded photograph.

Walking into the kitchen, Sophie smells the roasting meatloaf. Her mom takes the pan out of the oven and places it on the countertop next to a dish of foil-wrapped baked potatoes.

"Hi, Mom." Sophie inhales the aromas of the comforting home-cooked meal.

"Glad you came home in time." Sarah pulls the oven mitts decorated with red roosters off her hands. "I hope your dad is finished in the garage."

"He closed the hood on the car. That's a good sign." Sophie's eyes roam over to the basket of warm dinner rolls.

"Everything's ready, so I'll call him in." Sarah sees Sophie's shopping bag. "Did you find something for your costume?"

"I got my wig," Sophie says, showing the black locks. "It's the last thing I needed. I'll wash up before dinner."

Having just taken a few steps down the hall, she overhears her dad and mom talking in the kitchen.

"Sarah, I'm finished in the garage. Is Sophie ready to eat?"

"Yes. She's putting her things away. Did you fix your photo?"

"Not yet. Sophie saw it on the table and asked about it."

"Simon…" Sarah's voice becomes labored. "You know she is old enough now to know about what happened to us during the war. You can't keep her sheltered from the world forever."

The words float past Sophie like fog. She goes to her room and puts the shopping bag in her closet. She takes the silver charm bracelet off and hangs it on the bulletin board where a black-and-white picture of the Cinematics Club is pinned up. *That's the photo of us from our first shoot.* That night seems like it was so long ago—their own special world.

23
Stars in the Sky

"Attention, class." Ms. Kahn walks to the front of the room and checks the clock on the wall. "There are twenty minutes left for the last section of your midterm. I know that we are almost done for the day and your minds are on the Halloween dance tomorrow, but hang in there! We have journeyed through so many incredible periods of art, from Impressionism to Surrealism. I am going to show a slide of one painting. Please write down the artist, the title, the period, and a description, noting its importance."

Sophie turns and catches Matthieu looking over at her. She playfully covers her exam with her arm and throws a *you better not be trying to see my answers* look at him. Matthieu covers his exam and raises his eyebrow like they are playing a tennis match with secret flirty glances.

Ms. Kahn flips the light switch off, and a slide of a swirling indigo night sky projects onto the screen. She drops a hint to spark her students. "The artist who painted this wrote, 'But the sight of the stars always makes me dream.'"

The light grazes across Sophie's face as she is drawn into *The Starry Night*. She remembers the day Matthieu emerged from the magical projection. She gets lost in the painting for a moment, then glances back at her test and hastily finishes her Van Gogh answer.

The bright yellow fluorescent overhead lights flash on. "That's time!" Ms. Kahn announces, triggering a collective exhale of relief across the classroom. "Please turn in your exams and have a great weekend. Hope to see *everyone* at the dance tomorrow!"

The students whizz past Sophie and Matthieu as the last bell of the school day rings. Still seated at his desk, Matthieu starts to pull up his plaid long sleeve, exposing the start of a black ink line at his wrist. There are no notes to help him cheat written on the inside of his forearm, only a secret message for Sophie and the Cinematics Club.

She follows the black line with her finger, pushing his sleeve up until the words are fully revealed.

You're invited. Tonight.

✱✱✱✱✱✱

"I better get an A on the chemistry midterm. I even answered the *extra* extra-credit questions." Susan shuts the car door.

"Su, I don't know what you're stressing about. You did the practice test, like, a hundred times," Sophie reassures her as she grabs her black cardigan from the seat. "Mr. Hart already wrote you a recommendation for the summer internship at EnBioTek."

"I know," Susan agrees, putting on her jean jacket. "I just can't make any mistakes that might affect my college applications."

"That's not even until next year," Anisha says, looking out into the peaceful canyon. She is captivated by the hillside covered with green moss. "Right now, let's just celebrate the end of midterms and the dance tomorrow!"

CJ's sputtering Vespa chugs up Matthieu's driveway and parks next to Sophie's wagon. His passenger pulls off a red-and-blue-striped helmet.

"CJ! Oscar! You made it!" Sophie exclaims.

"I can never have too may parties to go to, right?" Oscar gives Sophie a hug, making sure she doesn't touch the almost-faded bruise on his cheek.

Wispy clouds start to sweep across the sky as evening approaches. Matthieu walks out of the carport with an unusual look of anticipation on his face.

"Do you have what you promised?" Matthieu asks CJ, like it's something illegal.

CJ reaches into his backpack, covered in mod band patches, and pulls out a VHS tape. He sees that he has the club's attention. "I just have the rough cut…of our awesome movie!"

A collective scream echoes through the trees as the members of the Cinematics Club embrace CJ, raising the tape up like a trophy. They follow Matthieu into the house like they have already won the Noble High assembly prize.

The boisterous club gathers in the living room, where their film first started. The warmth from the fireplace is inviting as they get comfortable on the floor. Matthieu pops the tape into the VCR and presses play.

CJ flops onto a blue Moroccan floor pillow, waiting to watch the greatness of their first film.

The movie starts with a close-up of Anisha and Sophie bathed in darkness except for a band of light that falls across their eyes. The club is glued to the TV screen as emotions flash across their faces, from thrilled excitement to cringing embarrassment. Suddenly, the black-and-white picture breaks up with a stuttering *crunch...crunch....crunch.*

CJ lunges for the VCR. "NOOOOOOOOOOO!"

Matthieu fumbles to hit the eject button and wrestles the cassette from the machine. The crinkled black tape dangles from the cartridge like limp spaghetti.

"*Dude*, your machine ate our film!" CJ barks, trying to feed the crumpled tape back into the cassette.

"Does this mean our movie is dead?" Anisha sighs, imagining her acting career ending before it started.

"I don't know what happened!" Matthieu hits the machine. Disappointment at letting his friends down pours across his face. "Sorry, everyone."

"Don't sweat it. It's just a copy." CJ reclaims his cool by putting on his black retro sunglasses. "I know my uncle will be at our club meeting on Monday. We'll still have time to finish it before the assembly in December."

"You're right," Sophie agrees. "Well, what should we do now?"

Leon races into the living room, followed by Genni carrying a fluffy space-themed towel. His small bare feet patter across the stone floor as he practices karate chops.

"Leon, watch out for those kicks!" Matthieu grabs hold of him by his bite-size white karate uniform.

Genni catches Leon and hypes up the excitement for his least favorite activity. "It's bath time! Go pick out some toys, and I'll be there in a few minutes." He races off to his room.

Genni opens a closet and gathers a vibrant rainbow palette of paper lanterns. "Hey, Cinematics, I have a surprise for you!" She unloads the lanterns on the kitchen countertop, then pulls her copper-red hair up and skewers it with a pair of chopsticks to secure it in a loose bun. "Oh, Matti, your father called. There's a big storm up in San Francisco, and the film shoot shut down. His plane coming home is delayed until late Saturday night. I think the rain is heading down our way."

Matthieu is privately relieved that his dad won't be here so their secret plans won't be interrupted.

"I think he heard you." Sophie points to Buster the cat, standing in the doorway of Marc's office.

Buster's big eyes look even sadder at the mention of Marc's absence. He slowly ventures a few steps toward Sophie, who freezes like a statue—not to make any sudden moves. Buster's furry gray striped body brushes Sophie's leg, and then he scurries back to the office.

"I can't believe he came up to you. He doesn't like anyone but my dad." Matthieu is amazed.

Sophie shrugs her shoulders and smiles. Somehow she senses that the cat is reassuring her about the night she found the photo of Balafre in Marc's office.

"Are the lanterns for Saturday's dance?" Oscar asks, curious about the brightly colored decorations.

"Dance?" Genni asks, puzzled. "What dance?"

"The big Halloween dance. It's exactly twenty-four hours away and counting!" Oscar answers, excited. "We're all going…except for you, Matthieu, right?"

"What? Why aren't you going?" Genni is surprised by the news.

Matthieu remains evasive. "I'm not into those things."

"Not into *those things*…hmmm." Genni brushes aside his stubbornness and spirals blissfully into nostalgia. "My high school Halloween dance, the Ookie Spookie Soirée, was so far out! I remember it like 1966 was yesterday. I went as Domino from *Thunderball*, and my date dressed as James Bond." She sighs. "Our first dance together was to 'Wild Thing.'"

"I looove that song by X! *Wild thing!*" Susan sings, flipping her head from side to side.

Genni quickly snaps back to 1985. "Thanks…I feel ancient now. Anyway, we'll talk about the dance later, Matthieu."

Sophie has already accepted that Matthieu isn't going with her to the dance. She focuses on the bright magenta lantern on the counter. "Genni, what are these pretty lanterns for?"

"Well, I thought these would be a nice way to celebrate your movie and the end of midterms." Genni passes one of the lanterns to each of the Cinematics. "They are also to wish Anisha a happy Diwali."

"Oh…thank you!" Anisha accepts a blue lantern.

"What's *Dee-vali*?" CJ asks, looking at his yellow paper globe.

"In India, it's the festival of lights," Anisha explains. "It is about light winning over darkness, good over evil."

Looking through the walls of glass, Sophie sees dusk approaching. The setting sun illuminates the sweeping clouds, fiery streaks of pink painted across a blue-gray sky. She looks into her lantern. "Do they glow?"

"I thought of that!" Genni passes out tiny lights. "You can put these inside the lanterns. We don't want to start any fires in the canyon."

Anisha and Susan dance around with their glowing lanterns.

"They are so pretty. Thank you, Genni!" Sophie's face lights up with a magenta glow.

"You are so welcome." Genni smiles.

"Why don't we go up the hill? You can see the whole valley at night," Matthieu says, holding a green lantern. "CJ, I'll race you to the path—rockers vs. mods." He dashes out the door.

"I'll beat ya!" CJ races out with his yellow lantern.

Anisha, Susan, and Oscar follow CJ, and Sophie is the last of the pack.

"I forgot my sweater. I'll meet you outside," Sophie yells out the door, then returns to the living room to get her cardigan.

"Sophie, wait!" Genni calls out. "Matthieu never mentioned anything about a dance. I just want you to know that you, this club…they mean more to Matthieu than he probably says. He has bounced around a lot, and having friends—*real* friends—is new for him. He thinks he's an outsider and has always shied away from school activities. Just don't give up on him."

Sophie gives an understanding nod. "Thanks, Genni. I better catch up with everyone." She closes the door and stands on the concrete steps lined with five carved pumpkins—one for each member of the Bernard family, including a mini cat-o'-lantern for Buster.

Where is everyone? Sophie wonders, walking past the swaying wind chimes hanging from the tree. She catches sight of the colorful lanterns on the fire road and climbs up the small hillside steps. At the top, a hand reaches out to help her up.

"We've all been waiting for you." Matthieu pulls Sophie close as she steadies herself on level ground. "Come on." He leads her by the hand to join the club down the path.

Sophie sees the beautiful colorful lanterns glowing in a row, a brilliant rainbow in the dusk. The club is huddled together under the stars and the approaching full moon. The Valley spreads out in all directions, dotted with streams of traffic and tiny lights. They look out at the world below them. Is it theirs to go along with or to make something better?

"You are so lucky, Matthieu," Oscar says. "I would look at this every night."

"Yeah, it is kinda great," Matthieu says, realizing that this is home now. "I'm glad that you're all here tonight." His gaze falls on Sophie.

"We have gone over our plans for La Luna. I just hope we'll be ready to catch Balafre once and for all tomorrow." Doubt is starting to seep into Sophie's mind like that anxious feeling the night before a final exam.

"Ready? Are you kidding?" CJ says, not flustered at all. "I was born ready!"

"CJ, how do you make everything seem all right?" Susan wonders, put at ease. She lets out a laugh. "And *how* did you beat Matthieu up the hill wearing sunglasses at night?"

"Su, just one of my many skills." CJ pushes his sunglasses up on top of his head to reveal his tender eyes to her.

"Oh no! The clouds are moving over the moon. It's going to rain," Anisha calls out.

Sophie points up to the night sky. "Hurry, there are six stars in the sky. Pick a star and make a wish!"

The six members of the Cinematics Club look up at the tiny points of light flickering in the darkness. They all hold up their colorful glowing lanterns and close their eyes as their wishes float up and away. Sophie opens her eyes to find the clouds forming a blanket over the Valley, one she wants to grab and wrap herself in.

24

School Spirits

Sophie leans toward her bedroom mirror. She sweeps a few strokes of kohl liner across her brows as INXS's "To Look at You" plays on her radio. Her eyes shift back and forth from the taped-up photo of *Blade Runner*'s replicant Rachael to her reflection as she makes her best attempt at Joan Crawford–style arched eyebrows. She pulls her hair back into a tight bun and puts on the black pinup wig, styled with large curled bangs. Picking up a tube of lipstick, she paints her lips crimson red.

Slipping on the 1940s embellished black blazer and matching pencil skirt, Sophie takes a look at her completed costume. *I bet no one will recognize me. Tonight, that's a good thing.*

The song fades away, and the DJ's voice blares from Sophie's clock radio.

"This is Sven Synth from LA's *cutting-edge* radio station, KNXS. It's Saturday night, you groovy ghoulies, and I'm at the most exclusive invite before midnight. That's right—it's the Noble High Halloween dance! I'm broadcasting live from six to eleven. Keep your radio tuned to this five-hour party—my lips are sealed for the surprise band performance at ten thirty.

The doors open in just ten minutes—I hear a pack of teen zombies pounding on them now! But first, a word from tonight's sponsor, Drink 'n' Dunk coffee shop."

Sophie shuts off the radio and takes one last look in the mirror, dressed in black from head to ankle boots. She takes the charm bracelet Anisha gave her from the bulletin board and slips it on. She puts on her vintage black gloves and applies one last coat of ruby red to her lips. Holding the lipstick, she draws a heart on the mirror and then turns off her bedroom light.

C u - c k o o ... c u - c k o o ... c u - c k o o ... c u - c k o o ... cu-ckoo...cu-ckoo...

Following the chirping sounds into the living room, Sophie sees a wooden bird popping in and out of the little carved cottage on the wall.

"The cuckoo clock works?" Sophie is amazed.

Sarah's absorbed in her photo album as she answers, "Isn't it great? Your father finally got it to work. Shouldn't you be at the dance? It's already six o'clock."

"I didn't want to be there right when it started. You know—fashionably late," Sophie says.

Sarah finally looks up and is awestruck by her daughter's transformation. "I…I can't believe how you look. I haven't seen that suit since my mother wore it when I was a child. She was so beautiful. You remind me of her, of Ursula."

"Uh…thanks, Mom," Sophie says, unsure how to respond. "I do think my costume looks cool. I tried to come up with something special. I know that there will be so many people at the dance dressed up as superheroes."

"There is more rain heading this way tonight. Is Matthieu coming to pick you up?" Sarah asks.

"He isn't sure if he's going," Sophie responds vaguely, inching away from the hot seat.

Sarah chalks it up to passing young love. "Well, better not be home too late. Your costume is very nice." She straightens the jeweled lapels and wide shoulder pads on the suit jacket. "Sophie, I'm glad you have your own mind. We need *real* superheroes, not just the ones in movies."

Sophie hugs her mom, concealing the real mission of the night. Closing the front door, she checks her purse for her school ID and minty breath spray.

She drives off to the school dance, listening to KNXS broadcast Missing Persons' "Destination Unknown." The bright moon shines upon the rain-slick streets, leading Sophie down a road of electric blue.

✶ ✶ ✶ ✶ ✶ ✶

Sophie drives past a serpentine line of students anxiously waiting outside the beige Noble High gymnasium. She can hear the speakers thumping and marvels at the strobe lights flashing in the clerestory windows. She parks her wagon and walks through the lot, alive like a rowdy tailgate party—a blur of teens making out and drinking in their hatchbacks.

"Have your school ID cards out! No weapons, no firecrackers, and no narcotics!" the security guard at the gym entrance yells out, the size of the wrestler Andre the Giant.

Sophie has always imagined what going to an exclusive private party might be like, and this is the closest she has gotten to an event with a doorman and red velvet ropes.

"Psst...over here!" CJ signals to Sophie.

Sophie sneaks out of line, not wanting to attract attention. She meets him around the side of the building.

"CJ! Your hair!" She runs her hand over his buzzed mohawk. "Mad Max, you look like you just walked out of the apocalypse."

"Thanks." CJ is dressed in a distressed black leather jacket over a long draped shirt, pants, and Docs. "You should know better—replicants don't wait in line. Oscar showed me the side door and gave me these special passes. Come on!"

"Are Susan and Anisha here?" Sophie asks, following CJ to the VIP door.

"I just got here. They're probably inside already." He knocks three times, and a hand extends from behind the door. CJ passes over the orange construction paper invitations pasted onto index cards.

"Hark! Who goes there?" a voice asks. Oscar steps out from behind the VIP door, outfitted in his pirate-influenced Adam Ant costume. There are tiny ribbons braided into the front of his hair and a red bandana tied around the elbow of his long black tailcoat.

"It's the Cinematics Club, of course," Sophie says, modeling the shiny charm bracelet over her black glove.

CJ and Sophie follow Oscar behind the stage curtain, where dance committee students race back and forth with destroyed Halloween decorations in their hands. They peek out the side of the black curtain to get a bird's-eye view of the action.

The bleachers-and-hoops gym has been transformed into a room bathed in black. Pulsating beams of light sync with the dancing crowd.

"I'm going to look for Susan. I'll see you down there." CJ descends the stage steps, taking pictures of people dancing.

"Meet me at my car at nine and we'll leave for La Luna," Sophie calls out.

Sophie and Oscar scan the dancing costumed crowd. Mixed in with the unicorns, Run-DMCs, and Draculas, there are the many versions of Madonna, particularly the *Desperately Seeking Susan* look with the pyramid jacket, bustier, and black mesh.

"This is so amazing!" Sophie takes in the joy and energy of the dancing crowd. Her eyes catch the giant lighted pumpkins that decorate the stage.

"Do you know him?" Oscar points to the boy with a brown mullet waving a white flag.

"The one dressed as Bono?" Sophie squints. "Oh, that's David Cooper. He's in my English class, and he writes for the *Knightley News* school paper. He's always speaking out about social issues like freeing Mandela." She notices Oscar's interest in David. "Let's go down and dance!"

Sophie and Oscar weave through the crowd to Pat Benetar's "Invincible," and she leads them into David's circle.

"David, love your costume!" Sophie yells above the music. "This is my friend Oscar."

David nods in respect and continues to move with his flag of peace.

"I better find Susan and Anisha," Sophie says in Oscar's ear, and disappears incognito through a circle of dancing girls who have tossed aside their high-heeled pumps.

Sophie emerges from the crowd at the bake sale table, which is covered with cotton cobwebs and giant plastic spiders. Ms. Kahn, outfitted as the *Mona Lisa* in a draped black dress and a gold frame, hands shocking orange-frosted cupcakes to a couple dressed as Pee-wee Herman and Dottie. She turns to Sophie and looks at her like she's a stranger.

"Ms. Kahn, don't you recognize me? It's Sophie."

"Sophie? I never would have guessed! Who are you?"

"I'm Rachael. She's, like, a robot from that movie *Blade Runner*," Sophie says, striking a model pose. "It's futuristic sci-fi."

"You look very mysterious, just like someone from those old black-and-white movies." Ms. Kahn picks up an empty tray to remove from the table. She reads the little cardboard sign: SPOOKY SESAME TREATS BY SUSAN TRAN. "These went fast."

"That's my friend who made them!" Sophie says as she spots Susan and her date approaching the table.

"They all sold?" Susan is surprised and pleased.

"You're a hit!" Sophie hugs her. She always looks forward to those doughy sesame balls filled with sweet bean paste and coconut that Susan sometimes brings for lunch.

"Sophie, this is Tai. He lives in Orange County," Susan says, sparkling in her silver lamé dress.

Tai waves to Sophie. He is head-to-toe club-cool Mad Max, from his short spiked hair and black leather jacket down to the rolled cuffs of his black pants and his shiny pointy-toed shoes.

"Hi, Tai!" Sophie waves back. "Su, have you seen CJ?"

"No, I haven't."

Sophie looks at Tai and wonders if CJ will even have a chance to dance with Susan.

A bright spotlight shines toward the stage as Principal Patterson bursts through the black curtains. He grabs the microphone like he is living out his 1950s teen rebel dreams. Dressed in a a motorcycle jacket, he has greased-back hair and flashes a white smile.

"Welcome to the 1985 Halloween dance, a night you will *never forget!*" The roar of the crowd and the thunder of feet stomping on the floor erupt like an earthquake shaking the gym. "I want to introduce our judges for the costume contest."

He shuffles through his note cards and reads, "We have Ms. Kahn judging for creativity, Mr. Hart judging for technical aspects, and Mrs. Sanchez awarding best couple's costume. Please give them a round of applause!"

The teachers climb up onto the stage and wave at the cheering students. Mr. Hart does a cool salute, dressed as *The Thing*'s MacReady in a ski parka, wraparound sunglasses, and fake icicles hanging from his beard.

"You've got some tough critics up here!" Principal Patterson announces, approving of his judging panel's impressive costumes. "There is still time to enter our costume contest. Put your name on the sign-up sheet located below our stage by eight o'clock, and our awards ceremony will take place at ten o'clock *sharp*. Of course, we will close out the night with our surprise band performance at ten-thirty!"

"Did you enter the couples' contest?" Sophie asks Susan.

"I do want those Cure tickets!" Susan leads Tai toward the sign-up sheet.

CJ miraculously reappears and snaps a picture of Sophie.

"Where have you been? There's Susan and Tai." She points.

"Oh." CJ looks conflicted, not knowing how to act. "I'll just go over and say hi—no big deal, right?"

Mr. Hart and Ms. Kahn come down to the dance floor to take pictures with students as the principal revels in the cheers of the crowd.

"Mrs. Sanchez, our ace softball coach, will make the next announcement." Principal Patterson hands her a note card, turns up his jacket collar, and walks like a cool cat off the stage.

Mrs. Rita Sanchez, sparkling as Sheila E. in a skintight iridescent suit and a short haircut with frosted tips, races to the side of the stage. She teeters back on her stiletto booties, dragging her husband out as *Purple Rain* Prince.

Sophie dreads softball, not because of any dislike for Mrs. Sanchez but because of her lack of athletic ability. Embarrassment bubbles up in her when she sits on the cold bench, usually the last to be picked for a team. At least Mrs. Sanchez is giving her a passing grade of C, even though she often reprimands her for wearing black tights under her Noble High shorts.

"How are we doing tonight?" Mrs. Sanchez revs up the crowd like it's a softball game. She glances down at the cue card. "My husband and I will be judging the couples' costumes, and here's a sneak peek at our first two entries. Competing for this year's prize is—come on out—Naveen and Anisha as Indiana Jones and Willie Scott from *Temple of Dooooom*!"

Naveen beams with pride in his archeologist attire, complete with whip fastened to his belt. Anisha is thrilled to be in the spotlight, dressed in a choli and a lehenga—an Indian embroidered white cotton crop top and an ankle-length skirt—with costume jewels draped around her head.

"Woo-hoo!" Sophie yells out from the dance floor, trying to drown out the nasty hecklers hiding in the crowd.

Mrs. Sanchez looks at the note card again. "Our next entry is called Best Friends Forever. From the movie *The Legend of Billie Jean*, let's make some noise for Amber and Brittany!"

Amber struts out in a white T-shirt with big lettering that says FAIR IS FAIR. She does a high kick, followed by Brittany wearing a cut-up wet suit top and khaki pants, her eyes painted with bright yellow and peacock-blue eye shadow. They raise their clasped hands in the air, declaring their unbreakable bond, as the Noble Knights cheerleaders rush the stage.

"Mr. Sanchez, let's get the party on the dance floor!" Rita tosses her note card out into the crowd. "It's time...*for the confetti drop*! Hit it!" Mrs. Sanchez dances with her husband to Sheila E.'s "A Love Bizarre."

Streams of colorful paper confetti rain down on the partygoers. Sophie looks around at all the happy students and teachers enjoying the dance. In that moment, she feels eerily alone and wonders, *Where did everyone go? Why couldn't Matthieu be here?*

Swept up into the swirl of dancing bodies, she hears a voice, garbled like someone speaking underwater. Her eyes focus on a boy's mouth moving in front of her. "Sophie? Sophie? Is that you? Do you want to dance?"

"Oh, hi." Sophie's eyes suddenly focus on her classmate Chris, and she scrambles to get the words out. "Sure...uh... let's dance."

Chris moves from side to side, happily throwing his arms in the air to Phil Collins's "Sussudio." Wearing an I LOVE TOXIC WASTE T-shirt, he smiles. "This was an easy costume. I'm the guy from *Real Genius*!"

"It's great, Chris." Sophie enjoys dancing for the first time tonight.

Chris makes small talk, excited to be with Sophie. "I haven't seen you at the Photo Hut lately. I wondered where you were."

"Our club is finishing our movie, and I just got busy with school and stuff." Sophie dances, keeping an eye out for the Cinematics Club.

"Yeah, I get it." Chris tries to stay in time with Sophie. "I'm filming with the AV Club tonight. I have a break and was hoping…um…that I would see you. This is the *best* party I've ever been to. So-So-Sophie!" he sings, making the song his own. He takes a chance and does a spin, almost crashing into her.

"It is incredible." Sophie moves to the music.

A guy in a red-and-green-striped Freddy Krueger sweater races up to them. Out of breath and in panic mode, he blurts out, "Chris, you gotta help us! The principal is in Sven Synth's DJ booth, and he wants us to get some close-up shots of him on the turntable."

"Uh, sorry, Sophie, I gotta go." Chris answers the AV Club's call of duty. "Wait for me…I'll be back!"

Sophie sees Anisha and Naveen wading through the dancing crowd like they are making their way through a jungle.

"I finally found you!" Anisha hugs Sophie.

"You and Naveen looked so cool on stage!" Sophie says.

"Thanks," Anisha says doubtfully, "but we have a lot of competition, especially from the homecoming king and queen."

Sophie puts out positive vibes. "Mrs. Sanchez was really impressed, and she is the judge. I know you're going to win a prize!"

"I do want that tux rental!" Naveen focuses on the practical prize. "We'll look sharp for the prom."

Susan and Tai join the group. "Finally, we found you!" Susan says.

"Where are CJ and Oscar?" Sophie asks.

"Here they come!" Susan announces.

They form their own bubble and dance in a circle to The Cure's "Close to Me."

"I requested it for you!" CJ shouts across to Susan.

"Thanks, CJ! You're the best!" Susan calls out, jumping up and down to the song.

"I haven't seen that creep Lee anywhere," Oscar says, relieved and feeling free. He catches a secret glance from David. "Everything came out good tonight."

"I'm so happy for you, Oscar. Everyone is having a great time," Sophie says, hiding her uncertainty of what lies ahead for the rest of the night.

* * * * * *

"Attention! Attention!" Principal Patterson speaks into the microphone as he adjusts the big headphones over his ears. "This is your principal, about to go live on KNXS. I want the world to hear the best high school on the planet!"

Sven Synth cues up records on his turntables and flips the red on-air light on. "It's eight-thirty, and we're halfway through the Noble High Halloween dance! I've got Principal Patterson trying out his mad DJ skills. Passing the mic!"

The principal pops a breath mint. "Hello, Los Angeles! This is Noble High's Principal Patterson." Looking out at all his students and teachers, he quickly amps up his cool factor. "That's right! Principal P. is on the mic and ready to spin the next record. Sven, let it drop!"

"You heard Principal P.—get on the floor and dance to this *hot, hot* track by Depeche Mode, 'Shake the Disease!'"

The moment Sophie hears the song, everything outside of the Cinematics circle melts away. She knows her time at the party is slipping away, so she enjoys every moment dancing to the music despite Matthieu not being there with her.

"Sophie, I'm coming back. I have something for our mission." CJ breaks away from the circle.

Susan tries to keep track of CJ, wondering where he is going. "I'm getting thirsty. Tai, let's go get some punch," she says. Tai follows her as she makes her way back to the bake sale table.

Sophie wanders past the same cliques that have staked their space on the dance floor just like it's lunchtime on the quad. She escapes to the bathroom to touch up her lipstick. The peach-tiled bathroom is packed with girls having their own cry and gossip fest. Sophie squeezes in by the mirror and applies her red lipstick. Then she makes a quick exit in her disguise as the homecoming queen and her court, dressed as big hairspray supermodels, burst in for their own private party. She spills out into the dim, empty girls' locker room.

"I knew that was you, Sophie." Brittany sneaks a drag from a cigarette, sitting alone on the locker room bench. She projects a steely cool persona, lit by the glow from the cigarette embers. "I've seen you around. You're in a club or something, right?"

"Yeah, we made our own film," Sophie replies, guarded, wondering why Brittany is finally speaking to her.

"Good for you," Brittany says in a condescending tone as she exhales a stream of smoke. "Take it from me—your little club won't be there for you, especially that new guy." She drops the cigarette to the floor, grinding it out with her lace-up boot, and says with a spiteful smirk that's hiding something deeper, "He didn't show up, did he?"

Sophie slips away and circles around the gym, searching for familiar faces. Ms. Kahn takes the stage and makes the next announcement.

"We have a very talented singer from our vocal ensemble performing next. Please welcome Melanie Azimi, accompanied on keyboard by Justin Sakamoto. They will be performing 'Only You' by Yazoo." Ms. Kahn starts the applause as the two students step into the spotlight.

Justin, wearing a white suit jacket and black bow tie, sits down on the stool and starts playing the Casio electronic keyboard. Melanie, evoking angelic Audrey Hepburn in a soft powder-blue 1950s ball gown, looks out into the darkened gym and takes a deep breath. Bathed in purple lights, she grasps the microphone with a white gardenia corsage wrapped around her wrist. Closing her eyes, her voice cracks with nervousness on the first notes and then blossoms into a beautiful soulful voice.

Dry ice snakes around Melanie and Justin until they look like they are floating in the clouds. The smoke drifts off the stage and billows out across the gym filled with slow-dancing couples.

Wandering through the swaying students on the dance floor, Sophie is lost in the darkness, trying to forget Brittany's words. *He didn't show up, did he?*

She catches her breath as the lights flash like a lightning strike, illuminating a boy standing in front of her. Sophie freezes when her hazel eyes meet his blue eyes.

"I came through the storm *for you*," the boy with bleached ice-white hair says.

Another bolt of light flashes across his face as Sophie finishes his sentence. "Tears don't have to fall like rain."

Matthieu smiles, knowing he has found where he belongs. "I'm Roy Batty, Nexus-6 replicant from *Blade Runner*."

Sophie smiles back and reaches for his hand. "Hello, I'm Rachael, Nexus-7 replicant. Roy Batty, let's dance to this last song before it's time to go."

He hesitates, confessing, "I…I don't really know how to dance."

Sophie places his hands on her waist and wraps her arms around his shoulders, draped in his trench coat.

"Just follow the beat." Sophie says, taking in Matthieu's new look.

Matthieu and Sophie sway gently back and forth to the synthesizer.

"What changed your mind about the dance?" Sophie asks.

"I didn't want to let you down again," Matthieu says, self-conscious about his movements. "We'll have this dance."

Sophie feels his hands pull her closer, his heart beating in time with hers. They dance together, buried in each other's embrace, as the music and lights fade away. They kiss as Melanie sings, "Only you."

Melanie and Justin take a bow as the stage lights come up. The crowd erupts in applause, breaking the moment for Sophie and Matthieu.

"Oops, I got some lipstick on you," Sophie laughs, pointing to the stain on his lips.

A pumped-up jock, dressed in a one-piece white spandex jumpsuit like the gymnastics hero from *Gymkata*, passes by and notices the red smudge on Matthieu's lips. He gives a thumbs-up and snorts, "Hey, dude, great vampire costume! You bloodsucker! Ha!"

Sophie and Matthieu look at each other and crack up. Matthieu wipes his coat sleeve across his lips to clean off the lipstick and takes Sophie's hand. "Let's find CJ. It's time to catch Balafre."

$$* * * * * *$$

"What happened? You're soaked!" Sophie exclaims.

"Look—there's a freak storm outside!" CJ props open the VIP door of the gym.

Sophie peers out to see thunder and lightening moving toward the hills. "It's passing."

"CJ, you can ride with me," Matthieu says, looking at the sky.

"Look, nothing is going to get in the way of our plan." CJ shakes the rain from his head. He reaches into his backpack and passes Realistic TRC-84 walkie-talkies to Sophie and Matthieu. "These are for our mission. This is how we'll communicate with each other."

"Where did you get these?" Matthieu asks, impressed by the gear.

"Special loan from Video Vault," CJ says. "Now, just pull up the antenna and press this side button when you want to talk. Let's do a test."

Matthieu presses the speaker button, and there's a crackling noise. "Sophie, CJ—can you hear me?"

"Roger!" CJ confirms into the walkie-talkie.

"Hear you loud and clear!" Sophie replies. "Let's go!"

Oscar, Anisha, and Susan push aside the black curtain and rush up to them backstage as Tina Turner's "We Don't Need Another Hero" plays.

"Hey, are you leaving now?" Oscar asks.

"Maybe you'll be back before the dance is over?" Anisha hopes.

"Sven Synth is going to perform with his old band, Velvet Laser," Oscar reveals the secret.

"Yeah, we're leaving for La Luna." Sophie hugs Anisha, Susan, and Oscar. "I can't promise we'll be back. I just know that we have to get Balafre once and for all."

"CJ, do you hear it? They're playing our song from *Mad Max*!" Susan makes her move and takes off her charm bracelet. She places it on CJ's palm. "Take this—it symbolizes the Cinematics Club. It's for good luck."

CJ clips the bracelet onto his dog tag necklace. He is supercharged and clutches the charm. "Thanks, Su. You know we'll be all right."

Sophie, CJ, and Matthieu exit through the VIP door and walk past a group of junior-high students trying to talk their way into the dance.

"This is really my ID! I just look a lot younger in person," a boy pleads, dressed as LL Cool J in a white Kangol hat and tracksuit.

Sophie gets inside her wagon, dropping her purse and walkie-talkie on the front seat. She watches as Matthieu drives off. Just as she starts her engine, CJ pulls up on his scooter. She rolls down the window, and he hands her a VHS tape.

"Take this," CJ calls out above his sputtering motor.

Sophie looks at the label on the side of the box. "This is our movie!"

"Yeah, it's our movie, but that scumbag doesn't know it. I say you swap the reel he wants for this."

"CJ, I think he knows the difference between a reel and a videotape," Sophie says.

"Well, keep it with you, just as a backup."

CJ secures his helmet and slips the walkie-talkie inside his leather jacket. He signals to Sophie, and she follows him out of the Noble High parking lot and toward their secret mission.

25

All Roads Lead to La Luna

The thunder and lighting have passed, leaving the slick Valley streets with a glow from the rainstorm—bouncing the colors of the green, yellow, and red streetlights across the pavement. Sophie tries to concentrate on the plan to catch Balafre, but the last few months flash through her mind like she is watching everything rewind back to the night when she first saw Matthieu at the box office. Specific memories come into focus: the night swim, filming at Matthieu's house, discovering the reel, the black-and-white photo of Balafre, the scar that is still an open wound.

Sophie drives down the busy boulevard and passes the neon marquee of La Luna, announcing in red lettering: TONIGHT! TWO SCREENINGS OF THE ROCKY HORROR PICTURE SHOW! She follows Matthieu's silver Spider as he turns the corner. His peroxide-white hair peeks out of the convertible. CJ's Vespa swerves past her to catch up with Matthieu, resembling a *Mad Max* desert wasteland chase.

A massive crowd waits outside the theater, spilling out into the street. Sophie is jammed in bumper-to-bumper traffic. She hears a voice transmitting from the walkie-talkie.

"Hello, can you hear me? The alley is blocked!" Matthieu says with urgency. "There are barricades *everywhere*."

She grabs her walkie-talkie and presses the side button. "I can't get through—there's too much traffic. I'm gonna pull off and park."

Static pops from the walkie-talkie. "What?" CJ takes command. "Sophie, wait! Stay on target!"

"Sophie!" Matthieu implores. "Keep following me."

But Sophie has made up her mind. "I know what I'm doing." She tosses the walkie-talkie back onto the seat and turns off onto a side street.

Sophie pulls into a parking spot on a leafy street lined with bungalows, decorated with Halloween pumpkins. She grabs her purse and throws in the VHS tape CJ gave her. The moon is bright as she races up the block, leaving the walkie-talkie crackling on the wagon seat.

"Sophie…Sophie!"

She rounds the corner back to the boulevard; the Saturday-night foot traffic is just as jammed as on the road. Sophie looks around for any sign of CJ or Matthieu as she runs past the shops. Everyone is having a good time. People dart out of Popsicle with see-through bags of colorful candy. Students in Halloween costumes who couldn't sneak into Noble High's dance bum around outside Chelsea Loft. As Sophie approaches La Luna, she sees people swarming around the theater, dressed up as the campy characters from *The Rocky Horror Picture Show*: the small-town Brads and Janets, the hunched Riff Raffs, and the fishnet-wearing Doctor Frank-N-Furters.

Sophie wades through a crowd of people singing "Time Warp." Making her way toward the alleyway, she bumps into a familiar face.

"Oh, hi, Angela! You made it!" Sophie is taken by surprise.

"I didn't think I would *ever* come to the Valley, but this is really cool!" Angela admits, super-psyched by the excitement. She is dressed as Columbia, wearing a gold glitter tailcoat, a top hat, and hot pants. "You look fab!"

"Thanks. Glad you came," Sophie huffs, trying to catch her breath. "Sorry I can't stay—there's something at the theater that I need to take care of."

She pushes on through the *Rocky Horror* fans. Not wanting to come off as rude, she yells back to Angela, "Enjoy the show!"

As she ducks and squeezes through the crush of people, her black wig becomes lost amongst the Riff Raffs singing and thrusting their pelvises.

Sophie reaches the alleyway, which is blocked off with wooden barricades, just as Matthieu warned. With her wig gone, she must go on without her disguise—just her now, just Sophie. She squeezes between the barriers and cautiously steps around the giant rain puddles that have formed in the broken craters in the asphalt. The alley is deserted, the neon glow of the theater sign reflecting off the brick wall. Sophie calls out, "Matthieu? CJ?"

Dylan spots Sophie and races down La Luna's back stairs, his keys jangling on his belt. "Moonlight, you've got to get out of here. The delivery is coming any second now!"

"I'm not leaving! This is our last chance to get Balafre!" Sophie stands firm.

"We've got this!" Dylan keeps a watchful eye out, waving Sophie away.

"I've heard that before," Sophie whispers to herself as she crouches down out of sight, hiding beside the dumpster graffitied with KILROY WAS HERE. The chill of the night falls upon her. She is unsure what will happen next or what has become of CJ and Matthieu. Shivering, she looks up at the moon and makes a wish.

The blinding glare of headlights shines toward the alley as a van approaches. Dylan walks toward the barrier and moves it aside. The Reel World Ltd. van slowly pulls into the alley, its muffler rattling loudly. Usually laid back, Dylan protectively walks alongside the van like a secret service agent, ensuring the safe transport.

The door of the van creaks open. Rikki hops out, wearing his black Searing Magmä T-shirt over a long-sleeved thermal shirt, and gives Dylan a bro handshake.

"I've got *Doctor Zhivago* for you." Rikki gives Dylan a *you know what I mean* look. He slides open the side of the van and pulls out a small 8mm metal reel case.

Dylan takes the container carefully. He knows the importance of the film; it is evidence of crimes that cannot be erased by time. As she watches from the shadows, Sophie's heart pounds and her throat tightens in anticipation.

Another van sneaks through the barriers, kills its headlights, and pulls up behind the delivery van. Rikki sizes up the sinister vehicle—its corroded blue paint, smashed metal bumper, and blacked-out windows.

"I'll handle this," Rikki assures Dylan. He walks over to the van, his broken arm and leg clearly healed, and knocks on the driver's darkened window. Channeling his Searing Magmä stage persona, he shakes out his black mullet and puts on a deep, menacing Viking voice. "Hey, I don't know who you think you are, but you better turn this pile of garbage around."

The van's engine starts up and idles. Confident he has made his point to the driver, Rikki throws a thumbs-up to Dylan. Then the van's door violently swings open, knocking Rikki to the ground with incredible force.

Stunned by the blow, Rikki writhes in pain on the pavement. He howls, "Ahhhh! *Judas Priest*—my arrrm!"

Dylan, clutching the film reel, rushes over to Rikki. Suddenly a body flies out of the van's open door, landing on top of Dylan. The figure, disguised in a black knit ski mask, punches Dylan in the stomach and grabs the reel from his hands.

Sophie, frozen in her dark hiding spot, watches as their plan to catch Balafre explodes in front of her eyes.

In the chaos, a silver convertible zooms past the barriers and rear-ends the idling blue van. Matthieu jumps over his windshield, leaps onto the front hood—his trench coat soaring like a cape through the night—and chases after the guy with the reel.

A cold surge shivers down Sophie's spine when she sees Balafre move into the driver's seat of the blue van.

"Stop the van! Don't let him get away!" she cries out.

Dylan lunges into the van to grab Balafre. CJ blazes up on his Vespa and skids to a stop in front of the van. Still wearing his helmet, he races around to the other side door and launches like a missile into the van.

Sophie bolts up into the light, her brain surging. *Not waiting on the bench this time!* She's determined to get Balafre. But then her attention is jolted, hearing a struggle up on La Luna's back stairs. Peering through the gaps in the steps, she catches sight of Matthieu locked in battle with the masked figure. On the top landing, Matthieu wrestles to get the reel back and snatches the mask off the guy's head. Matthieu takes a blow and loses his balance, falling backward and dropping the mask.

"Matthieu!" Sophie screams as he tumbles halfway down the cold metal stairs before he's able to grab the railing and catch himself. Dazed by the fall, Matthieu props himself up.

"Can you see? Are you okay?" Sophie helps Matthieu down to the bottom step, blood streaming from the gash above his right eye. She squats down and checks his brow, the blood staining his white hair like fresh snow.

"I'm okay. I grabbed his mask, but I didn't see his face," Matthieu says, still dizzy, sliding down onto the soaked pavement. He wipes the blood away from his eye with his coat sleeve, already marked with Sophie's red lipstick.

Before Matthieu can get back on his feet, Sophie dashes up the stairs, ripping the back slit of her skirt. She runs past the ski mask that has fallen on the step. With her adrenaline fight response in high gear, she climbs to the top landing. With nowhere to escape, the figure, his back turned, desperately grapples to open the locked door to the projection room.

Sophie grabs the VHS tape from her purse and uses it to whack the guy on the back of his head. As he wobbles around, she frantically digs back into her bag and grasps a tube, blasting his eyes with her minty breath spray.

The boy frantically rubs his burning eyes, which are swelling up. He lifts his face up, flushed and spotted with acne.

"Lee?" Sophie gasps in disbelief. She knows that this is the end of the road; there is no more time for cat-and-mouse games. Determined to get an answer, she demands, *"Why? Why are you doing this?"*

The boy, whose usual reflex would be to lash out, lowers his head. He clutches the reel, his hands protected by his BMX bike gloves, and lets out what he has held in for so long.

"You don't understand. He's…he's my grandfather."

Everything seems to fade away as those words rain down on Sophie. Everything finally makes sense; it's like putting the last piece into a puzzle. At first her impulse is to stand up to him and fight back, but then she is overtaken by a different feeling. She hears the shame in his voice, the legacy he believes he is destined for.

"Lee…you *don't* have to be him. You *don't* have to do this." Sophie sees the remorse in his eyes and extends her hand toward him. She implores, "Please…give me the reel."

Lee hesitates, struggling to release himself from the chains of his family's dark secret. Sophie is the first person he has opened up to, even if it was just for a few seconds, and she is offering him a chance at redemption. Wanting to free himself, he loosens his grip and hands Sophie the reel. Then Lee climbs over the railing and dives off, landing in the dumpster below. His fall is cushioned by the mound of cardboard boxes in the trash, and he bounds out and flees away into the night.

Matthieu scales the back stairs and throws his arms around Sophie like he is shielding her from fire with his trench coat. "Are you all right?" He frantically looks around to find that they are the only ones on the landing. "You—you got the reel!"

Sophie sees the red neon glow flashing off and on across Matthieu's face, flushed with excitement.

"Yes! The reel is safe!" She clutches the metal canister, unsure how to explain what just happened between her and Lee. "That guy just left it and disappeared. What happened to Balafre?"

They look down at the alleyway where the blue van idles, rocking violently back and forth.

"Let's get down there!" Matthieu takes Sophie's hand, eager to finish their mission.

Bathed in the red neon light, they descend the staircase. A roar of voices radiates from inside the blue van. They run up to the window. CJ is in the driver's seat as a lookout, his attention ping-ponging back and forth from the windshield to the action inside the van.

"What's going on? Did you get Balafre?" Sophie anxiously asks.

"Things are *totally* under control," CJ says with complete assurance while nervously eyeing the commotion inside the van. He glances into the side-view mirror and spots someone running into the alley. "Hey, Matthieu, there's someone coming. Go put the barrier back."

Matthieu races around the van just as a woman runs past him, her glittery hat and jacket shimmering.

"Angela!" Sophie exclaims. "You can't be here!"

Out of breath, she doubles over, then looks back behind her. "Someone dressed as Riff Raff is chasing me. I'm trying to get away from him." Angela crouches down beside the dumpster, trying to shake the costumed stalker off her trail.

Matthieu, pulling the wooden barrier back into place, steps out in front of the clueless guy. He is dressed in a long black tailcoat and a bald cap with stringy blond locks that flow from the back.

"The alley is closed," Matthieu barks. "VIPs only."

"No waaay!" Defeated, the stalker sheepishly walks back to the crowd down the street.

Matthieu races back to the van just as CJ bounds from the driver's seat.

Suddenly the side doors swing open with a loud clang. CJ, Matthieu, and Sophie peek around from the front of the van, awaiting the next move.

"Rikki, wait for my signal!" Dylan yells, jumping out from the van doors into the alley. His dark brown hair is dripping with sweat from the scuffle, and his black dress shirt is in crumpled disarray. He takes a defensive position with his arms outstretched, preparing for the final capture. "I'm ready when you are!"

CJ, Sophie, and Matthieu huddle together in front of the blue van.

Is this really happening? Sophie wonders. She didn't exactly have an idea what capturing a Nazi would actually be like. It was more of a rough sketch than a finished drawing—call it being naive…call it right against wrong…call it the happy ending she always loves just before the movie credits roll. Now that she is here, standing at the edge of this cliff, all she wants is for it to be over. A jolt of panic seizes her. *What have I done? What are Mom and Dad going to do when they find out? Have I put all of us in danger?*

Sophie looks at CJ, excitement all over his face. She glances back at Matthieu, and he whispers in her ear, "It's because of you that this is happening. You never gave up." His blue eyes are certain and unwavering.

CJ, Sophie, and Matthieu lean out together to get a better view. Dylan and Rikki lock arms around their prisoner, his skeletal hands bound by a rope that is also wrapped around his thin waist. Up close, Sophie looks at Balafre's profile and is surprised by his slender frame and normal appearance—thin gray hair, wrinkles, the jowls of an elderly man. He looks like anyone you might pass on the street—a grandfather dressed in a plaid sports coat. She gazes at the scar across his forehead as he turns to face her. For the first time, she looks directly into his eyes. They show no signs of guilt or conflict; they're just black and hollow. He has lived in plain sight for so long, where he has survived by blending in and banking on the fact that people would forget the past.

Sophie's world turns to black and white. She pictures herself in the film reel, captured in the Paris roundup. Surrounded by frightened Jewish families, she stares straight into the Nazi's eyes. Her fear drains away, replaced with a surge of courage in her heart. She looks at Balafre, unflinching, promising herself that what he has done will be known.

Then a rush of headlights brings Sophie back into the world of vivid color. A black-and-white Crown Victoria police car, lights and sirens blaring, speeds toward them from the other direction of the alleyway. The cruiser comes to a screeching stop in front of the van.

"Don't move!" Agent Sampson yells, leaping out of the driver's side. Standing firmly in his pressed uniform and badge, he points his gun at the three struggling men. His partner, Agent Marconi, thrusts his pistol forward as well, shielding himself behind the car door.

Dylan and Rikki stand frozen like statues, still holding Balafre. Squinting in the blinding light of the police car's high beams, Matthieu and CJ slowly raise their hands above their heads as Sophie clings to the reel.

"You!" Agent Marconi yells to Angela, who is still crouched, trembling, by the dumpster. Impatient, his mustache twitching, he calls, "Get over here!"

Angela, still shocked by the events unfolding in front of her, walks furiously in her Mary Jane dance shoes, teetering across the broken asphalt.

"I don't know what all this is about," she explains, her voice quivering. "I'm here for *The Rocky Horror Picture Show*!" She joins the lineup and raises her hands above her glittery top hat.

A gray Chevrolet Caprice sedan skids to a stop, leaving a smoking trail of tire tread marks down the alley. A tall man, his angular face accentuated by his strong jawline, darts out of the sedan and strides over to the police officers.

"Detective Lt. Deckard," he announces in a voice rugged from years of uncovering the truth on the streets of LA. He stands confidently with his gun holster strapped over his white shirt, his steely eyes surveying the scene in front of him. His eyes lock onto his subdued target. "Agent Sampson, take him into custody."

The police officer puts cuffs on the captive and escorts him to the police vehicle. Matthieu watches Balafre, silent and shackled, being secured in the back seat of the police car. Agent Sampson locks the door and tosses aside the rope Dylan and Rikki used to restrain the prisoner. In his native French, Matthieu shouts out to the captive, "*Lâche*!" The word— *coward*—travels with the force of a rock and penetrates the window glass, drawing the eye of the stone-faced Balafre.

Deckard turns his attention to the rest of the ragtag group. "Okay, I don't know how you got mixed up in this. Just drop your hands and stay where you are. I'll need to get your statements for our report. We've been on the trail of this Nazi war criminal for several months. Balafre, aka The Scar, has used many aliases since he fled France in 1945. Through our intel, we learned that he'd finally come out of hiding in his attempt to destroy two film reels. They are the only recorded evidence of his crimes, thanks to our informant—the brave man who shot the films while in a secret U.S. army unit."

A man emerges from the back seat of the detective's Chevy Caprice. He walks with measured steps to the police car and looks through the window at the aloof, handcuffed Balafre.

"I've waited so long for this day," Max Greenfeld says with a deep sigh. It's like he's been holding his breath since he first filmed the horrific scenes in Paris through his Revere 8mm movie camera. "After I returned to the U.S. from the army, the film reels went missing. It was only recently that they were discovered in a film vault—they'd been mistakenly sent to Hollywood."

Max approaches Sophie, who hands over the canister.

"Sophie." Max smiles. "Didn't I tell you? It's La Luna. There's something magical here, something that brought us all together." He glances back at the neon theater sign, then continues, "All of you did something *extraordinary* tonight." He holds the reel close as the emotion wells up in his voice. "Thank you."

"Max, was it you who sent the reels here?" Sophie asks, anxious to unravel the mystery.

"Yes, Sophie. It was me all along," Max confesses. "I have been searching for the reels and for The Scar. I knew he was alive all this time. Once I discovered that Balafre was in Los Angeles, I planned to lure him here to La Luna. Detective Deckard has been working with me on the investigation so we could finally capture him. I had no idea that you and your friends would ever be in harm's way."

"Mr. Greenfeld, sir…let me explain," Dylan interjects. "We had our own plans to nab Balafre. As you can see, everything worked out great. Don't you worry, Mr. G.—the other reel is safe and secure upstairs." Confident that he has made his point, Dylan inches in the direction of the theater. "I really need to get back up to the projection room now. I'll get you the other reel!"

Deckard, not amused, commands, "Don't you move until I'm done."

"We're cool, man," Rikki reassures Deckard, cradling his sore left arm. "We're all cool."

Another man bounds from the back seat of the detective's sedan. Instead of a gun, he holds a Nikon camera with a zoom lens, moving like a sleek panther as he shoots. The flashbulb emits white strobes of light as the shutter clicks in rapid fire.

Click, click, click, click: *The Scar.*

Click, click, click, click: *the police and Deckard.*

Click, click, click, click: *Max holding the film reel.*

Click, click: *two guys, a girl, and a van.*

As the camera pans by CJ, Sophie, and Matthieu, a voice shouts out from behind it:

"Charles! Sophie! Matthieu! WHAT ARE YOU DOING HERE?"

"Uncle William?" CJ blurts out, equally surprised. Only his family calls him Charles, and usually when he's in trouble.

Detective Lt. Deckard pops a piece of gum into his mouth and asks, "Will, do you know these kids?"

William Omolo, aggravated, lowers the camera from his face and replies, "Yeah—that's my nephew and his friends from school." He has spent many years doing ride-alongs with the police, slowly gaining their trust. This exclusive access allows him to be the first photographer on the scene to capture breaking news stories. Clearly embarrassed and angry that

CJ and his friends are caught up in this investigation, William becomes flustered, not knowing what to ask first.

"Charles, what the hell are you doing here? You all could have been hurt, shot, killed! What am I going to say to your mom and dad?" William's cool on-the-job reputation shatters as he fumbles to change the film in his camera. "And don't even try to come up with excuses while I'm speaking. I can see the gears spinning in that head of yours."

William turns to the detective. "Deckard, I'm the mentor for their school photography and film club. I had *absolutely* no idea that they knew anything about this operation." He points to the surrounding buildings. "My nephew works at that video store over there, and Sophie works at the movie theater."

CJ, still wearing his scooter helmet, can't hold back and asks, "Is this why you've been MIA for the past month?"

"Yes," William confesses. "This is the big story I've been working on. I couldn't tell anyone."

"I need to take care of Balafre. I've got the FBI, the CIA, and the DOJ all clamoring for him. We have no reason to take these kids in. We just need to get their statements, and then they can go," Deckard assures William. The detective signals to the officers. "Agent Marconi, Agent Sampson—let's get this area secured and finish up. I'm calling for backup to transport the prisoner."

Deckard walks over to his sedan and calls in his updates over the CB radio.

The back door of La Luna's projection room swings open, and Robert Garcia rushes down the back stairs, unknowingly kicking Lee's black ski mask into the dumpster below. He runs up to Max with a metal canister. Trying to catch his breath, Robert gasps, "Max, Max! Don't leave! Here's the film reel."

"Robert, thank you." Max holds both reels, now returned to their rightful place in history. "These films will be used as evidence to put away that murderer once and for all." Clutching the reels, he walks to the detective's car and gets in the back seat.

Robert is relieved that Max's plan has worked. But when Max told him about the plan to ensnare The Scar, he emphasized that nothing would interrupt the operations of the movie theater. Now he takes a good look around the alley at the surreal scene playing out behind the theater—the vans, the police cars, and the large group of people. He spots Dylan and shouts, "Dylan! What are you doing down here? We have a theater full of people waiting to see the movie!"

"Sir, you're going to have to wait till we finish with our interviews," Agent Marconi interjects as he begins taking statements from Dylan, Rikki, and Angela. Agent Sampson questions Sophie, CJ, and Matthieu.

Robert takes a deep breath and pulls it together. He straightens his tie and suit jacket and calls out to Dylan, "I got this! I'm going up to run the projector. I'm not letting the audience down!" Determined to finish his mission for the night, he turns around and races up the back stairs to start the show.

Speaking into his shoulder microphone, Agent Sampson radios the police station. "We have a 10-15, prisoner in custody, at La Luna Theater. We need to transport the prisoner's van. Requesting a tow truck." He looks at the state of Matthieu's face, examines the streak of blood across his brow, and asks, "Are you hurt? Do you need an ambulance?"

"No, I'm okay," Matthieu says, shaking his head, strands of his white hair falling across the gash.

A loud thundering noise rumbles overhead as helicopter searchlights slice through the night sky. The intense beams circle around, shining down on the alley. As the choppers hover above, swirling cyclones of air surround them. The chilling wind blows straight through Sophie's bones, and the deafening sound of the chopper blades closes in.

Matthieu takes hold of Sophie's left hand, clutching it like he never wants to let go. He'd been set adrift from France when his mother passed away, a ship lost on rough seas. Los Angeles—the hills, his family, Sophie, and the Cinematics Club—have finally anchored him.

Sophie grabs hold of CJ's left hand. The three of them stand united in the eye of the storm, feeling protected by an invisible force field. A flurry of action swirls around them.

Agent Marconi, finished with his interviews, flags the tow truck driver pulling up behind Matthieu's car. "The convertible is drivable. The blue van is the one we're impounding for evidence." Straining to be heard above the loud copters, Agent Marconi calls to Rikki and Matthieu, "We're towing the van now. You're free to go."

Matthieu turns to Sophie, determination in his eyes. "I'm not leaving. I am coming back." He slowly releases her hand and races over to his convertible, its front fender and headlights smashed. He whizzes out of the alley in reverse. Unseen without headlights, Matthieu swerves his Fiat back onto the street, searching for a parking space.

A guy in navy coveralls hooks up Balafre's beat-up van to the tow truck and hauls it away.

Rikki thrusts his arms up in the air, forming a V for victory, and shouts to the moon, "I'm never gonna forget this night!" Ignoring his sore limb, he throws his arms around Dylan in a big bear hug. Weeping tears of joy, Rikki rests his head on Dylan's shoulder, proclaiming, "I love you, man." Then he walks proudly to the Reel World van and fires up the engine. Rikki, fist pumping out the window, rolls back down the alleyway.

✳ ✳ ✳ ✳ ✳ ✳

The helicopters circle like sharks waiting for their prey. The wind whips across Sophie, tossing her hair around her face as she keeps an eye on Balafre, sitting motionless in the back seat of the squad car. CJ watches his uncle maneuvering around undetected as he photographs Balafre's capture. William aims his Nikon, zooming in and out, advancing and retreating, photographing the real emotions and moments that will be remembered from this night.

The choppers swoop down as an armored military vehicle pulls up. A squad of black-clothed officers, their faces concealed, jumps out. With synchronized movements, they swarm around the police car and swiftly usher Balafre inside their black van. The darkness now captured and sealed inside, the stealth truck speeds away.

The choppers zoom back up into the air, following the armored transport with laser-focused searchlights. The turbulent wind dies down, and CJ removes his helmet. He spots a polished sports car barreling up to Deckard's sedan.

"What the—" Detective Deckard exclaims, reaching for the pistol in his shoulder harness.

A guy jumps out of the Toyota Supra dressed in a black dinner jacket and a Casio Databank calculator watch.

"Hello, don't shoot! I'm Steven Tran." He waves in front of him a laminated identification card. "Here's my badge. I work as an aerospace engineer at DynaRocket."

"This alley is closed for a criminal investigation," Deckard shouts. "You'll need to leave immediately!"

Aimee peeks her head out of the car window. "Sir, we're here on an urgent police matter," she firmly responds—she has a great deal of practice politely dealing with stressed members at the Racquet Centre.

"My sister Susan phoned me," Steven explains. "She's friends with Sophie, Matthieu, and CJ. She was worried that they were in danger." Steven points toward Sophie. "I brought that girl's father with me. We all know about the plan to catch the Nazi."

Deckard's retracts his hand from his shoulder holster and grips his throbbing temples. His patience hits the boiling point, and he yells, "Is there anyone who *doesn't* know about this ultra-secret operation?"

Simon squeezes out of the back seat of the Supra. He looks frantically around, scanning the officers and police cars.

"That's my daughter!" He rushes over. "Sophie!"

Sophie can't believe her dad is here, dressed in his usual navy-blue pants and striped dress shirt, and is unsure of what his reaction will be. She runs up to him, and he hugs her tightly, the instinctive way a parent protects his child. There is sadness in Simon's voice as he repeats her name.

"Sophie…Sophie…Sophie."

He knew it was only a matter of time before his daughter finally breached his bubble, entering the cruel world he has tried to protect her from.

After a night of costumes and disguises, angels and monsters, a cyclone of emotions has built up inside her. Sophie feels the weight of her body like she has just crash-landed back on Earth.

In her dad's embrace, Sophie exclaims triumphantly, "Dad, we did it! We got him!"

******

The road back to La Luna becomes an obstacle course for Matthieu, who has to weave through the stream of *Rocky Horror* fans throwing their own party on the sidewalk. He runs past the swaying, towering palm trees as their fronds rain down onto the street. He can't hold back the electric-charged happiness he feels surging through him, unable to hide the big smile lighting up his face. He races up to CJ, leaning against his scooter with his helmet hanging on the handlebar.

"Hey! This has been the greatest night!" Matthieu says, shaking CJ's shoulder. "My father will never believe we were here!"

"Your dad will have proof." CJ gestures to his uncle, who is aiming his Nikon right at them. "This was a truly righteous evening!" He basks in the success of their mission, then begins to wonder what Susan is doing at the dance.

Matthieu looks around to find Sophie and is surprised to see that her dad had arrived. He watches as Simon stands protectively by Sophie. His smile fades away, and he is seized with insecurity. Matthieu retreats, hanging back by CJ.

Simon glances over and catches sight of CJ, who waves to him. He doesn't recognize the boy with the white-blond hair, but something about him triggers a memory of his childhood in Germany. The color reminds Simon of his big brother Heinz, who had the fairest blond hair in his family. Heinz was a teenager when he was taken away by the Nazis and put into forced labor. Simon and his family never saw him again.

"CJ! Matthieu!" Sophie calls out, waving them over.

William puts his camera equipment into his bag and walks with CJ over to Sophie.

"Hi, I'm William Omolo. I'm CJ's uncle," he says, introducing himself to Simon, Steven, and Aimee. "I'm photographing for the *Los Angeles Daily Tribune*."

Detective Deckard gathers Agents Sampson and Marconi by his vehicle and reviews all the information they have gathered from the scene. He clears his throat—his voice is getting increasingly hoarse—and announces, "Can I get everyone's attention? Thank you for your cooperation this evening. The officers have taken your information and statements for our report. Now I need everyone to clear the scene. Will, you can drive with Marconi. Do all minors have parents or guardians present to get them home safe?"

"I came on my scooter." CJ points out his Vespa to the detective. "I'm just going to go back to our school dance."

"I don't think so." William throws his camera bag over his shoulder. "We're going to follow you home." He gets into Officer Marconi's police car.

"It looks like everyone is okay, so we'll be on our way." Steven Tran waves goodbye and gets into his car. He checks his watch and says to Aimee, "It's almost eleven. Susan should be leaving the dance. Let's swing by and see if we can find her." The headlights of his Supra ignite, and the sunroof slides open.

"Look at that moon tonight!" Aimee says, leaning her head back against the seat, as the Supra jets away.

"I'm taking my daughter home," Simon tells the detective.

"Dad, what about Matthieu?" Sophie asks.

"Matthieu, why don't you come with Sophie and me. I'll drive you home." Simon steps toward him, a gesture of acceptance. "I'm not angry at you. What you did was…" Simon searches for the right word. "Brave."

Matthieu looks Sophie's dad in the eyes. His pained look dissolves. "Really? You're not mad?"

"The man you helped capture tonight is evil. Doing good when most turn their heads away—that is heroic. That is something to be proud of." His tone shifts, circling back to stern dad mode. "But as Sophie's father, this is the *last* secret mission my daughter or your club will get mixed up with. Are we clear?"

Matthieu nods as he follows Simon and Sophie back to her wagon.

******

Deckard observes the last two people lingering around and walks over to Dylan and Angela. "We've got everything we need. You can go."

He takes one final look around the scene and signals to Officer Sampson, who dashes back to his squad car. The Chevy Caprice speeds away. Officer Marconi's police car tails CJ's scooter.

An eerie quiet takes over the alleyway. Dylan lights up a cigarette and takes a puff before passing it to Angela.

"I *knew* I shouldn't have come to the Valley." Angela calms her nerves with a drag of his cigarette, which she holds between her red-polished fingernails. Her hand trembles as she passes it back to Dylan.

He is struck by her classic Hollywood beauty, a cross between Josephine Baker and Francine Everett. Dylan inhales and passes the cigarette back to Angela. He doesn't let the opportunity go to waste. Smoothing out his shirt and brushing his hair back, he regains his cool. "I'm Dylan, by the way. I work here at the theater as a projectionist, but I'm studying filmmaking. I've already directed my first movie. Cameron—*James* Cameron—loved it. Have you done any acting?"

"Uh, no." Angela gives him a suspicious glance; she knows when she's hearing a pickup line.

"I'm in preproduction for my sequel, *RoboCruisers 2*. I'm looking for my lead actress. Can I get your number?" Dylan takes the last puff of the cigarette and flicks it away.

"Do you think I can still get into *Rocky Horror*?" Angela asks, pulling the movie flyer from her sequined clutch. She scribbles her phone number on the back of it and dangles the sheet in the air.

Dylan takes the paper and tucks it away in his pants pocket. He extends his arm to Angela and says, "Come with me. I'll get you into the movie through my secret entrance."

He escorts her up the back stairs of La Luna to the rear projection room door. Dylan is captivated by Angela in the pulsing red light of the neon sign—a muse, her Gina Rowlands to his John Cassavetes.

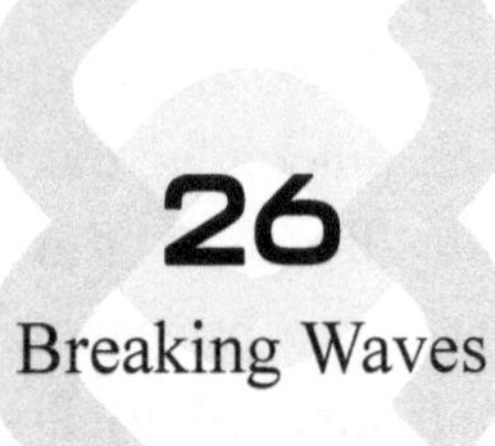

26
Breaking Waves

Simon drives Sophie's Jeep through the dark canyon. Without the distraction of the radio, an obvious silence hangs in the car. A hollow hum fills the air, infused with an earthy citrus scent from the walnut trees. Sophie, sitting beside her dad, catches her reflection in the side mirror. Her eyeliner has smeared, and now she looks like a German Expressionist portrait by Kirchner. Her face captures the night of triumph and tears. She glances at Matthieu in the rear-view mirror. He stares out the window, the cool air blowing against his face. Sophie's attention wanders over to her dad.

Simon's left arm rests on his rolled-down window as he steers with his right hand. As far back as Sophie can remember, he has been a one-handed driver. Even someone as serious as Simon has adopted the laid-back West Coast style. He could drive the canyon with his eyes closed, knowing each curve by heart.

Sophie reaches for the radio and turns the station away from KNXS, knowing her dad doesn't like her music. She changes from FM to AM, rapidly turning the knob past the static until she finds the news station.

"Good evening, Los Angeles, this is Frank Foster," the broadcaster announces in a deep voice. "We have a breaking news story. A wanted Nazi war criminal who has been in hiding for decades was captured tonight in the Valley. He is in custody after being apprehended by the police and—" The broadcaster takes an unexpected pause before continuing, "Am I reading this right?" His voice shifts from puzzlement to excitement. "The Nazi was apprehended by the police and students from Noble High. We'll have more on this incredible story as details come in. And now, a message from our sponsor."

Simon turns off the radio as he drives up the hill to Matthieu's house. He parks at the top of the driveway and turns to Matthieu in the back seat. "Let me speak with your father first." He gets out of the wagon and walks toward the house, passing the wind chimes swaying from the trees.

Sophie watches her father enter the courtyard as Marc steps out of the house to meet him. There is a polite introductory handshake between them. She can't make out what they are saying to each other. Tired and uncomfortable, she releases her seat belt and takes off the blazer over her black tank top. She twists around to face Matthieu.

"Do you think your dad already knows?" Sophie asks, leaning over the leather seat.

"If he does, I don't know what he's going to do." Matthieu unbuckles his seat belt and leans in toward Sophie. He wraps his arms around her shoulders and pulls her toward him.

Sophie slides between the front seats and into the back beside Matthieu. Out the rear window, she sees a fallen uprooted tree brought down by the storm. Its branches fan out like a tarantula. A bird with brown-and-white feathers swoops down below a limp limb. As its head swivels back and forth, a light catches Sophie's attention—the brilliant yellow eyes of a burrowing owl. It calls into the night, then finds its way back home.

Sophie reaches over the back bench into the trunk and retrieves the metal box containing Balafre's forged IDs.

"Here, give these to your dad," Sophie says, placing the box on the seat.

Matthieu embraces Sophie, and she rests against his chest. They watch through the car window and try to decode the exchange between their fathers.

$$* * * * * *$$

Marc looks over at the Jeep and then returns his attention to Simon. Wearing a T-shirt, he folds his arms in front of him, shielding himself from the chill. As he listens, Marc reaches out, grasping Simon's shoulder to steady himself. Like the earth is shaking beneath him, he loses his footing and crumples, collapsing onto the stone steps. Marc cradles his head in his hands, feeling the enormity of the news. The pain of losing his family as a child has never left his body. It has always been there.

Matthieu, seeing his dad lose his composure and fall down, bolts from the back seat. He races to his dad, clutching the metal box.

Sophie gets out of the car as well and stands at the door. She watches Marc sob, covering his face with his hands. She instantly recalls the William Turner painting *The Shipwreck* with its dark tumultuous sea. Sophie no longer strains to understand the pain as words fill her thoughts.

One crosses the ocean, and the memories cross the water with them. Sometimes the memories wash ashore as warm gentle waves. Other times they come crashing in like a violent storm, pulling one down as to not forget.

Marc gathers his strength and pushes himself off the steps. He stands up and embraces Matthieu protectively and triumphantly. His face flushed with drying tears, Marc extends his hand to Simon again in a gesture of gratitude. Accepting that his past is now part of his present, he walks into the house clutching the metal box.

Simon looks closely at Matthieu, seeing beyond his bruised face. All of his preconceived ideas about Matthieu have disintegrated. Simon shakes his hand and walks back to Sophie, who is still waiting by the Jeep.

"It's been a long night. Let's go home." Simon gets into the car and starts the engine.

Matthieu, with his long trench coat and his hair that glows in the moonlight, looks over at Sophie. He puts his hand over his heart and nods. Sophie mirrors his movements as a way of saying *I love you.*

The Wagoneer drifts slowly down the canyon. The traffic is sparse on the main boulevard. Everything looks the same as always—the traffic, the convenience stores—but something has changed tonight. Sophie can feel it.

Stopped at the traffic light, she looks over at her dad, who is lost in his own thoughts. Would now be the time he opens up to her about his past, his childhood?

Sophie looks up at the green stoplight. "Dad, we can go."

"Uh…thanks," Simon says, pressing on the gas. "Your mother is going to be very worried about where we've been. I think it's best if we just talk about everything tomorrow."

Looking out at the clear night sky, Sophie smiles. That's what her mom always tells her when it comes to her dad: *Let's not worry him. We'll talk about it tomorrow.* Sarah is the easygoing one compared to her father. She is the peaceful negotiator and doesn't mind when Sophie spends time on Melrose or working on the Cinematics Club film.

Sophie realizes that at least for tonight, her father's past will remain hidden. And that is okay. All that really matters is that he is here, as he always has been.

27
And the Winner Is…

The headlines are splashed across all the newspapers and TV news shows for weeks:

BALAFRE, WANTED NAZI, IN CUSTODY
AFTER FORTY YEARS!

THE SCAR, WORLD WAR II CRIMINAL, NABBED
IN LOS ANGELES

NO MORE HIDING FOR THIS NAZI—CAUGHT AND
CAPTURED ON FILM!

The stories focus on Max Greenfeld, the secret footage he shot during the war, and his decades-long quest to find Balafre. There are nonstop TV interviews with Detective Lt. Deckard. Standing in front of a huge bulletin board covered with images, Deckard gives his play-by-play of the capture. But besides the photos William Omolo shot the night of Balafre's arrest, the Cinematics Club's involvement remains recorded only in their own memories.

The alarm clock beeps at six thirty a.m. Sophie springs from under her Marimekko comforter and accidentally kicks one of her fuzzy bunny slippers across the bedroom carpet. The slippers were a Hanukkah present from Susan. She looks up at her Picasso calendar featuring *Seated Woman (Marie-Therese)*, a cubist portrait from 1937 of Picasso's young muse painted in blue, yellow, and red. It's Friday, December twentieth, the last day of school before the holiday break. The date is marked with a magenta heart and a scribbled note: "Winter Wonder Assembly!"

Sophie puts on the outfit she has planned for the official premiere of the Cinematics Club movie. After changing into her oversized white shirtdress and black vest, she dabs a few drops of plumeria perfume behind her ears. Her brother bought her the fragrance from his summer trip to Hawaii, along with a typical airport ALOHA T-shirt. Pulling her hair up into a ponytail with a few wavy strands falling behind her ears, she reaches into her jewelry box. She selects a pair of long chandelier earrings that remind her of the ones Isabelle Adjani wore in the French film *Subway*. This is a very special occasion. The excitement is bubbling in her stomach. She takes a final look in the mirror and then slips on her wrist-length black gloves and her C charm bracelet.

Sophie glances over at the framed picture on her dresser. It is a black-and-white photo Mr. Omolo took of CJ and Matthieu. The image of them in the decisive moment of triumph never made it into the *Los Angeles Daily Tribune*. Thinking back to that night, she can't believe two months have passed since Balafre's arrest.

Soon after that October night, a brown box was left at her front door. Her father went out to retrieve the morning newspaper and was surprised to find the package containing the exact amount of cash he had unknowingly paid Balafre for Sophie's car. Simon never questioned where the money came from, believing in good luck, but Sophie knew the source of the mysterious windfall.

Once Balafre's van was impounded by the police, a large stash of cash was discovered. When Detective Deckard questioned Sophie about Balafre, there was one last item she needed to reconcile, and that was the money her father had paid for the Wagoneer.

$$* * * * * *$$

Listening to Scritti Politti's "Perfect Way," Sophie pulls her Jeep into her usual Noble High parking space next to Matthieu's Fiat and CJ's Vespa. The only activity planned for the half day of school is the Winter Wonder Assembly, a showcase for Noble High's clubs.

Sophie finishes the last bite of a toasted English muffin and wipes away the crumbs that are stuck to her lips with a tissue. Looking in the rear-view mirror, she applies a sweep of berry-colored lipstick. She locks the car and slings her purse over her shoulder—free from carrying a heavy stack of textbooks.

Inside the Noble High gym, there is a giddy buzz of students and teachers already in vacation mode. Talk of family trips and shredding the slopes circulates around. Huge glitter letters float above the bleachers: WINTER WONDER 1985.

Sophie grabs a program from the table by the entrance. She quickly scans the agenda until she finds the Cinematics Club. A happy glow colors her pale cheeks. She wanders along the beige walls, looking at the poster board presentations that are set up on long tables. There are game competition photos from the Chess Club and an assortment of cabbages and broccoli grown by the Future Farmers of the Valley.

A pack of girls in silver metallic cape dresses and hair rollers whizzes past Sophie. They are from Mr. Romanoff's Theater Club, which is going to perform Grease's "Beauty School Dropout."

Sophie stops by the Chemistry Club's table, where students are gathered around a large poster board display covered with pictures of icebergs and charts. Susan checks her note cards and gives a smile when she spots Sophie.

"Hello, I'm Susan from Mr. Hart's Chemistry Club." She points to a *Nature* magazine cover pasted on the display. "One of the major scientific headlines from this year is the discovery of a hole in the ozone layer over Antarctica by the British Antarctic Survey, England's polar research institute." Susan's hair has grown to a shoulder-length bob with wispy bangs. She conducts the presentation in a fluorescent pink sweater with a starburst crystal pin.

CJ slides up next to Sophie and whispers, "My uncle is here, and he brought the movie. Matthieu is saving our seats under the basketball hoop. Look for the giant snowflake hanging from it." He's dressed in his film wardrobe, and he loosens the black tie over his dress shirt and suspenders. CJ's mohawk has grown out to a short cut. He smiles and waves to Susan before dashing off.

Sophie pulls an instamatic camera from her purse and snaps a picture of Susan pointing to a chemistry formula: CCl_2F_2.

"Man-made chlorofluorocarbons, or CFCs, are depleting the protective layer of ozone that surrounds the Earth. We can help stop the destruction and save our planet." Susan shuffles her note cards and looks up at the three freshman students directly in front of her. "If you'd like to join the Chemistry Club, we have a sign-up sheet on the table. Thank you."

Sophie starts the applause, and the few attentive students join in before going over to the sign-up sheet.

"Su, you did great!" Sophie gives Susan a big hug.

"You think?" Susan smiles and files the note cards away in her backpack. "I'm *so* glad I'm done!" Looking around, she asks, "Where's CJ?"

"His uncle is here with the movie. I'm sure CJ went to go set it up." Sophie scans the chairs that are set up on the gym floor. "Matthieu is saving our seats under the hoop with a snowflake."

"Let's go! I can't wait to see the film!" Susan grabs Sophie by the hand and notices her sparkle. "I love your earrings!"

"Thanks!" Sophie says. Following Susan's lead, she zig-zags through the excited Christmas sweater–clad crowd. "I can't wait till everyone sees our big-screen debut! Have you seen Anisha and Oscar?"

"No sign of Oscar, but I saw Anisha and Naveen at the Junior Medic Club. Their table is way in the back," Susan says, pointing toward the bathrooms. "They were doing blood pressure readings on teachers. Anisha's mom came. She was super happy and taking pics. You should have seen the shocked look on Mr. Weber's face when they said his blood pressure was, like, *crazy* high."

Sophie spots the Fine Arts Club table and lets go of Susan's hand. "Su, I just want to say hi to Ms. Kahn. I'll meet you at our seats, okay?"

"Sure." Susan pulls a strawberry-scented lip gloss from her backpack. "See you there!"

Ms. Beverly Kahn stands proudly by the Fine Arts Club display. There are several canvases by promising students who could be the next David Hockney or Georgia O'Keeffe—water-color landscapes of sandy beaches and vivid acrylic abstract self-portraits. Ms. Kahn is dressed in an elegant jumpsuit perfect for an evening gallery opening. Her blush and lipstick match the glittering red beaded top with butterfly sleeves.

"Ms. Kahn, happy holidays!" Sophie waves as she approaches.

"Thank you." Ms. Kahn gives Sophie a hug. "I am very pleased by how well your class did on your exams."

"I am *so* glad they're over for this year," Sophie sighs. "I'm waiting to hear back from Mr. Everett about the summer internship at the museum."

Ms. Kahn pulls a letter from a folio. "Actually…I was very impressed by your report on Japanese art and its influence on Gustave Klimt, so I sent a copy to Mr. Everett. I just received this letter this morning. Mr. Everett has selected students for the 1986 summer internship program."

"And?" Sophie asks, eager and impatient.

Ms. Kahn breaks into a smile and presents the letter. "Congratulations, Sophie. Your name is on the list!"

Sophie throw her arms around Ms. Kahn. "I can't believe it! Thank you…thank you!"

"Mr. Everett will mail out the official letters in the spring. This will be a valuable museum experience and something to look forward to next summer!" Ms. Kahn beams, seeing Sophie's bright potential. She tucks the letter back into her folio.

Sophie can't help but grin as a man walks toward them.

"Bev, this should keep you going through the assembly." William Omolo hands Ms. Kahn one of the Drink 'n' Dunk coffee cups he is carrying. He maintains his professional demeanor but still flashes a wink at her.

"Thank you, Will. That's very nice of you." Ms. Kahn smiles back at him with her red lips and warms her hands around the steaming cup of coffee.

"Sophie, the film is all set up," Mr. Omolo says, then takes a sip from his cup. He is wearing a loose gray suit with a white scarf that drapes down from his shoulders. "I'm going downtown for a City Hall reception this afternoon, but I couldn't miss being here. I'll be rooting for the club."

"I'm looking forward to this," Ms. Kahn says, opening the program. "You have a very good chance of getting an award this year, since the AV Club has always won in the movie category."

"I'm so excited for the school to see our film!" Sophie's exhilaration turns to slight disappointment. "We're the last club on the program, though."

"Well, you know how the saying goes," Mr. Omolo says encouragingly. "Saving the best for last."

Sophie takes in Mr. Omolo's words of wisdom and goes off to find her club.

"Do They Know It's Christmas?" rises up from the speakers, signaling the start of the assembly. Teachers and students scramble for their seats, filling in the bleachers and the chairs lined up on the gym floor. Teachers, the top athletes and academics, and presenting club members are seated on the floor, while the bleachers are filled up by the rest of the student body, leaving the nosebleed seats to those who want to remain off Principal Patterson's radar. Sophie spots the snowflake hanging from the basketball hoop, the beacon that leads her to the Cinematics Club.

"Sophie! *Finally!*" Susan jumps up from her aisle seat to let Sophie in.

"I know! I made it here just in time!" Sophie slides down the row of folding chairs below the bleachers.

"Hey, Ani, I saw your mom at the Junior Medic table," Susan says, passing around breath mints. "Is she staying for the movie?"

"Uh, no," Anisha sighs, disappointed. "I understand—she has to go to work. And she doesn't think much of the acting thing anyway. She thinks it's a waste of time." Speaking in her mom's critical voice and crossing her arms over her chest, she huffs, "*Acting is* not *a profession. You must think of your future.*"

"I hear you." Susan can relate, given how her family expects her to follow in her older siblings' footsteps.

"You're really good in the film," Sophie affirms.

"Well, I think this may be my first and last acting role," Anisha says, accepting the reality. "At least I tried. Right?"

CJ tucks his feet under his chair to let Sophie pass by. He's focused on writing his acceptance speech in his program. "I'd like to thank my mother, my father, and our club mentor, William," he recites. "I'd like to thank those who inspire me: photographer William Claxton, poet Langston Hughes, and much respect to ska music and to the directors—"

"Do you think everyone is going to stay till the end? They put us last, *after* the AV Club!" Anisha pops a wintergreen candy into her mouth. She slips off her white lab coat and gets comfortable in her white sweater and gray acid-washed jean skirt.

"Seriously? Of course everyone's going to stay till the end. That's when they're giving out the awards," Oscar replies snappishly. He refuses to think the worst—that no one will stick around to see their film. He stands up to smooth out the black vest over his white dress shirt and adjusts the black fedora over his gelled hair. "Sophie, I'm working at two. *Enemy Mine* is opening!"

"Cool! I'll be there at two too!" Sophie slides past Oscar and gives him a high five.

Matthieu, wearing the charcoal-gray trench coat, takes his sketchbook off the empty metal chair beside him and tucks it into his khaki military-style canvas backpack, decorated with Midnight Oil and X band pins.

"I was saving your seat," Matthieu says. His bleached hair has almost completely grown out, back to his regular brown. He leans toward Sophie, and his blue eyes widen as the scent of plumeria fills the air. Matthieu wraps his arm around her shoulders and whispers in her ear, "The club is coming over to my house at seven."

Sophie's mind drifts back to the news about the internship and her face lights up, ready to burst with the news.

Matthieu suspects something is going on by the way Sophie keeps grinning and flecks of green light up her hazel eyes. He tilts his head and asks, "Quoi de neuf? What's up?"

"I got it!" Sophie says, still amazed to be able to say those words out loud. "I got the summer internship at the museum."

"C'est magnifique!" Matthieu hugs Sophie. He brushes a strand of her hair away from her eyes. "Another reason to celebrate tonight."

"What?" Susan shouts out from the end of the row. "That's awesome, Sophie!"

"This is going to be the best summer!" Anisha proclaims.

"Righteous!" CJ, psyched, finally lifts his head out of the program. He has assembled a choice look for the special day: a vintage two-tone suit with ankle-length pants. An intense confident attitude takes over as he puts on a pair of square black 1960s sunglasses. "Cinematics, let's show them something they've never seen before. This is our time!"

The Weather Girls' "Dear Santa, Bring Me a Man This Christmas" blasts from the speakers. The cheerleaders, dressed in red-and-green leotards with tinsel sashes, do handsprings across the floor. Bodies fly through the air until they all assemble into a pyramid. Amber and Brittany propel themselves to the top. Students erupt into applause, stomping their feet on the wood floor. During the thundering roar, Principal Patterson makes his grand entrance.

"Hello, Noble Knights! Welcome to Winter Wonder 1985!" Principal Patterson yells into the microphone, his words echoing through the sound system. "Before we say adios to this year, we must celebrate our impressive achievements here at Noble High!"

A small earthquake erupts across the gym floor with another round of stomping feet and cheers.

"A big thank you to our sponsor, A Taste of Class Tux Rentals. For this special occasion, they generously provided me with this stylish suit." The principal does a model strut in his white suit, accented with a red bow tie, cummerbund, and lapel carnation.

The enthusiastic jocks seated in the front row respond with raucous hoots and catcalls. Principal Patterson, emboldened like a frat brother, smirks and nods back. Looking out across the gymnasium, he shouts, "Thank you to our exceptional teachers, students, and club mentors who have made this a great year! And to our *most triumphant* Noble Knights football team, who have crushed our competition and are going on to the state championships!" Working up a sweat now, he hollers into the microphone, "We have an incredible lineup this morning. To kick off our program, let's give a big round of applause to our king of chemistry and outdoor exploration, Mr. Hart, and the Noble Hikers Club!"

The cheerleaders, led by Amber and Brittany, escort the principal to the faculty seats, throwing their tinsel sashes out into the audience. One of the sashes lands around Mr. Hart's neck. His students follow him to the court floor, wearing club T-shirts printed with a wizard on top of a mountain peak. Moving with his wooden hiking stick in one hand and the microphone in the other, Mr. Hart describes the exhilarating trek around the Yosemite Valley loop trail. The club members pass the microphone as they share their observations, their snow-filled memories, and their epic lodge shenanigans.

Mr. Hart chuckles and interjects, "No snowmen were harmed on this trip. Enjoy the photos!" The overhead florescent lights switch off. Talking Heads' "Road to Nowhere" plays as the club's slideshow projects on a giant screen.

******

Sophie tries to catch herself from checking her watch for the hundredth time. *Only ten thirty?* The restless anticipation for their movie screening makes it impossible to concentrate. Her attention wanders away from the *Grease* musical performance. She looks over at the Cinematics, curious about what they are doing. Matthieu, blocking out the mundane high school experience, listens to music on his Walkman. Sophie leans slyly toward his headphones and is taken by surprise when she hears Depeche Mode's "Shake the Disease."

Matthieu's cheeks flush—he can't hide the fact that he is listening to Sophie's music now. It is undeniable that he will forever think of her when he hears that song.

Sophie smiles, rests her head on his shoulder, and glances back down the aisle.

CJ pulls up his suit sleeve, and Oscar draws a pen tattoo of the Cinematics Club logo on his right inner forearm.

Girls twirl around in silver salon capes and wigs piled up with large rollers. Anisha and Susan playfully sway and sing along to "Beauty School Dropout."

Sophie claps for their performance as the fluorescent lights come up. Susan and Anisha crack up at their goofiness.

The theater students quickly move away the 50s diner booth from the *Grease* musical number. Amber and Brittany make their encore appearance like ice queens from planet popular. They strut to the center of the gym dressed in matching white shiny satin coats, scrunchy socks, and pumps. Their plastered-on grins can't hide the sneering looks they share with each other.

"That was *really, really, REALLY good*," Amber remarks through clenched teeth. She cackles into the microphone. "Let's just hand out the awards now!"

"Only two clubs left before the awards ceremony," Brittany adds, puckering her lips. "I know we can't wait to see the Halloween dance music video by the AV Club."

"Brittany, you took the words right out of my mouth. There will be a quick intermission now, so everybody *should* stick around until the *very* end," Amber says, winking to the jocks.

The cheerleading squad swarms Amber and Brittany, accompanying them to their pre-party in the locker room.

There's a cacophony of moving chairs and feet as people disperse throughout the gym. Some rush to the bathrooms while others bolt for the exits.

The way Brittany intentionally omitted mentioning the Cinematics Club did not escape Sophie's attention. She knows it wasn't by accident. Before, something like that would have festered, distracting her. But now she wasn't about to let Brittany get into her head.

CJ, still wearing his dark shades, stands up and rallies the group. "Everyone ready?"

Sophie closes her eyes and takes a deep breath. She exhales, opens her eyes, and speaks with certainty. "Let's go!"

The Cinematics Club walks together across the gym, finding Mr. Omolo by the audiovisual and sound mixing equipment.

"This is your big moment," Mr. Omolo says, pointing to the film projector loaded with their movie. "I'll be with you for the introduction. Did you rehearse? Who will be speaking?"

"We all have something to say," Sophie assures him. "We'll keep it short."

"Yeah." CJ tucks his shades inside his jacket pocket. "We want everyone to know that each of us is a part of this movie."

"I'm just going say what's in here," Oscar says, patting his heart.

"This has been an"—Mr. Omolo searches for the right word—"*unbelievable* semester. You've gone through a lot." His thoughts wander for a moment, and he shakes his head. "I'm surprised I didn't lose my job. In any event, I'm very proud that you stuck together and actually listened to my lectures. Everyone should be very impressed by the film you created. I know I am."

"Thanks, Mr. Omolo!" Anisha smiles with satisfaction, fired up by the pep talk. "You've been such a great teacher. I would never have tried acting or learned about making a movie without you."

Matthieu, sensing that the time to say something is fleeting, adds, "Whatever happens now, we know you believe in us. Thank you, Mr. Omolo."

A reserved monotone voice comes over the speakers. "We will resume our program in five minutes. Please return to your seats for our final two club presentations, followed by the Winter Wonder awards."

"Look!" Susan points toward the big screen. "The AV Club is lining up over there."

"Then let's be ready." Mr. Omolo leads the way to the side of the gym, beside the giant projection screen.

The AV Club is comprised of six students led by Noble High's tech guru, Fritz Meyer. Hailing from West Germany, he ensures that Noble High is supplied with the latest video cameras and equipment. He has a slicked-back blond ponytail and forgoes any formal title, going only by Fritz. The AV Club students operate on their own self-autonomous status. They zip around campus, wheeling carts loaded with slide projectors and televisions. Since they assist teachers with their audiovisual setups during classes, they are never stopped for hall pass checks or asked for tardy slips.

"Sophie!" Chris waves, his voice crackling with nervous energy. "I finally get to see your movie!" Adrenaline surging, he jogs over to her in his black nylon parachute suit with teal flaps and asymmetrical zippers.

"I can't believe we're finally here!" Sophie says. She notices that the AV Club is dressed in matching outfits. "Impressive, you even planned what to wear. You look like a cool Euro band."

"Really? You like it?" Chris asks, curiously sliding his jacket's zippers open and closed. "Fritz thought it would make a strong impression. It's kind of flashy."

Matthieu stands beside Sophie. He unsuccessfully acts aloof, yet his gaze keeps returning to Chris, tracking his attention toward Sophie. He finally interjects, "It reminds me of Devo. They all dress alike in their videos."

"That's cool. I like Devo, *for sure*." Chris nods. "I think Fritz was going for that German band, Kraftwerk." He moves like a robot, modulating his voice like a computer. "Po-cket cal-cu-la-tor."

Matthieu realizes that Chris is not his adversary and can't help but laugh along with Sophie. He extends his hand to Chris. "Good luck."

"Hey, thanks, dude," Chris says, shaking Matthieu's hand. "We've never had a competitor for the movie award. May the best movie win."

Returning from intermission, Principal Patterson walks out to the center of the floor. There is a noticeable difference in the size of the audience. The bleachers are empty, leaving the floor seats filled in. Principal Patterson masks his displeasure with the disappearing student body by doing the 60s Cool Jerk dance to get the crowd animated.

"Welcome back, Noble High!" Principal Patterson yells enthusiastically into the microphone. "Thanks to our ace students with the fortitude to persevere to the end of our assembly. It is my pleasure to introduce our first club in the movie category. I know I have been anxiously waiting to see what Fritz and the AV Club have created!"

Joining the principal in the spotlight, Fritz is trailed by a stream of students in black sports suits, their frizzy mullets tamed into ponytails.

"Thank you, Mr. Patterson," Fritz articulates into the microphone, carefully choosing his words. "The AV Club presents the Halloween dance in a music video format. My team has learned the latest cutting-edge processes using VHS camcorders. The video is a feast for the eyes." Fritz, bowing his head and waving his hand, signals the start of the presentation.

Everyone holds their breath until the sound of an electric guitar strums, playing Oingo Boingo's "Dead Man's Party." A spiraling title fades up to fill the screen—NOBLE HIGH HALLOWEEN DANCE 1985—and then drips aways like slime. The video captures the dizzying night, the cameras zooming in for close-ups: Principal Patterson spinning records with Sven Synth; the Madonna-wannabes' lace-and-fishnet dance-off; the blur of shockingly bright makeup and monster masks.

Syncing with the blare of horns, the video ends with a giant lit pumpkin exploding into a fireball. The audience breaks its silence, erupting into loud cheers.

"What was that?" Matthieu asks, narrowing his eyes in distaste. "The whole video focused on the popular people."

"The exploding pumpkin was cool," CJ responds objectively.

"I saw Oscar," Susan adds. "And there was that *split second* of Anisha and Naveen winning the the couples' costume contest."

"It's just different from our movie, that's all," Sophie says, trying not to worry about the competition.

Fritz and the AV Club wave to the audience and walk off to the side of the screen. Clapping enthusiastically, Principal Patterson returns to the center of the gym. Shaking his head in exuberant disbelief, he announces, "That was in-cred-i-ble. Fritz and the AV Club, you have outdone yourselves once again!" Catching his breath, he says, "And now, without further ado, please welcome our last movie contender. This is a new club mentored by *Los Angeles Daily Tribune* photojournalist Mr. William Omolo. Give a round of applause for the Cinematics Club!"

The Cinematics Club lines up under the big screen as Principal Patterson passes the microphone to Mr. Omolo.

"Thank you for the nice introduction. My name is William Omolo. The Cinematics Club celebrates the arts of photography and film. This movie was created, written, and filmed completely by these students. I'll let them give you their final thoughts." William passes the microphone to his nephew and returns to the side of the screen.

"Hello, my name is Charles James. This is a film about good versus evil…and it has a great chase scene too!"

"Hi, I'm Susan Tran. I worked on the script and was the wardrobe stylist." She sees a glimmer from the C charm hanging from her wrist and smiles. Looking over to CJ, she catches his eye and says, "We learned a lot making this movie. It's about taking chances."

"I'm Anisha Patel," she says, hoping nobody notices her voice wobbling with nerves. It steadies and she proceeds, "This is my first acting role. I really liked being part of a film shoot. I hope you enjoy the movie."

"Hey, I'm Oscar Garcia." He runs his hand over his fedora and lowers it down, resting it over his heart. He proclaims, "This movie is from la corazón, the heart."

"My name is Matthieu Bernard," he says without any embellishment. "Art speaks for itself."

Sophie, the last one to speak, takes the microphone from Matthieu. She feels the sea of eyes staring back at her. *Let's go. You can do it.*

"Hi, I'm Sophie Alexander. The title of this film is *Gen1 Society*. It's a spy thriller about a group of first-generation Americans on a secret mission." She looks out into the audience and spots Ms. Kahn beaming. Sophie smiles back and concludes, "This is *our* movie. We are the Cinematics Club."

Sophie hands the microphone back to Principal Patterson as the yellow-tinged ceiling lights switch off. The Cinematics Club converges by the side wall, looking up at the big screen.

In the darkness, the title card appears: THE CINEMATICS CLUB PRESENTS: GEN1 SOCIETY. Heaven 17's "Let Me Go" plays as the story unfolds in shades of rich black and crisp white. Sophie watches the film, and the drab gym fades away. She recalls creating every scene playing across the screen. Those moments, like the jump into Matthieu's pool, flood her memories in vivid color. Light from the water, in deep blues and greens, dances and reflects off their faces.

Glancing over at the rest of the club, who are also captivated by the movie, Sophie feels an electric charge connecting them. It is an energy that has brought them together and one that is preserved on film. Like a light shining into a dark cave filled with hidden wonders, their characters reveal glimpses of their true selves.

The movie closes with credits, including Buster the cat. The gym's bright lights switch on. As the mediocre applause fades, one person's clapping lingers.

"Mom?" Anisha gasps in disbelief, squinting at a woman dressed in white.

Raya Patel walks toward her daughter, unable to fight the tears welling up in her eyes.

"Mom...I thought you went to work," Anisha says. She desperately tries to decipher her mom's conflicted expression. That look can only mean that Anisha has brought shame upon her family, and being grounded would probably be her next starring role.

"You were *so* radiant up there," Raya says, wiping tears from her cheeks. Standing there in her nurse's uniform, she sighs and reveals, "I wanted to be an actress when I was your age, but my parents would not hear of it. In India, the movie theater was a magical palace where people threw coins at the screen. I dreamed of one day being an actress like Nargis."

"Really? So you're *not* mad?" Anisha asks.

"I know I've been hard on you," Raya confesses. "In your movie, I saw the spark in your eyes. I see it now. It is the same fire I had...before I let it go out."

"Are you staying for the awards?" Anisha asks, still in shock.

"Yes, I changed my shift to the afternoon." Raya smiles. "How could I miss your big premiere?"

✳✳✳✳✳✳

The Winter Wonder awards ceremony looks like the mega prize reveal at the end of a TV game show. Two cheerleaders wheel out a Christmas tree on a dolly draped with fluffy white cotton. The pine boughs are decorated with blinking lights and shiny silver award ribbons. Pictures are snapped as students race up to receive accolades for Most Innovative Club, Best Academic Achievement, and Best Presentation Table. It is no surprise to anyone that the Best School Spirit award goes to the cheerleaders. That is, except for Oscar.

"Seriously? That's *so* lame!" Oscar gripes, caught somewhere between anger and annoyance. "This is rigged! If it wasn't for the Halloween dance committee, the most exclusive party of the school year wouldn't have happened."

"Oscar, don't let it bug you," Sophie says.

"Yeah. It's totally bogus," CJ remarks. He stands up straight and smoothes out his suit, waiting for their category.

"We're up next—Best Movie," Matthieu says, eyeing the last ribbon hanging on the Christmas tree. "It's ours. I can feel it." He removes his trench coat to reveal an Edwardian-style fitted white dress shirt with a black polka-dot tie in a four-in-hand knot.

Sophie turns to Matthieu, caught off guard by his absolute certainty and his polished outfit. She looks into his eyes. "I think you really want this award."

"We have one last prize to hand out," Principal Patterson says, his voice gravelly now from all the shouting. "Our presenters are Mr. Hart and Mrs. Sanchez!"

Mr. Hart escorts Mrs. Sanchez to the center of the gym.

"Well, Rita, this is it! This is the final award and the last time we'll see everyone in 1985!" Mr. Hart exclaims. He has dressed up his hiking outfit with a brown leather bomber jacket and a hunter-green cashmere scarf. "I'll be taking off to Patagonia."

"Mr. Hart," Mrs. Sanchez says. "Let's hand out the award for Best Movie." She is ready to dance right into 1986, wearing a shimmering black strapless minidress with a rose at the waist. Her eyes pop with blue-and-purple eye shadow. She waves her red-painted nails. "Can we have the AV Club stand here on our right and the Cinematics Club line up to our left?"

The two clubs flank Mrs. Sanchez and Mr. Hart. Sophie feels like she is in a weird, surreal talent show at the mall. Mr. Hart peels open the last envelope. He slowly pulls out the card and hands it to Mrs. Sanchez.

"And the winner for Best Movie is…" Mrs. Sanchez says with dramatic hesitation, heightening everyone's anticipation.

For a second, time stands still—no one breathes or moves. The gossiping stops, and students' mouths hang wide open. Sophie rubs her hands together, drying off her clammy palms. From the corner of her eye, she catches CJ mouthing his acceptance speech.

"The AVeeeee club!" Mrs. Sanchez hollers as she waves the card decorated with calligraphy. "Let it snow!"

Tiny white streamers drift down. Cheers flood the gym as students play in the paper snow that covers the floor. The AV Club accepts their silver ribbon and poses for pictures in their coordinated outfits.

"It's all about the playback. You can quote me for the school paper," one of the members says, wearing the silver ribbon, as the photographer takes the winning club picture.

"Well, that's a wrap for the Winter Wonder Awards!" Principal Patterson shares in the celebration, raising a glass of eggnog topped with a mountain of whipped cream. "Thank you to all of our outstanding clubs, and a toast to the winners!

Have a great winter holiday, happy new year, and see every-one in 1986!"

The Cinematics Club stands frozen. The letdown clouds Sophie's mind as the paper snow falls, sticking in her hair.

Fritz and the AV Club exchange handshakes with the Cinematics Club, rousing them back to the real world of Noble High. It is a gesture of goodwill toward their first and only competitor.

"I don't understand how they snubbed your movie," Fritz says. "Your choice to shoot in black and white was brave. It evoked the French New Wave of *Diva* and the suspense of Hitchcock's *The 39 Steps*."

"Thank you," CJ says, shaking Fritz's hand, speaking film-maker to filmmaker. "I respect that our films each had their own look and vision. I picked up that the exploding pumpkin had a bigger meaning…bigger than all of us."

CJ leaves Fritz, contemplating his next video vision.

Mr. Omolo takes the Cinematics Club aside, gathering them into a huddle for a pep talk. "Don't take this as a defeat. You put your film out there, and it made an impression. In Swahili we say, kila ndege huruka na mbawa zake: every bird flies with its own wings." He checks his watch. "I'm sorry to leave you now, but I have to be at City Hall. Happy holidays."

Mr. Omolo walks off to visit Ms. Kahn at the Fine Arts Club table before leaving Noble High.

"Merde," Matthieu laments, swallowing the bitter pill of a bruised ego. He takes off his polka-dot tie and slips it around Sophie's neck. "You look much better in this." He averts his eyes, trying to hide his disappointment.

"Don't be sad," Sophie replies, fixing the silk tie loosely around her neck. "I know you really wanted to win the award even though you act like it's dumb and doesn't matter."

The AV Club is still buzzing in party mode. Fritz takes action shots of the group holding camcorders like they are a rock band posing for an album cover. The Cinematics Club watches the photo shoot, accepting the reality of being the Winter Wonder losers.

"Hey, are you hungry?" Chris asks. "We reserved the Capri Room at Napoli's. Wanna join us for some pizza?"

28
The Setting Sun

Valley holiday parade banners hang from the lampposts that line Ventura Boulevard. The warm afternoon sun beams into the store windows, which are decorated with festive Christmas lights and shiny tinsel garlands. Shoppers dash along the street, toting gift-wrapped boxes with large bows. Sophie, CJ, and Susan walk down the boulevard to their work shifts.

"I can't believe we couldn't find a place to park in the lot." Sophie holds a small pizza box, swerving to avoid a crush of mallrats racing to make their bus.

"It's these crazy last-minute shoppers. They took all the spaces." Susan navigates around a woman clutching stuffed gift bags.

They pass by Popsicle's window display, where supersize inflatable reindeer lead a green gummy bear driving a red-and-white 1960 Nash Metropolitan.

"That is such a cool car!" CJ exclaims, carrying his scooter helmet. He grabs a blue jelly bean sample from the huge candy cane dispenser outside the store.

Arriving in front of Video Vault, Sophie and Susan laugh.

"Is this your holiday helper?" Susan puts her arm around the giant cardboard cutout of *The Terminator* wearing a red velvet Santa cap.

"I'll take all the help I can get!" CJ steps through the open door wearing his retro sunglasses. "I hear we're already sold out of *Beverly Hills Cop*." Kids are running laps around the racks, knocking videocassette boxes to the ground. CJ grins and says with the utmost composure, "I'll see you later at the party. I better get down to business."

Walking away from the video store, Sophie and Susan hear CJ yell, "Hey, you brats! All of these boxes better be back on the racks or you are banned from renting movies *for life*!"

"Very impressive." Sophie nods in approval. "He sure took care of business."

Susan walks up to the door of Ciao Gelato. "I wanna change before the party. I'll see if Steven or Andrea can pick me up after work."

"Okay," Sophie replies. "I'll see you at Matthieu's." Something is on her mind, and she works up a way to phrase it. "Hey, Su, I know that we're all such close friends…but would you be weirded out if CJ likes you?"

Susan releases the door handle and turns back to Sophie. "I've tried to figure out if he likes me. I thought he was *finally* going to say something at the assembly. I've been dropping hints, like when I gave him my bracelet at the dance, but he hasn't noticed any of them. Did he say anything to you?"

"It's not that he's said anything," Sophie explains. "It's just the way he's always asking about you and the way he looks at you. It's just a feeling."

The words give Susan a boost. "Thanks, Sophie. Why are these things so complicated? Well, let's see what happens tonight at the party."

Susan opens the door to Ciao Gelato, and the smell of waffle cones and mint gelato waft into the air.

* * * * * *

The wailing guitar of Bryan Adams and Tina Turner's "It's Only Love" beckons Sophie to Chelsea Loft. The large steel-frame windows are filled with stacks of TVs, spray-painted Day-Glo colors and flashing HELLO, 1986. Mannequins dance on top of the TVs in electric-blue bubble dresses and loose-fitting suits. Sophie doesn't linger, resisting the temptation to be sucked into the store, and walks straight to work.

La Luna's marquee announces, ENEMY MINE PRE-MIERES FRIDAY! Now that school is officially out for winter break, there is a long line of kids snaking around the theater for the three p.m. showing. Sophie ducks down and dashes past the empty box office, avoiding being detected by the rowdy moviegoers.

The lobby looks like a sci-fi North Pole. Placed between an artificial snow-frosted Christmas tree and an animated Santa Claus, an alien creature with big black eyes holds a sign adver-tising La Luna gift certificates. Sophie races up to Oscar, who is behind the candy counter firing up the popcorn machine.

"Hey, no outside food!" Oscar jokes, spotting the Napoli's pizza box in Sophie's hands.

"You got me!" Sophie laughs. "I brought some leftover slices for Dylan. Is he upstairs?"

"I saw him out in the alley." Oscar places a cardboard standup sign on the counter as popcorn ricochets around the machine behind him.

"What is *alien goo* popcorn?" Sophie raises her brows, curious about the new promotion.

"This is my creation!" Oscar pulls out a paper cup and opens the see-through door of the popcorn machine. He scoops up some hot popcorn, sprinkles in candy, and then squeezes a drizzle of caramel sauce on top. He enthusiastically tilts the paper container toward Sophie. "See how the chocolate and caramel ooze together with the popcorn? This is going to be a bestseller!"

"Totally cool, Oscar! I better find Dylan. I have to open the box office soon."

Sophie breezes through the dimly lit empty auditorium and down the sapphire-blue carpet. It's peaceful and quiet, the moon and star reliefs illuminated along the walls. She props open the back door and squints to adjust her eyes to the bright sunlight.

Dylan is seated on the back stairs. Fully absorbed, he writes in a book while a cigarette dangles from his lips. Underneath an unbuttoned gray vintage blazer, he is wearing a black Searing Magmä T-shirt.

"I brought you Napoli's." Sophie hands the pizza box to Dylan.

"Thanks, Moonlight." Dylan takes a last puff on his cigarette, coughs, and flicks the butt away. "I'll eat this upstairs."

"I thought you were quitting?" Sophie asks, pointing to the smoldering embers on the pavement.

"That's my New Year's resolution." Dylan stacks his notebook on the box. "I'm sketching storyboards for *RoboCruisers 2*. Rikki's working on the music. I can't wait till

I finish the final cut and screen it for my film school graduation in June."

"I'm sure it's going to be awesome," Sophie says with encouragement, though her eyes reveal a glint of melancholy.

"Oscar told me that your movie club didn't get the prize at school." Dylan stands up and stomps out the cigarette butt with his black distressed boot. He looks out into the car-congested parking lot and observes, "If I know anything, it's this: don't wait for others to see your greatness."

Sophie sighs, nodding.

"Look where we are. In this alley, all these people are running around and don't have a clue. But we know what happened here." Dylan walks up to Sophie. "The world is a better place because of us."

Sophie smiles and walks toward the theater's back door.

"Hey, Moonlight, one more thing." Dylan reaches inside his jacket pocket. He pulls out a tiny red gift box and hands it to her. "Happy holidays. Angela picked it out from her shop."

Sophie opens the small box to reveal an Art Deco crescent moon pin. The blue zircon stones sparkle like the crystal-clear sea. "It's so beautiful. I love it! Thank you and Angela." She pins it to the collar of her shirtdress. Dylan hikes up the back stairs as Sophie returns to the theater.

Rushing back through the lobby, she opens the manager's office door. The desk is covered with ledgers and newspaper movie advertisements. Robert finishes his phone call and places the receiver in the cradle.

"Hi, Robert, great news—there's a super-long line outside! I'm going to open the box office now." Sophie quickly grabs her name tag, the cash box, and the roll of red tickets. She stands by the door, suddenly noticing the glazed look on his face. "Is everything okay?"

"I just got off the phone with Max." Robert is still processing the news, and the words come out slowly. "He's in Washington. Balafre…The Scar…is going to be extradited to France."

"Really?" Sophie answers. "That's good, right?"

"Uh, yeah. Max mentioned something…something about a war crimes trial," Robert says, still in a daze. "Before Max ended the call, he said that it's time for him to pass the theater on to someone who is going to take care of it. He said that someone is me." Robert sits back in his leather chair and chokes up. "I've worked all my life for this."

✶✶✶✶✶✶

Sophie opens the tiny back door to the box office and sets up the cash box and tickets. She turns the sign on the window from CLOSED to OPEN, slides open the speaker, and says, "Welcome to La Luna. How many for the three p.m. showing of *Enemy Mine*?"

The line files by Sophie's window: junior-high first dates, sci-fi nerds, and after-school babysitters with kids. By late afternoon, the sky starts to dim. The blue fades to gray with a wash of soft pink. A faint breeze blows through the tall palm trees, a hint of a half moon peeking through the swaying fronds. The boulevard pulses with headlights from rush hour traffic.

The next group moves by Sophie's window, and she sells them the last tickets and puts up the SOLD OUT sign. She checks the ticket roll and grabs the yellow Walkman from her purse. She slips on the headphones and presses play, starting Cocteau Twins's "Donimo." Seeing the Winter Wonder Assembly program, she stuffs it deeper into her bag.

As the throng of people thins out, a figure stops for a moment. He is just another unknown face in the city, an everyday person getting off a job in worn coveralls and work boots. Sophie looks out her window and catches her breath. The boy's formerly shaved head has now grown in new light brown hair. But she remembers those eyes, the ones behind the mask.

No one at Noble High has seen Lee for months. It was like he disappeared off the planet, which brought relief to those he had tormented at school. Sophie never saw him after the night on La Luna's back stairs. She has never told anyone that Lee is Balafre's grandson or that he was the one behind the ski mask.

As he stands in front of her, Sophie sees the vulnerability in Lee's eyes. He remains frozen, feeling like his past is chained to him, forever following him like his own shadow across the terrazzo tiles. It doesn't cross Sophie's mind to panic or scream for help. She only sees a boy starting a new life for himself. She nods to him, and Lee reciprocates, a silent message they share from afar. As the holiday shoppers swell in front of the theater, Lee disappears into the crowd.

29

Stars Light the Dark Night

"Wait, Oscar, don't turn the dial. I *love* Friday night dedications!" Anisha pleads from the squeaky back bench seat of the Wagoneer. Feeling all the bumps in the road, she and Naveen bounce up and down as Sophie drives into the canyon.

Oscar pulls back his hand and reclines in the front passenger seat. His hair is gelled under his black fedora. He takes a whiff of his shirt collar. "I still smell like popcorn, chocolate, and caramel."

"Maybe you should bottle that," Sophie laughs. Speaking with a breathy voice like she is in a fancy perfume commercial, she purrs, "Sweet yet salty—Alien Goo cologne by Oscar."

Beep, beep, beep!

Shining its single round headlight, a midnight-blue Vespa whizzes past the Jeep as Sophie turns onto the dark Windswept Canyon Road. Static breaks up the radio reception. "This is Sven Synth at LA's *cutting-edge* radio station, KNXS. We're playing your love dedications tonight between six and eight. In love, out of love, or looking for love somewhere along the 101?

Call us at 555-KNXS! This next dedication is from Naveen at Noble High to Ani. 'Never Surrender' by Corey Hart."

"*Awwwwwww*," Oscar and Sophie coo in unison, causing Anisha and Naveen to blush. "Woo…woo…woo!"

Sophie slowly drives up the hill as everyone sings along to the song. She parks in Matthieu's driveway. Naveen, dressed in jeans and a graphic patterned sweater, spots Matthieu's Fiat and takes a closer look at the silver beauty.

"Sophie, what took you *so long*?" CJ playfully teases, securing his scooter on its stand with his creeper shoe. He pulls off his helmet and rests it on the handlebars. Noticing a missing Cinematic, he asks, "Where's Susan?"

"Steven is supposed to drop her off." Sophie steps out of the Jeep. She has changed into the outfit she wore for their first movie shoot: a black leotard with a long sheer ballet skirt over leggings. The crescent moon pin, attached to her top, sparkles like the light across the Pacific Ocean.

A red Toyota Supra revs up the driveway and comes to a screeching stop behind Sophie's Jeep. Steven gets out in his sporty pressed white shorts, polo shirt, and V-neck tennis sweater.

"Nice place." Steven leans against the open car door, taking in the secluded hillside. Then he sits back down in the driver's seat and starts the engine. Pulling a white card from his wallet, he passes it to Sophie through the car window. "Is Martin back from college?"

"He'll be home tomorrow." Sophie takes the card, running her finger across the embossed DynaRocket logo.

"Great. That's my new business card." Steven shifts into neutral. "He can call me. I'll introduce him to my boss."

"Okay. Thanks. I'll give it to him!" Sophie tucks the linen business card into her purse.

"Su, are you getting out of the car?" Steven wonders. "Aimee reserved the racquetball court for us, and I've got to jam down the hill now."

The passenger door swings open, and Susan steps onto the gravel. After an emergency fashion consultation with Sophie over the phone, she also decided to wear her film wardrobe: the black-and-white polka-dot romper over leggings, a tailored black blazer, and lace-up short boots. Her hair, pulled up into a ponytail with a red scarf, cascades down in crimped strands. Steven backs up, and his headlights pop up. Revving the engine, he waves from the window and zooms off down the driveway.

Sophie hugs Susan and is instantly hit with the scent of a woodsy floral perfume. "I can smell your Poison."

"Well, my sister did say it's irresistible," Susan whispers. "If this doesn't work, I don't know what will."

CJ walks toward Susan and becomes flustered, saying only, "Hey, Su, cool look."

Sophie, Susan, Anisha, Naveen, Oscar, and CJ walk through the courtyard filled with the music of the swaying wind chimes. The front door is ajar, propped open by a suitcase with a garment bag folded on top.

"Hello?" Sophie calls out, stepping past the luggage. She walks into the living room, which is toasty from the crackling fireplace. "Matthieu, we're here!"

"Well, hello, Cinematics!" Genni jogs out of Marc's office and waves everyone inside. "Please get comfortable on the couch. Marc is just leaving for the airport. The holidays are always a crazy rush...and where did Matthieu go?" Even though she is dressed in a sweatshirt and jeans, Genni still radiates California chic. She grabs a folder off the kitchen counter and peeks outside the front door.

Everyone settles on the couches by the cinder block fireplace. Sophie notices the new Lucite-framed photo on the TV. It is of the first Hanukkah the Bernards celebrated in Los Angeles. The picture captures Matthieu helping Leon light the menorah with the expansive canyon view beyond the large windows.

"Genni! Have you seen my passport?" Marc walks out of his office carrying a travel bag over his shoulder. He is dressed in a charcoal-gray suit, white dress shirt, and black tie.

"Your driver just pulled up," Genni reports. She shows him some papers in the folder, shifting into personal assistant mode. "These go in your carry-on bag. Here are your passport and plane tickets. I've typed out your itinerary for Paris and New York and confirmed your reservations." She tucks money inside his jacket pocket. "This is for the driver."

"*Mon amour*, you're amazing." Marc slips the documents into his bag. He gives Genni a tender kiss and embraces her. A conflicted look flashes across his face—he's hesitant to leave and unsure what awaits him in Paris.

Leon, in royal-blue corduroy pants and a striped burgundy shirt, runs proudly up to Marc, trailed by Matthieu.

"Daddy, I made this for you!" Leon gives him a handmade paper plane. "Matti helped me."

Kneeling down, Marc wraps his arms around Leon and kisses him on the cheek. "Thank you. I'll keep this safe." He puts the paper plane in his passport and stows it away inside his bag. Marc hugs Matthieu, who is his same height at nearly six feet.

The gray-haired driver, dressed in a traditional chauffeur's vest and cap, appears at the door to retrieve the baggage. Instead of rushing off, Marc turns back into the living room. He looks at Matthieu and his friends, who are hanging out by the fireplace. It is still incredible to him that they helped capture Balafre.

It was a lifetime ago that Marc's boyhood was destroyed. He spent so much time burying himself in his work while keeping the painful memories locked away. Now he has a chance to go back to Paris and tell the court what Balafre did to his family.

"Hello," Marc says, catching Matthieu's friends by surprise. "I'm sorry that I have to leave and won't be here for your film club party. Please know that I will view your movie when we come back from our trip." Marc spots the driver waiting by the front door and feels remorseful about his rushed goodbyes. "Thank you again for your friendship to Matthieu. I am sincerely grateful."

The Cinematics Club smiles as Marc makes his departure.

"Matthieu, are you going to Paris?" Sophie asks, puzzled.

"No, my dad is going by himself. He's finding out when Balafre is going to be put on trial so that he can be a witness. We're meeting him in New York for New Year's Eve."

Before Sophie can process the news, CJ blurts out, "Cool! You're going see that big ball drop in Times Square with, like, a million people!"

"My dad wanted us to be in New York to see snow and the city," Matthieu says, excited. "I'll takes lots of photos."

"You'll have a great time—all the art and buildings." Sophie draws her gaze toward the fire, hiding her disappointment. "I guess this means I won't see you for New Year's Eve."

"I wish you could be there too," Matthieu says, knowing how much she talks about Keith Haring and the art galleries there. "We'd be running around SoHo, taking pictures in front of CBGB."

"Well, since this didn't turn out to be our film award party, let's make this our New Year's Eve's party!" Susan exclaims.

"I like that!" Sophie says, shaking off the blues.

"That's an awesome idea!" Anisha agrees.

"How about a game?" Oscar suggests.

"I'm in!" Naveen says, raising his hand.

"For the record, we are *not* losers!" CJ stands up in defiance. He takes off his jacket and rolls up his shirt sleeves. "I'm in for a game. Who's on my team?"

＊＊＊＊＊＊

The party has moved outside to the backyard. The steam from the heated swimming pool rises into the cool night. CJ is lying on the diving board looking up at the nightglow. He sweeps his hand through the warm pool water. "Can I just sleep here under the stars tonight?"

Anisha, Naveen, Oscar, Susan, Sophie, and Matthieu are seated in a circle on the cement patio. They are munching from glossy black octagonal bowls of potato chips, round French butter cookies, mini toast crackers, and chocolate chip cookies.

"What do you think 1986 will be like?" Sophie gazes up at the moon. She leans back against Matthieu, feeling the warmth of his body as he folds his arms around her.

"Darn it! I left my *Missy Mode* magazine at home," Anisha laments. "There's a whole forecast based on your favorite color." She swallows a cracker and says, "I predict that we will ace our finals and SATs!"

Matthieu looks over at Sophie. As she twists her body toward him, his arms loosen around her waist. She watches the pool light reflecting on his face, defining his sharp jawline. She reads his serious expression and asks, already knowing the answer, "It's over, isn't it?" He nods in agreement.

The chatter around the circle falls to a silence.

"The party's over already?" Oscar asks, reaching for another chip.

"Our film club," Matthieu finishes the sentence.

"The Cinematics Club is over before I could even join?" Naveen is mystified.

"The spring semester is going to be hard." Susan tenses up just thinking about the workload. Brushing the cookie crumbs off her clothes, she says, "I know I'll be busy."

"We made the movie we wanted to make. That time will always be with us on film." Sophie smiles wistfully.

"But that doesn't mean *we* are over!" CJ sits up on the diving board and stretches out his arms. "This is our club." He jumps off the board and joins the circle of friends.

"Everyone hold hands," Sophie says, sitting between Matthieu and CJ. She radiates warmly to the circle. "Whatever happens in 1986, we have each other." The group nods.

"So, what game are we playing?" Anisha asks, getting up and pantomiming with her hands. "I love charades."

"How about hide-and-seek or a scavenger hunt?" Oscar throws out ideas. "I'll hide something in the backyard. Whoever finds it first is the winner."

"The backyard goes all the way up to the trail. That's all fair play." Matthieu points way up through the canopy of trees that surrounds the terraced canyon garden.

Oscar nods. "Okay."

"We can have two on a team," Susan says.

"Anisha and I are a team." Naveen clasps her hand.

"CJ, are you with me?" Susan asks, gauging his interest.

"Yeah, I'm with you!" CJ nods with absolute certainty.

"What should I hide?" Oscar ponders, looking around the circle. His eyes lock on a colorful object. "Susan, how about your scarf?"

"Okay. It's lucky—I wore it for finals." Susan unties the bright red sheer scarf and hands it to Oscar. Her crimped hair falls down around her silver mesh earrings.

"Let's go inside so Oscar can hide the scarf," Matthieu says, waving for everyone to follow. He grabs a flashlight from a basket and tosses it to Oscar.

"Call us when you're ready!" CJ grabs the bowl of tiny crackers and closes the glass door behind him.

******

Oscar slides opens the patio door and yells into the house, "I'm done! You can come out now!"

Everyone assembles by the pool. Matthieu closes the patio door, carrying a silver cassette player. He sets it on a small glass table between a pair of mid-century modern chaise lounges with vinyl straps.

"We'll look around the pool." Anisha grabs a cookie, passing another one to Naveen.

CJ and Susan whisper to each other and nod in agreement. CJ announces, "We're going to take the left side of the hill."

"Sophie and I will take the other side," Matthieu says, passing a flashlight to CJ.

"I'll be chillin' *right here*, but I'll signal the start." Oscar hands his flashlight to Anisha. Grabbing the bowl of chips, he gets comfortable on a lounger. He turns on the cassette player, and The Waterboys' "The Whole of the Moon" plays. After checking his pocket watch, which is chained to his belt loop, he calls out, "Everyone—on your mark...get set...go!"

The teams disperse to scour their territories. Matthieu surprises Sophie and sweeps her off her feet. Her sheer ballet skirt flows through the air. He creeps close to the pool edge. Wrapping her arms tight around his neck, she shrieks and giggles, "*Nooooo!*" Matthieu lowers her slowly down to solid ground. He flashes a mischievous smile, takes her hand, and guides her up the hillside terrace.

Matthieu and Sophie meander up the flagstone steps until the lighted pathway turns to crushed granite. As they climb the hill, the music from below fades away. The tranquil canyon comes alive with the rustling sounds of nocturnal creatures.

"I don't see anything yet." Sophie scans the evergreen trees and sage shrubs they pass. The minty fragrant scent of blue gum eucalyptus infuses the cool air. Climbing to the edge of the property, they approach the fire road.

Matthieu shines the flashlight back down the path. It flickers like a slowly dying flame, and he hits it against his palm. "The batteries are dying. This is the end of the line. We didn't find the prize."

A deer darts past them, and Matthieu pulls Sophie close. In the dimming light, the fluttering leaves cast shadows across his face. Caressing his cheek, she traces the outline of the leaf shadows until her finger brushes gently across his lips. Hearing voices getting closer, Sophie glances over to see CJ and Susan slowly making their way toward the top of their area. A birdcall pierces through the trees.

"I see something red!" Susan calls out, pointing the flashlight at a garden globe. "Look! My scarf is on top of that orb thingy!"

CJ rushes toward the reflecting ball that rests on an ornamental pedestal wrapped in creeping vines. Displaying its brown-and-white spotted wings, a burrowing owl swoops toward them. Its sharp claws grab the red scarf that is draped over the iridescent glass ball. Taking flight, the owl drops the scarf onto a eucalyptus tree branch.

"Are you serious?" Susan says, annoyed, peering at the tree leaning out over a dell. "That's my lucky scarf!"

"I've got this!" CJ says firmly, stretching out his right arm with the Cinematics Club pen tattoo Oscar drew that morning. He backs up a few steps and grinds his creepers into the dirt for traction. Then CJ takes a running leap and grabs hold of the branch.

"CJ, be careful!" Susan yells.

Grabbing the scarf, CJ calls out to Susan, "I've got it!" As he swings his body back toward the path, he loses his footing and slides down into the shallow dell. Susan drops the flashlight into the dirt, slides down the slope, and lands on top of him.

"Why did you do that?" CJ snaps, jolted by her uncharacteristically reckless action. He brushes Susan's hair away from her face, making sure she is not hurt. Clutching the red fabric, he proclaims, "I got your lucky scarf. We won!"

Susan brushes the dirt from her clothes and pushes CJ back against the side of the hollow. She shakes her head and takes matters into her own hands, kissing him. It feels like a lightning strike; at first he can't tell if it's real or if he has a concussion and is merely imagining it.

"CJ! Susan!" Sophie yells, looking down into the dell. "Are you hurt?"

Matthieu shines the flashlight in their direction, sweeping the beam across their faces.

"We're okay!" Susan yells back, waving her red scarf. She ties back her hair with the fabric.

"How did you get down there?" Matthieu kneels close to the edge and extends his arm. "Can you reach my hand?"

CJ clasps his hands together to give Susan a boost up. She steadies herself against the hollow and stretches her arms up, but she can't feel Matthieu's hand. "I can't reach you!" she huffs, falling back down to CJ.

Matthieu pulls off the sweater he's wearing over his The Clash T-shirt. He lowers it down, and CJ hoists Susan up again.

"I've got it!" Susan shouts, grabbing hold of the sweater, and Matthieu pulls her up to the path.

Sophie helps Susan up and hugs her, dusting the dirt off her clothes. She points the flashlight down into the dell.

"You'll need a rope. I can't reach the sweater." CJ squints into the flashlight beam, grasping at the sides of the hollow.

Susan removes her jacket and hands it to Matthieu. "Can you tie these together? Maybe that will work?"

Matthieu ties the sweater and jacket together and lowers down the makeshift rope. CJ grabs it and climbs out of the dell. He rolls over onto his back, takes a big breath, exhales, and grins.

"Next time we're staying by the pool," he says.

CJ, Susan, Sophie, and Matthieu snake down the terraced pathway until they return to the glowing blue-green pool.

"Where have you guys been?" Oscar yawns, reclining on the lounge chair. He looks at his pocket watch. "It's been forever, and I'm supposed to be home by eleven!"

"What happened?" Anisha sees that CJ's white dress shirt is covered with dirt.

"You know that scene in *Raiders* where Indiana Jones is escaping from that cave and jumps across that pit, barely hanging on to the edge?" CJ says.

"Yeah!" Naveen's eyes widen.

"Well, it was *just* like that," CJ says, smiling at Susan.

"Let's just say it was an adventure." Susan turns around, presenting her lucky red scarf tied in her hair.

"The stars are sure bright tonight." Sophie takes in the glittering sky above the canyon. She looks at the club and can't think of anywhere else she'd rather be. "Happy New Year. Here's to 1986."

30

Par Avion

"Su, the mail hasn't come yet!" Sophie says into her phone instead of the customary hello.

"What's that noise in the background, then?" Susan asks.

Hearing the jingle from the street, Sophie looks out her bedroom window onto another hot July afternoon. She sees a swarm of skateboarders and kids descending upon the red van parked across from her house.

"It's just the ice cream truck," Sophie reports. "I'll call you as soon as I get the package."

"It's been, like, a month since Matthieu left for Paris," Susan says. "Airmail takes so long. Sending packages to Vietnam takes forever!"

"All he wrote in his last letter was that I'd receive a package for my birthday." Sophie wedges the receiver between her ear and shoulder as she files away her museum internship notes into a folder. She is wearing a long white T-shirt—her handmade version of a Jackson Pollock drip painting splattered with turquoise and purple.

"I wonder what it could be?" Susan rattles off some options. "Well, maybe *parfum*…or one of those cute French striped shirts? A Jean Paul Gaultier?"

Sophie grabs the receiver with her hand again and giggles. "Su, I'm sure whatever Matthieu sends will be nice. Since he won't be back until September, I'm going to write him a letter now. I'll tell him what everyone's up to." She looks out the window to see the ice cream truck driving off with a skateboarder hanging on to its bumper. "How's the internship going at EnBioTek?"

"It's fine. I've got a badge, and I'm making lots of photocopies. The place is sooo big that I'm always getting lost!" Susan lowers her voice. "Everything there is very hush-hush, so I can't really say too much."

"Gotcha. I'll call you when I get the mail. Bye, Su!" Sophie hangs up the phone.

She turns on her teal clock radio, and Lone Justice's "Ways to Be Wicked" plays. She opens her desk drawer and retrieves her colorful stationery set decorated with neon palm trees. Selecting a purple pen from a cup full of markers, she pulls out a sheet of paper. Her gaze falls upon a framed photo—the one Matthieu took of them in front of Klimt's *The Kiss*. Seeing it only fuels her longing for him.

July 14, 1986

Bonjour, Matthieu,

I hope you get this letter. I am trying to use the French I have learned. (HA!) I usually want the summer to last forever, but since you're not here, I wish it was already senior year! I've always wanted to be in Paris on Bastille Day. It must be fun there.

My summer internship at the museum will be finished in a week. It is fun giving art tours to kids! They really like the big pop art canvases by Roy Lichtenstein that look like comic strips. Mr. Everett says that he will write me a letter of recommendation for my college applications.

Everyone says hi! Since I'm not working at La Luna anymore, Oscar took over working in the box office. He is really excited to be the chair of the Halloween dance committee this year. Susan is interning at EnBioTek and has super-secret assignments. CJ is doing ride-alongs with his uncle Will and taking lots of pictures. He has also started shooting his own music videos and is going to be a production assistant on Dylan's movie. Anisha is volunteering at her mom's hospital and is going to audition for the school play this fall. She's visiting cousins in Canada now. I'm including some pics.

Well, that's all the exciting news from the land of palm trees. Miss you and our walks on the fire road!

Je t'aime,
Sophie

After sealing the photos and letter inside, Sophie draws hearts and the words *par avion* on the envelope.

"Sophie?" Sarah knocks on her door. "A package arrived for you. Can I come in?"

"Sure, Mom!" Sophie bolts off the desk chair and flies to open her bedroom door. Sarah, wearing a floral summer dress, hands her a brown paper–wrapped box.

"Your father and I are going to the paint store and then to lunch at the Wise Owl. Do you want us to bring you back anything? A chef's salad with Roquefort dressing?"

"Uh…no, I'm fine." Sophie grins, her eyes fixed on the box. She looks up at her mom. "Sorry, what I mean is, I'll just make a sandwich. Thanks!"

"Okay, we'll be back later." Sarah smiles.

Sophie rushes across her bedroom and leaps onto her bed, clutching the shoebox-size package. She brushes her hand over Matthieu's handwriting and carefully opens the brown paper wrapping. Slipping off the box top, she peels apart the tissue paper. A postcard of the Eiffel Tower rests on top of a raspberry-colored beret. Sophie feels the wool fabric of the hat and puts it on. She turns over the postcard and reads Matthieu's note.

Sophie,

Greetings from Paris.

Are you ready to play a game for your birthday? There are three presents in the box. Please do the following in this order:

1. Put on this beret from the flea market
2. Start the mixtape I made for you
3. Open the envelope

I wish I could be there to see you and hear your funny laugh. I'll just imagine that I'm with you.

—Matthieu

Sophie picks up the plastic tape case marked SOPHIE'S BIRTHDAY MIX. She puts the tape into her mini stereo system and hits play. She closes her eyes, and the soul sound of David Bowie's "Win" fills her bedroom. Then she reaches for the envelope at the bottom of the box and opens the flap. Sliding out the contents, she catches her breath at the sight of an airline ticket.

Skyseat Airlines
Passenger: Sophie Alexander
Departure: Los Angeles, U.S.A.
Arrival: Paris, France

Ring...ring...ring...

Sophie's eyes remain locked on the airline ticket as she reaches over to pick up the phone. In a fog, she lifts the receiver to her ear and hears Susan's voice.

"Sophie? Did you get Matthieu's package? Was I right...*parfum*?"

THE CINEMATICS CLUB
WILL CONTINUE...

Thanks for Reading!

Thank you for supporting my work. As a new author, please share your review online and on social media with the hashtag: #TheCinematicsClub. If you fell in love with the book, please encourage others to read the story too!

Acknowledgments

The Cinematics Club is my appreciation for the people, places, and things that have shaped me and my life: family, friends, movies, music, fashion, and art. It is a love letter to the city where I was born—Los Angeles.

I want to thank my editor Alison Cherry for her helpful insights!

About the Author

Renee Windman, born in the City of Angels, is a visual story-
teller. She is an award-winning art director and designer skilled
in creating brands. Drawing from her love of movies, music, art,
architecture, and Los Angeles, she brings her immersive style
of vivid storytelling. *The Cinematics Club* is her debut novel.

Learn more and follow the club online at:

TheCinematicsClub.com
Instagram: @thecinematicsclub
Facebook: The Cinematics Club

www.ingramcontent.com/pod-product-compliance
Lightning Source LLC
Chambersburg PA
CBHW032012310726
48972CB00002B/378